# "MY PEOPLE EXPECT ME TO EXACT REVENGE,"

Colin growled.

Roanna paled, but did not give way. She faced him determinedly, her slender body held straight and firm, her features composed. Only the slightest tremor of her rose-hued mouth betrayed her trepidation. Deep inside, she understood the time had come for a final, desperate gamble.

"Then if I am to die, I have a favor to ask first."

The pretense had gone far enough. Colin could not bear for her to believe he truly meant to harm her. About to assure her she had nothing to fear, he was abruptly and shockingly forestalled.

"I do not wish to die a virgin . . ."

Dear Reader,

We, the editors of Tapestry Romances, are committed to bringing you two outstanding original romantic historical novels each and every month.

From Kentucky in the 1850s to the court of Louis XIII, from the deck of a pirate ship within sight of Gibraltar to a mining camp high in the Sierra Nevadas, our heroines experience life and love, romance and adventure.

Our aim is to give you the kind of historical romances that you want to read. We would enjoy hearing your thoughts about this book and all future Tapestry Romances. Please write to us at the address below.

The Editors
Tapestry Romances
POCKET BOOKS
1230 Avenue of the Americas
Box TAP
New York, N.Y. 10020

# Forbidden Love

## Maura Seger

A TAPESTRY BOOK
PUBLISHED BY POCKET BOOKS NEW YORK

**Books by Maura Seger**

Defiant Love
Rebellious Love

Published by TAPESTRY BOOKS

An *Original* publication of TAPESTRY BOOKS

A Tapestry Book published by
POCKET BOOKS, a division of Simon & Schuster, Inc.
1230 Avenue of the Americas, New York, N.Y. 10020

ISBN: 0-671-46970-3

First Tapestry Books printing July, 1983

10 9 8 7 6 5 4 3 2 1

Printed in the U.S.A.

*For Michael,*
*always*

# Forbidden Love

# Chapter One

"MY LADY, ARE YOU SURE YOU REALLY WANT TO GO outside?" the maid asked cautiously.

Roanna's wide, amber eyes flashed her answer before she spoke. "Of course I do. I've been cooped up in here for weeks."

"Ten days, my lady. Not weeks."

A slight pout rounded the generous mouth that was usually set quite sensibly. "It seems longer. I'm perfectly well now and it's such a beautiful day. I can't bear to stay inside a moment longer."

"Perhaps you should just check with the Lady Brenna . . . ?"

"No!" Roanna insisted hastily, well aware that her sister-in-law would want her to remain abed several more days. Grateful though she was for the expert

1

nursing that had seen her safely through a bout of fever, Roanna was now more than ready to be free of supervision.

Outside beyond the wooden palisade that was the main line of defense for their temporary home, a fresh summer day beckoned. Swallows and warblers sped busily around their nests caring for their young. Gnarled oak trees in full leaf bent heavily over the nearby river that rushed chortling and sparkling through sylvan glades. Shy deer peered from cover at the strange goings-on of the humans recently come among them.

It was a morning for meandering strolls, pensive pauses, sun-dappled thoughts. Roanna ached to be out enjoying it.

"I won't be gone long, and I'm not going further than the riverbank in clear view of the guard towers, so there's no reason to mention my plans to anyone."

The maid looked doubtful. She was one of the few Anglo-Saxons trusted to serve in the house of the new Norman lord, and she took her responsibilities seriously. However cruel and rapacious many of the conquerors might be, they were a reality that could no longer be denied. Upon their favor depended all the necessities of life.

The fact that she served a master who was unfailingly kind and just only strengthened her determination to do nothing to jeopardize her fortunate position. If the Lady Roanna wandered off and got into any trouble, his lordship's wrath would be terrible.

Roanna, sensing the conflict in the girl, smiled reassuringly. "My brother is supervising the castle construction as usual, and will be there most of the day. I'll be back long before he returns."

Before the maid could debate the matter further, she was distracted by her ladyship pulling clothes out willy-nilly and beginning hurriedly to dress. At nineteen, Lady Roanna was radiantly beautiful even despite her recent illness and had an excellent sense of fashion, but she tended to be just the least bit disorganized.

As she attempted to put her white linen camise on backwards, the maid intervened.

"If you would allow me, my lady . . ."

Roanna permitted the assistance gratefully. She was somewhat weaker than she cared to admit. Simply standing in the center of her small chamber in the wooden round tower required sufficient concentration without having also to dress herself.

Having enjoyed the luxury of her first full bath since becoming ill, her honeyed skin glowed warmly. Large, tawny eyes fringed by heavy lashes were brighter than they had been in some time. Her upturned nose and full, rather mischievous mouth softened the strong line of her brow and chin. Beneath a long, graceful throat her shoulders were delicate. Slim arms held up the silken fall of her golden hair as the maid straightened the camise. It fell softly over her high, firm breasts, narrow waist, and rounded hips, ending halfway down her slender thighs.

After the camise went a silk tunic the color of yellow irises. It was embroidered at the neck, wrists, and hem with violet stitching that matched the surtunic worn over it. The bliaut was laced tightly enough at each side to leave no doubt as to the perfection of Roanna's form.

When a comb had been run through her thick, waist-length tresses and her head covered by a transparent veil secured by a golden circlet, she was ready. Thanking the maid, Roanna stepped quickly from the room. Before any further effort could be made to dissuade her, she sped down the circular wooden staircase and through the main hall.

The bailey just beyond thronged with activity. The knights and squires who served her brother were busy with their endless practice for battle. Their shouts and grunts rang out with the clash of steel and the whinnying of horses as they worked with tireless patience to keep themselves in peak condition.

Surrounding them along the edges of the palisade, armorers and tanners worked in their separate domains built against the inside of the protective wall. At a respectable distance, the more mundane tasks of chicken and pig tending, weaving, and food preservation went on.

Crossing the bailey, Roanna paused to look back at the castle rising remorselessly on a hillock dominating the countryside. Already the shape of the outer curtain could be clearly seen. Two narrow walls of locally quarried sandstone mortared with lime were being filled in with densely packed rubble. Workers scurried along the scaffolding that surrounded them. Where the walls had reached their full height, battlements with narrow archery slits were being built.

Beyond the outer curtain with its moat and gatehouse would stretch a narrow open field that gave way quickly to an inner wall punctuated by further guard-posts. Inside that would be the great hall, chapel, family quarters, kitchens, well, and all the other accommodations required by a noble household.

When it was finished, the castle would present an essentially impenetrable defense against which even the most fervent enemies would be helpless.

Not that they were expecting any real trouble. The Anglo-Saxons who surrounded them certainly nursed grievances and hatreds in the aftermath of the Conquest, but they were too wise to attempt an all-out assault on the Norman fighting machine that had proved its implacable strength at Hastings.

Roanna frowned slightly as she considered the subtler forms resistance took, causing her brother no end of headaches but appearing to present no real danger in themselves.

As she waved to the guard manning the temporary gatehouse, she noticed that the small, rarely used confinement cell was occupied. Her sister-in-law had mentioned the previous evening that a persistent poacher had been caught and was awaiting trial.

Brenna gave the information calmly enough, but Roanna wondered at her feelings. Anglo-Saxon herself, but wed to a Norman before the Conquest, her sister-in-law left no doubt that her loyalty was to her lord. But she still felt deeply for her people, who were often bewildered and frightened by the vast changes occurring around them.

Several times, her gentle influence had stayed

Guyon's hand in punishment, with the result that most of his new vassals were becoming inclined to respect and accept him. But the poacher languishing in the cell had defied all efforts at reason.

The man publicly proclaimed that the Norman forest laws which restricted the taking of game were ridiculous and that he for one would never obey them. He went on blatantly behaving as if the conquerors simply did not exist, until at last Guyon was forced to arrest him.

What he would finally do with the man Roanna did not know. Her brother was ruthlessly fierce in battle and awesomely skillful in negotiation, but he had little stomach for the giving of justice which led to executions. Killing a man in combat was one thing; ordering him to swing from the end of a rope was quite another.

Much as she sympathized with her brother's dilemma, she knew there was nothing she could do to help him. By birth and training, he was conditioned to the responsibilities of his position. He would fulfill them admirably, no matter what the personal cost.

But perhaps she could ease his burdens to a tiny degree by finding some of the succulent wild strawberries he liked so much. Pleased with this task, she made her way toward the riverbank, going slowly to savor the warmth of the sun on her face.

The air, fragrant with the scents of thyme and honeysuckle, caressed her gently. Butterflies flitted past. As she neared the river, Roanna stopped and sank quickly to her knees. A red-furred vixen and two pups had come down to drink. For long, sweet moments she watched the foxes until they loped off back into the forest.

Breathing deeply, Roanna settled on a rock near the water. She tossed her heavy hair back over her shoulder, heedless of how this motion revealed the gentle swell of her breasts pushing against the restraining silk. Cupping her hands, she bent to slake her own thirst.

The sheer pleasure of returning health flowed through her. Aware of her good fortune in surviving an illness that had carried off several strong men, she wondered how she might express her gratitude to Brenna.

Between Roanna and her sister-in-law was a deep and abiding love that left no room for the conflicts that might have otherwise plagued two women thrown together in such proximity. Brenna was her brother's wife. To Roanna, that said it all. She had the absolute right to manage the household and receive the deference of all who lived there.

That her sister-in-law was also a kind and gentle woman possessed of rare serenity and sensitivity only made it all the easier to accord her the position she deserved. Roanna thought her brother infinitely fortunate in his choice of a consort, and did not hesitate to tell him so.

However, Brenna did have one small shortcoming. She loathed doing household accounts, something Roanna liked little better but could at least tolerate. Making up her mind that she would offer to take over the task, she lay back in the sun-warmed grass. For a brief while she watched the meanderings of a caterpillar making its way over a nearby rock. But shortly the unaccustomed exertion of her walk took its toll on her still recovering body and she drifted off to sleep.

For the first time in too long, her dreams were pleasant. Gone were the dark and fearful images that had tormented her all during the months of preparation for the invasion, when her brother and sister-in-law were separated and she ached for them both. Banished also was the agonizing dread for Guyon's safety that had awakened her in a chill sweat night after night until she learned at last that he had survived the battle and been reunited with his wife.

Even after she came at their mutual persuading to join them in the family's new home, Roanna was still often restless in the night thinking of the frightened, angry people among whom they now made their lives. She and her brother shared the trait of hiding their deepest concerns beneath an unruffled facade that inspired confidence in everyone around them. It was an invaluable skill that sometimes exacted a harsh price.

But the fever seemed to have burned away the last of her concerns. She slept as serenely as a child, only stirring occasionally when a feathery seed pod or wisp of grass ruffled her nose.

To the men crouched in the underbrush nearby, she presented an irresistibly beautiful and desirable quarry.

One of the bearded, battle-hardened warriors, older than the rest and given to speaking his mind, whistled softly, "Ever see anything quite that comely, my lord?"

The man beside him shook his head wryly. Despite his sometimes violent, always demanding life, Colin Algerson had a connoisseur's appreciation of lovely women. He had known more than a few himself, but never one quite as startling as the glorious creature before him.

Slate gray eyes deep set between arching brows and a straight, rather assertive nose drank in the sight of her. A grimace touched the chiseled mouth draped by the long, pointed ends of a mustache the same coppery hue as the hair that brushed his massive shoulders. His huge, powerful body stirred restlessly. At twenty-eight, with ten years' leadership of his family's lands behind him, he did not care to feel like a randy boy.

"She's right in our path, my lord," the older warrior reminded him. "Think we can get 'round without her hearing?"

"I'm not sure it will do any good if we can," Colin murmured. "You saw the guards on the palisade."

"Aye, more than we thought and more alert than other Normans we've encountered since Hastings," Alaric admitted. "Now that they've settled in a bit, most of that brutish lot seem to think no one would dare to challenge them. Their arrogance is our best weapon. But not with this bunch! They look ready for battle at a moment's notice."

Colin shook his head ruefully. "I'd heard about the high standard D'Arcy sets for his men, but I didn't quite believe it until now. Saving my laggard cousin's life is going to be more difficult than I'd thought."

The older man fought back the urge to suggest the

9

effort was not worthwhile. In the most revered traditions of Anglo-Saxon nobility, Colin was utterly loyal to his kinsmen and retainers. Bound by ties of blood or oath to follow him, they received in return his complete protection. Never mind that his cousin was a drunken rabble-rouser who had never shown the slightest respect for authority. Colin still felt compelled to try to save him.

But the plan they were counting on was now clearly impossible. Any attempt to enter the Norman stronghold would only result in their own deaths, inevitable against such overwhelming odds. All the courage or skill in the world would not make the slightest difference in the outcome.

"We'll have to try some other way," Colin muttered, his gaze again on the girl. Far in the depths of his silvery eyes, a light flared. "Who do you think she is?"

The older man shrugged. "A noblewoman, that's for sure. D'Arcy's wife maybe. . . ."

"No, she's supposed to be beautiful all right, but with dark hair, not golden like this one."

"Mayhap he keeps a concubine."

Colin laughed, only just managing to stifle the sound so as not to wake the object of his attention. "Not with his wife in the house. She's one of us, not some weak-kneed Norman wench. I warrant she'd have his head if he tried anything like that."

"Then what's left? Unless she's some forest creature sent to enchant us. . . ." Alaric broke off. Like most of his kind, he was deeply superstitious. It was not at all unbelievable that a beautiful spirit might appear to lead them astray.

Colin shook his head. Whoever the girl might be, he was quite sure she was mortal. Slowly, he said, "I've heard talk of a sister . . ."

"D'Arcy's sister?"

"The same. If she is, we may have found the answer to our problem." For the first time since spying the girl, a blatant male grin of anticipation curved his mouth. "Yes . . . she might do very well indeed. . . ."

Before the older man could ask what he meant, Colin rose cautiously from the underbrush. Motioning his thegns to stay where they were, he moved forward stealthily.

No sound warned of his coming. With agility unusual in so large a man, he crossed the small distance between them until he stood close enough to see the slight flush of her high-boned cheeks and the steady rise and fall of her ripe breasts.

His own breath tightened in his chest as he knelt beside her. For a moment he was content to observe beauty greater than any he had ever encountered. But mindful that she might wake at any instant, and that her scream would alert the guardsmen well within sight of the river, he forced his errant thoughts back to business.

The leather jerkin he wore left his powerful arms bare. Bronzed by the sun and heavily muscled, they were a formidable weapon in themselves. He was careful to use only a fraction of the strength he would have brought against a man as he simultaneously covered the girl's mouth and lifted her against him.

Roanna woke to a nightmare. Amber eyes darkened with shock as they focused on the barbaric giant

11

holding her. The uptilted slant of his silvery eyes, his high-boned cheeks, and the sharp angles and planes of his rugged face gave him all the fearful menace of a marauding Viking.

Vividly aware of the warmth of his huge body and the sun-warmed scent of his skin, Roanna lay frozen in his arms. But only briefly. The mocking smile curving his hard mouth turned her fear to anger.

Instinctively, she began to struggle. Her small fists pounded against his steely chest as she tried vainly to twist free of a grip that tightened remorselessly with her every movement.

"Stop that!" Colin hissed. "You'll only hurt yourself." The struggling hellion in his arms amazed him. Everyone knew Norman women were supposed to be insipid, spineless weaklings useful only as ornaments. Where then did this one get the nerve to fight him?

Roanna ignored the warning. She redoubled her efforts to get free, kicking out with long, slender legs honed since childhood by riding and vigorous work around her brother's household. If this English dolt thought he could hold her, he was very much mistaken. A D'Arcy to the core of her being, she possessed the fierce pride and determination that would never let her admit defeat.

Heedless of the bruises she was inflicting on her delicate skin, Roanna managed to turn just enough to get her knee in the most useful possible position. Only Colin's rigorous training and superb reflexes saved him from an injury as painful as it would have been embarrassing.

"God's blood!" he snarled, barely evading the blow, "Alaric may have been right. Perhaps you are the devil's spawn!"

Relentlessly, he dragged her back through the underbrush to where his men waited. They could not quite hide their astonishment at the sight of their lord struggling with a wisp of a girl.

Since reaching manhood, Colin had never been overcome by any opponent either on the training field or in battle. His immense size and strength coupled with superb fighting skills and keen intelligence made him unbeatable. Yet the instincts that demanded he treat her as gently as possible left him hard pressed to hold on to his outraged captive.

Biting down savagely on the hand over her mouth, Roanna tasted blood. She knew a moment's satisfaction as Colin grimaced. Certain that he would pull back from the pain, she took breath to scream. But despite his injury, the pressure of his grip only increased.

"Give me a gag," he grated, "and two lengths of rope."

The men hastened to obey. Within moments, Roanna's arms and legs were secured and a soft, but nonetheless effective strip of material was tied firmly over her mouth. She could breathe easily enough, but no sound other than a small snarl escaped her.

Colin looked down at her with grim satisfaction. In their struggle, her clothes had been pushed up, baring her long, slim legs to mid-thigh. With the thin fabric twisted around her, the ripe swell of her breasts and the narrow span of her waist were all the more evident. Her veil had come off, lost somewhere back where he had caught her, and her glorious hair tumbled free in the sunlight.

Towering over her, he laughed softly as he took in the enraged glare of her golden eyes. She reminded him of a magnificent, high-spirited falcon ready to leap back into the sky at the slightest opportunity. But there would be no such chance for freedom. He had already made up his mind what he meant to do with her, and he was not about to let a mere woman interfere with his plans.

Gesturing to his men to bring the horses, he lifted her easily. Roanna's further efforts at resistence were futile. The slight strength she had recovered since her illness was almost exhausted, and her bonds made it impossible to move. Helplessly, she had to suffer Colin's touch as he carried her to his stallion.

Alaric held her as he mounted, but all too quickly she was laid across the saddle in front of her captor, her body pulled tight against his massive chest. One corded arm wrapped round her back while the other lay insolently across her abdomen near the cleft of her thighs. Lean, brown hands grasped the reins as he gave the signal to move out.

As steathily as they had come, the band of raiders vanished back into the thick forest. Following paths only the most experienced woodsmen could make out, they put swift distance between themselves and the D'Arcy lands.

It was anyone's guess when Roanna's disappearance would be realized. But once the alarm was given, there was no doubt her brother would act swiftly. Colin intended to be well within the walls of his own fortress before that happened.

Roanna remembered very little of the ride. She was too conscious of the man holding her to notice more than the slightest details of their journey. Her heart beat painfully against her ribs as she grappled with fear surpassed only by rage.

Too late she realized how foolish she had been to leave the safety of the compound. The nearness of the guards had not helped her when confronted by an enemy who moved so swiftly and silently as to be all but invisible. Blinking back tears, she thought of her brother and sister-in-law remorsefully. It was all too easy to imagine how anxious they would be. Her impulsiveness would harm far more than just herself.

As to her own fate, she had little doubt that it would be grim. The dress and manner of the man who held her proclaimed him an Anglo-Saxon lord, one of the few to survive the debacle at Hastings. Dimly she remembered something about an ancient English family still holding lands to the north of Guyon's near the Welsh border. If her captor was of that clan, the chances of getting her back unharmed were dim indeed.

Sorrow filled her as she considered that her lack of prudence would be the cause of yet more violence in this blood-soaked country. Though she would most likely not live to see it, Guyon would not rest until he had exacted the full measure of vengeance from those who harmed her. His hopes of being able to rule peacefully would be shattered as he and his men plunged yet again into war.

A low murmur of contrition broke from Roanna, inadvertently catching Colin's attention. He glanced down in time to see the sheen of tears in the amber eyes that were quickly averted from him.

Unable to guess the train of her self-condemnatory thoughts, he presumed she was simply afraid. But the satisfaction he would have expected to find in her dread eluded him. Almost without his being aware of it, his arm tightened around her in a gesture that was oddly comforting.

Long before they reached the Algerson stronghold, Roanna's bound limbs were numb and her back ached mercilessly. What color had been in her cheeks was gone. Despite the balmy summer day, she shivered. But not for the world would she let Colin see her discomfort. When he lifted her from the horse, her eyes were as flat and hard as any determined warrior. Curious onlookers kept a respectful distance as she was carried into the great hall.

Placed at the center of the stronghold where it was surrounded by open fields and a double protective wall, the timber-frame structure was at least two stories high and large enough to hold several hundred people comfortably. Above wood plank walls covered with daub and wattle plaster, the slanted roof was finished with carefully fitted slate tiles and bracketed on either side with stone chimneys.

Around the hall, smaller, separate buildings of similar design housed the kitchens, laundry, latrines, bakery, and brew house. Close to a nearby stream stood a mill, drying kiln, and a large granary. The vegetable and herb gardens and the orchards lent fragrant scents to the soft summer air. From the stables the whinnying of horses, the lowing of oxen and cows, and the baaing of sheep and goats could be heard mingling with the raucous cluck of ducks, geese, and chickens housed in adjacent coops.

All the many functions essential to a large, prosperous community that was almost completely self-sufficient were well represented. Ample room was set aside for the workshops of blacksmiths, armorers, tanners, fullers, wheelwrights, weavers, and seamstresses. A little distance away stood private sleeping quarters for the family and high-ranking guests. Everyone else slept outside under the stars or, during a good part of the year, within the hall itself.

Inside the massive structure Roanna blinked to adjust to the dimmer light. The air was fragrant with the scents of drying herbs hung from the rafters. She could make out a vast expanse of packed-down dirt strewn with clean rushes. Tables and benches were set up in preparation for the evening meal. Against the walls, sleeping pallets and personal belongings were rolled out of the way.

Unlike most of the victorious Normans, Roanna had no contempt for the conquered English. Even without her deep affection for her Anglo-Saxon sister-in-law, she was far too intelligent to nurture prejudice against any people. But she was nevertheless surprised by the ordered luxury of her surroundings.

More than ever she was convinced she must be in

the stronghold of the Algersons, since they were the only surviving family in the area wealthy and powerful enough to maintain such standards despite the new regime.

Several men-at-arms had followed her captor into the hall. Set on her feet in their midst, her bonds at last released, Roanna glanced round warily. The warriors eyed her avidly, making no effort to hide either their appreciation or their curiosity. Only the copper-haired giant frowned as he surveyed her expressionlessly.

Under his scrutiny, Roanna had to fight down the urge to smooth her clothes and hair. Her dishevelement would have troubled her more had she realized the wanton edge it gave to her beauty. Colin found it difficult to hide his response to her, a fact which only worsened his mood.

Scowling, he demanded, "Am I correct in presuming that you are D'Arcy's sister?"

Roanna hesitated. Sheer cussedness made her want to refuse to tell him anything, but she realized her identity might offer the only protection she could find. Surely not even the formidable man before her would be anxious to incur her brother's wrath.

"I am Lady Roanna D'Arcy," she admitted reluctantly. "Who are you?"

Instead of answering at once, the battle-hardened warrior poured himself a mug of ale and drank most of it before looking at her again.

Roanna's brow furled at what she regarded as discourtesy. After the long ride on the warm summer day, she was easily as thirsty. A Norman, she thought stiffly, would have offered a lady refreshment before partaking of anything himself. But not, honesty forced her to admit, if he regarded that woman as an enemy.

In fact, the ale was being drunk more for the pause it offered than for itself. Colin needed a moment to get his contrary thoughts back under control. He had felt a definite twinge of disappointment when the girl confirmed his guess about her identity.

If she had been anyone else, he would not have hesitated to satisfy the urges she provoked. Always presuming, of course, that she could be coaxed into sharing his desire. Colin had no taste for unwilling women, but his considerable expertise had long ago convinced him that there were very few such creatures.

D'Arcy's sister, however, required frustratingly different treatment. Scowling, he turned back to her.

"I am Colin Algerson, Lord of Hereford." A slight, mirthless smile curved his mouth. "And you, my lady, are hostage for the safe return of my cousin, who languishes in your brother's prison."

Long years of self-discipline enabled Roanna to hide her surprise, and her relief. Hostage. That was far better than what she had feared. To be seized for revenge would have subjected her to all manner of horrors. But the taking of hostages by both Anglo-Saxons and Normans was a time-honored ploy well regulated by secular and religious law. The details of her treatment were clearly understood by both sides. Instinct told her that Colin was not a man to ignore the proprieties. For the moment, at least, she was safe.

With the realization that she had less to fear than she had thought came a resurgence of anger. It was all very well for this savage to announce she was a hostage. That didn't mean she would accept her captivity docilely. How dare he so upset her life just when she was once again beginning to enjoy it? She longed to let the arrogant cur know what she thought of him and his plans. If only she were a man. . . .

Roanna's gold-flecked eyes sparked mutinously. Her back stiffened as she drew herself up to her full height, a rather wasted gesture since though she was taller than most women she came barely to Colin's shoulders. For just a moment, the broad sweep of his chest tapering to a taut waist, lean hips, and long, sinewy legs revealed by his short tunic made her forget what she meant to say.

Annoyed as much by her own weakness as by him, she sneered, "I should have known one of your kind would not dare to challenge my brother openly. How much better for you to hide behind a woman's skirts and try to get your way by treachery."

The deliberate insult wrung shocked gasps from the men-at-arms. Their lord was a proud man who did not take any slur to his honor lightly. Hardly breathing, they waited for his response.

Beneath his rugged tan, Colin paled in fury. He took a step forward before reminding himself that she was only a woman and he could not avenge the affront as he normally would. The blow he would have struck any man who so dared to anger him would have snapped Roanna's slender neck.

Unbidden he felt a spark of admiration for her courage. He had expected a Norman wench to be tearfully cowering. Instead he found himself confronted with a gloriously beautiful she-devil who stared at him scornfully and did not hesitate to speak her mind.

So struck was he by the extraordinary combination of loveliness and bravery that, had no one else been present, he might have been tempted to forgive her insolence. But half a dozen of his men had heard the insult. He had no choice but to punish her immediately.

A flick of his hand was sufficient to summon two of the guards. Already regretting her hasty words, Roanna's throat tightened painfully as he said, "You appear determined to make things hard on yourself, my lady. So be it." Turning to the men, he ordered, "Take her to the confinement cell."

Hard hands grasped her arms, pulling Roanna in the direction of the door. She had only a glimpse of Colin's rigid expression, his eyes cold and his manner implacable, before she was yanked from the hall.

# Chapter Two

THE CELL WAS NOT AS BAD AS ROANNA HAD FEARED.
Set some little distance from the hall near the bar-
racks of the men-at-arms, it was a small wooden hut
sturdily constructed and entered only by an iron-stud-
ded door secured by a heavy bar. A tiny window,
also barred, admitted some light along with the busy
sounds of men and women at work in the bailey.

The walls were dry, their daub and wattle plaster
keeping out any dampness. The floor was strewn with
straw, which she inspected gingerly before determining that it was in fact clean. A blanket lay folded in one
corner, but she ignored that for the moment. After
depositing her in the cell, the guards returned with a
pitcher of water, then left for good after slamming the
bolt into place behind them.

For a while Roanna paced the narrow space aimlessly. She was irritated with herself and uneasy at being confined. The long days of her illness through which she had been restricted to her room in her brother's keep had been bad enough. To such a vigorous girl, imprisonment in the tiny cell was almost intolerable.

Drawing a deep breath, she told herself she should be glad it was no worse. The cell that held Colin's cousin was not likely to be as comfortable. Guyon was a just and merciful man, but he was so angered by the poacher's intransigence that he would give no more thought to his well-being than was absolutely necessary. In all likelihood, the prisoner shared his lodgings with rats and various other vermin. Whereas here, no matter how acutely she listened, she could make out no presence but her own.

Toward dusk, her solitude was interrupted by an old woman escorted by the guards who brought her a bowl of stew and bread. The food was hot and smelled enticing. Roanna accepted it gratefully, though her smile was returned only by a grudging nod.

With her stomach filled, some of her anxiety eased. Settling back against a wall of the hut, she smoothed her clothes as best she could and combed through the worst tangles in her hair with her fingers. That done, her eyes began to close. It had, to put it mildly, been an eventful day. With her small store of strength long gone, she slipped easily into sleep.

For several hours the summer night remained balmy. But after the moon set, a chill wind blew up. A current of air pushing out of the northern lands that remained perpetually encased in ice mocked the time of year with its sudden, frigid blast. Roanna stirred restlessly. Without waking, she groped for the blanket and wrapped it around her.

As the temperature continued to drop, peasants in their huts woke grumbling to light fires. Animals in the forests burrowed deeper into their lairs. Such abrupt changes in the weather were not uncommon, but coming after so many weeks of blissful breezes and bright sunshine the sharp cold was a shock.

In the cell, Roanna was losing the struggle to keep warm. Her clothes were thin, and the blanket, which should have been more than sufficient, was instead proving inadequate. Lost in her dreams, she imagined herself back at the keep, ill with the fever that had so weakened her. Tossing on the straw, she wondered faintly why Brenna did not come to help.

In his own quarters, slightly apart from the great hall where most of his retainers lay, Colin slept fitfully. He had retired later than usual, after gently refusing the company of a comely serving girl who had shared his bed several times before to their mutual enjoyment and who made it clear she would like to do so again.

Lying with his arms behind his head on the large bed carved from the trunk of an ancient oak tree, he had hoped to sleep deeply. But the memory of mocking amber eyes, honey-spun hair, and a slender, ripe body kept him from rest. Cursing softly, he tried without success to put his enticing captive out of his mind. But when he finally did manage to sleep, thoughts of Roanna followed him into his dreams.

Deep in the night, he came abruptly awake. His hand reached automatically for the longsword lying beside the bed as he tried to determine what had disturbed him. Moments passed before he realized the cause.

It was cold. Inured to physical discomfort, Colin could not imagine why the sudden change of weather should bother him. Until he remembered the girl in the confinement cell.

A low curse broke from him. Springing from the bed, he crossed the room in rapid strides, pausing only long enough to pull on a tunic. The thegns keeping guard on the palisade grinned at each other as they observed their lord's hasty progress. But their smiles vanished when they heard the angry oath he uttered upon thrusting open the barred door.

Roanna lay crumbled on the hard floor. Her legs were drawn up and her arms wrapped around herself in a futile effort to keep warm. At Colin's order, a guard came running with a torch. By its flickering light, he could see that her skin was ashen and her brow damp with perspiration. She moaned softly when he touched her but showed no awareness of his presence.

Dread stabbed through Colin. The prison he had meant to be no more than a brief, salutory lesson had turned into a deadly menace. Silently he castigated himself for being misled by the girl's brave spirit into thinking her less delicate than she must be. Remorse made him exceptionally tender as he lifted her slight weight and carried her swiftly from the cell.

The private quarters next to his own were kept cleaned and aired for honored guests. By the time he deposited Roanna in the center of the large, soft bed, serving women had scurried to light the braziers and bring fur throws. An old grandmother revered for her healing skills was summoned and set quickly to work brewing herbs to cast off fever and ease breathing.

Colin, who had considerable experience himself in helping the sick and wounded during war campaigns, had no illusions about the seriousness of Roanna's condition. His lean, skilled fingers found signs of swelling beneath her throat. A hand placed below her left breast determined that her heart was beating unusually fast. Since reaching the bower, her color had faded even more and her soft, ripe mouth was already cracked and dry.

Fighting down the foreboding that threatened to paralyze him, he moved swiftly. In any illness of this sort, time was of the essence. Without waiting for the servants who had hurried off to fetch more blankets and extra peat for the braziers, he stripped Roanna's sweat-soaked clothes from her.

The slender, perfectly proportioned body that was thus revealed to him shook even his determined detachment. He had beheld many beautiful women over the years, but never one who so effortlessly moved him.

A wry smile softened his harsh expression as he considered that his heart was now beating at least as fast as Roanna's. His hands trembled slightly as he drew the covers over high, firm breasts whose velvety nipples beckoned his mouth, a tiny waist he was certain he could easily span, and gently rounded hips tapering into slender thighs separated by a cluster of golden curls.

Reminding himself sharply that the girl was ill because of his thoughtlessness, he tucked the furs firmly around her, blocking out all but her lovely face and the tumult of silken hair. When the old woman entered carrying a cup of broth, he was seated beside the bed with one of Roanna's small hands clasped in his.

"Try to get as much of this down her as you can, my lord. 'Tis the best I know for fever."

Nodding, Colin eased an arm around Roanna's shoulders and gently lifted her. With the woman's help, he managed to get a fair amount of the medicine into her. Their patient protested faintly, probably because with her swollen throat it was painful to swallow. But Colin persevered until the cup was empty.

Looking down at the small figure on the bed, the old woman tut-tutted softly. "I've seen this sickness before. Strong men fall to it. But for a girl . . ."

"She's going to recover," Colin insisted tightly. "Whatever it takes."

The old woman was not about to contradict her lord, but she privately thought the lass's chances were slim. Shaking her head, she left the chamber glad that the responsibility was not her own.

In the hours that followed, Colin was forced to consider that the old woman might be right. Roanna's fever worsened steadily. She twisted violently on the bed, lost in her own distorted dreams. Several times he had to restrain her forcibly from tossing off the covers. There was some small satisfaction in the fact that she seemed to respond to his touch and the sound of his voice, but as the night lengthened and she showed no sign of improvement he realized desperate measures would have to be taken.

Near the main well behind the great hall there was a deep pit dug into the ground. At its bottom, wrapped in multiple layers of straw and burlap, lay slabs of ice preserved from the winter. Dispatching several strong men to pull one up, he set the serving women to scouring a large trough. When the ice was smashed into tiny chunks with hammers and picks, cool spring water was poured over it.

Shutting the chamber door firmly behind the last of the wide-eyed servants, Colin lifted Roanna from the bed. He ignored her indistinct protest and determinedly lowered her into the bath.

Over and over he cupped water into his big hands and ran it gently over her dry, heat-infested body. Over and over he spoke to her reassuringly, telling her she would get better, not to be frightened, to trust him and let him do what was necessary.

Long after it had begun, he dared to hope his desperate effort was having some effect. Roanna lay quietly in his arms, her silken skin gleaming with diamond droplets, her eyes closed and her lips softly parted. Her breathing seemed easier and the muscular tension associated with fever had left her limbs. She rested languidly against him, her head cradled by his shoulder almost as though they had just made love.

With her skin now so cool from the bath, it was impossible for Colin to tell whether the fever was abating. Taking a chance that such was the case, he lifted her from the water and gently toweled her dry. Slipped back into the bed, she was covered snugly before he sat down beside her to continue his long vigil.

Too quickly, Colin realized that his treatment had worked but had brought with it another danger. Far from being too hot, Roanna was now shivering with cold. More blankets piled on top of her did no good. She continued to tremble uncontrollably.

Colin stared down at her hesitantly for a long moment before finally accepting what must be done. Stripping off his sandals and the tunic that had become wet from her bath, he slid into the bed beside Roanna. Her slim, petal-soft body fit perfectly against his lean hardness. With a pained sigh, he reconciled himself to an acutely uncomfortable night.

Cradled against him, taking warmth from his body, Roanna at last slipped into restful sleep. Colin had to envy her blissful unawareness as he fought a relentless battle with his own desires. How easy it would be to take advantage of her helplessness. How tempted he was to stroke and caress and taste the feminine perfection next to him until all thought of honor vanished in the firestorm of need.

But the mere thought of taking a woman who could not share the pleasure disgusted him. Whatever his body might wish, his mind overruled it sharply. Comfort and protection he would give her, but nothing else.

Shortly before dawn, Colin managed at last to fall asleep. He lay on his back with Roanna's head nestled into his arms and one slim hand at rest over his taut abdomen. In sleep, their legs entwined and their bodies moved even closer, until they were knit together as intimately as sated lovers.

Roanna murmured contentedly, her breath teasing the burnished hairs of his chest. She was dimly aware of an extraordinary sense of well-being. Not even when she was a child secure in her brother's love had she known such peace. Her eyelids fluttered as she smiled and snuggled even closer.

Turning slightly, her lips brushed a velvety hardness that seemed underlaid by iron. Puzzled, she moved her mouth again, chasing the sensation.

Deeply asleep but by no means impervious to such a caress, Colin moaned. He rolled over, his hand gently cupping her breast. The delightful sensation that darted through her penetrated even the haze of Roanna's slumber. She woke with a jerk.

"W-what . . . who? . . . *Oooh!*"

"Mmmm," Colin muttered groggily. Softness engulfed him. He savored the sweet scent of perfumed skin, the delight of ripe curves and slender limbs, the provocative hardening of her nipple beneath his fingers. Instinctively, he drew her closer, his head unerringly finding the silken hollow between her breasts even as his eyes remained closed.

Roanna froze in shock. What was happening to her? How had she ended up naked in bed with her brash, arrogant English captor? Had he dishonored her? Horror at the thought that she might have been so taken advantage of stiffened every muscle in resistance. Even if the damage was already done, she was

damned if she would let him take his pleasure of her
again.

"Stop it! Don't you dare! You . . . you swine! Cur!
Leavings of a worm! Let me go!"

Colin frowned. Something had gone wrong with his
marvelous dream. The delicious bundle of feminity in
his arms had turned into a clawing, snarling cat. He
opened his eyes warily, only to be struck by the full
impact of exactly where he was and what he was
doing.

"What the hell? . . . Oh . . . Roanna . . ."

"Yes, Roanna! Your so-called hostage! Whom
you're supposed to treat honorably! And instead
you . . . you . . ." Words failed her. Flushing, painfully, she hid her face.

Beating down a treacherous desire to laugh with
sheer relief at her recovered spirit, Colin thoughtfully
finished the sentence for her. "And instead I kept you
warm."

"W-warm? . . ." Very reluctantly, Roanna looked
up at him through thick, golden lashes. Surely she
misunderstood? Her flush deepened as Colin climbed
matter-of-factly out of bed. She refused to give him
the satisfaction of looking away, although the sight of
his unclothed maleness sent shock waves rippling
through her.

Roanna had spent her life surrounded by supremely
fit men who were often seen in various stages of
undress. But nothing had prepared her for Colin.
From the top of his burnished head down broad
shoulders, sculpted arms and torso, slim hips, and
long, corded legs, he was magnificently male.

Only a livid scar running the width of his massive chest marred the perfection of his virile beauty. As he turned to pull on his tunic, her gaze lingered appreciatively on the taut line of his buttocks. A wanton desire to reach out and touch him proved almost impossible to overcome.

"You took a fever," he explained calmly when he was dressed. "I found you in the cell after the weather turned cold. An ice bath got your temperature down, but afterward you were racked by chills no amount of blankets could ease. You didn't quiet down and sleep peacefully until I held you."

A rueful gleam appeared deep within his silvery eyes. "At least you had no difficulty sleeping. I, on the other hand, spent a rather restless night."

Roanna was perversely glad to hear it. Any suggestion that she had lain naked in his arms without the least effect would have offended her deeply. She was about to suggest that he had deserved his discomfort when Colin forestalled her.

His expression had changed as he surveyed the still-pale, fragile-looking girl. He was remembering how she had come to be so ill, and berated himself yet again for being so careless with her well-being.

Sitting down on the edge of the bed, he said quietly, "I am very sorry about what happened. I never meant for you to be more than slightly discomfited by being in the cell. Had I known you were so delicate . . ."

"I am not delicate!" Roanna flared, outraged by the mere suggestion. Relenting a bit, she realized his apology stemmed from genuine remorse. Much as she

32

would have liked to see him suffer for his rough treatment of her, she could not allow him to take the blame for something that was in no way his fault.

"It's just that I had been ill for a while and should not have gone out yesterday. I thought I was completely recovered, but now it seems that wasn't the case." Reluctantly, she admitted, "I probably would have gotten sick again no matter where I was."

Colin looked at her for what seemed like a long time before he murmured, "You are very generous. I could have gone on thinking it was my fault."

"Well, it wasn't, so stop worrying about it."

"I intend to," he agreed, recovering what she had already come to think of as his usual self-assurance. "However, I shall not forget your foolishness in going out too soon. Perhaps your kin have no control over you, but here things will be different." Ominously, he added, "You will do exactly as you are told, including staying in this bed until I say you may leave it."

A dozen angry responses sprang to mind, but for once in her life she had the sense to keep silent. Common sense warned that Colin Algerson was not a man to push very far. Her brother and sister-in-law, who loved her, were susceptible to her whims. But this man . . .

Biting her lip, Roanna realized that she had come around once again to wondering what it would be like to be loved by him. Damn him! He had no right to slip into her very thoughts and make a mockery of her self-control.

Glaring at him, she became aware of a certain quiet

watchfulness in his manner. He was waiting for her to make some outburst, which would provide him with an excuse to enforce his authority over her. Refusing to give him the opportunity, Roanna kept stubbornly silent.

Colin frowned, then shrugged. She was even more willful than he had thought, but he couldn't find it in him to condemn such spirit. With his opinion of Norman women undergoing a rapid reevaluation, he contented himself with a grim reminder.

"Don't forget what I said. Try to move out of that bed and I guarantee your exquisite bottom will be sore for a week!"

He was gone before Roanna could do more than snarl at the blatant reminder of how familiar he now was with her body.

The next few days passed very slowly. By the simple expedient of not providing her with any clothes, Colin made sure his orders were obeyed. Confined to the guest chamber, allowed to rise only long enough for carefully supervised baths during which half a dozen braziers were kept lighted despite the return of summer temperatures, Roanna quickly learned the true meaning of boredom.

She slept as much as possible and ate the delicious meals provided to her, but there were still long hours of the day during which she tossed restlessly under the eye of one or the other serving women set to guard her.

Finally taking pity on her, they suggested all manner of diversions. But Roanna had no fondness for the

usual pastimes of a noble lady. She despised needlework, had a poor hand at sketching, and thought her
inept assaults on the lute or harp should not be
inflicted even on an enemy.

The old woman who nursed her finally allowed her
to help mix medicinal herbs. Since proportions had to
be meticulously measured, she found some distraction
in this task. But it was completed too soon, leaving her
once more at loose ends.

On the third day, Colin at last deigned to visit. His
arrival brought a rush of male vitality into what had
been a purely feminine domain. Roanna had to force
the smile from her lips by reminding herself that he
was the cause of all her problems.

As she barely acknowledged his presence, the serving women scurried away, after making sure their lord
was comfortably seated and did not require ale or
other refreshment.

Crouched in the center of the bed with the covers
pulled up to her chin, Roanna looked him over warily.
Sunlight filtering through the windows burnished his
shoulder-length hair. The bronzed skin stretched tautly
over his lean, hard body shone with health. Sharp
lines were cut into his face, reminding her that though
he was still a young man he carried heavy responsibilities. But his eyes betrayed not a shadow of self-doubt
as he returned her gaze in full measure.

Clad in a sweat-stained tunic that left his powerful
arms and legs bare, he had obviously been working
hard. The wide leather belt strapped around his slim
waist held a longsword. On the other side, a dagger lay

close at hand. She wondered if he had come from the training field, but resisted the urge to ask.

Instead, she demanded coolly, "Have you dared to get in touch with my brother yet?"

Colin took his time answering. He was content to savor the sight of beauty that had haunted his every waking thought and made his dreams endurance contests. She was even lovelier than the image indelibly burned into his brain. The brief smile he had glimpsed in those remarkable eyes made him long to soothe and please her. Wryly he reflected that a man would put up with a great deal to win this one's favor.

His bland response gave no hint of the turmoil of his thoughts. "It took a while to arrange safe conduct for my messenger, but your brother now knows your whereabouts and my demands."

Some of Roanna's bravado faded. Her shame at the worry she was causing her family had not eased. "W-what did you tell him?"

"That you will be released when my cousin is safely returned, and that in the meantime you will not be harmed." More gently, he added, "I told your brother the truth, Roanna. You need not fear you will be mistreated."

Actually, the thought had not occurred to her. Even brief exposure to Colin was enough to assure her of his honor. However much he might hate the Normans for what they had done to his country, he showed no tendency to take those feelings out on her.

Unwilling to reveal how much faith she had in him, she muttered, "There are all sorts of ways of mistreating people. You've left me shut up in here for days with nothing to do!"

The accusation, so sincerely uttered, surprised Colin. The serving women had orders to tell him if Roanna refused to eat or if she showed any signs of becoming ill again. When they said nothing, he presumed that all was going well. But now it seemed she had not enjoyed her leisure.

"But you had only to ask if you wanted something, and it would have been provided."

"Would it?" Roanna scorned. "So far I have been offered pretty pieces of needlework, drawing paper, and musical instruments, the refuges of women who have nothing of worth to offer. Meanwhile, I will wager that everyone else on this demesne is working hard to prepare for winter. Do you have any idea how useless I feel?"

"I don't understand. . . . Are you saying you think I should put you to work?"

"Of course! Anything would be better than sitting around here all day feeling about as lively as an effigy carved on a sarcophagus."

Colin shook his head, more in bewilderment than rejection. "But you are a lady. I cannot work you like some ordinary prisoner."

"I am hardly asking to be put out in the fields! I just want something useful to do."

In her anxiousness to convince him, Roanna sat up straighter in the bed. The sheet slipped slightly, baring her smooth shoulders against which golden curls lay temptingly. Colin stifled a groan. He could think of something extremely useful for her to do, but doubted she would view the suggestion kindly.

Though she had come a long way since his first impression of her as a weak, fearful woman, he could not yet credit the sincerity of her plea. Suspiciously, he suggested, "This desire to work wouldn't have anything to do with some idea of escape, would it?"

Shock widened Roanna's eyes. Was he seriously suggesting she didn't understand the etiquette of being a hostage?

"I am perfectly aware of my position here," she informed him coldly. "You refrain from harming me and in return I don't make trouble. Will your cousin, I wonder, behave as well?"

"I doubt it," Colin admitted, relenting slightly. "He's never behaved well in his life."

"Then why are you trying to free him?"

"Because he is my kinsman, sworn to my service. I have no choice but to protect him. But when he gets home . . ."

Roanna nodded understandingly. "He may wish he was still a captive."

"It doesn't matter what he wishes," Colin said grimly. "He will pay for his foolishness. There are enough problems with the Normans without provoking more."

Roanna did not want to talk about the conflicts between their two peoples. Deftly, she turned the subject back to the matter at hand. "Now, about what I can do . . ."

Colin sighed. "I'm sure your skills are extensive."

Ignoring the sarcasm, she informed him, "I'm very good at preserving foods, spinning, dying, and weaving. I can read and do accounts and . . ."

His rugged face abruptly brightened. "You do accounts?"

Apprehensively, Roanna nodded.

"That's marvelous! I can manage fine with letters, but numbers are always a struggle. More than one good priest gave up on teaching me."

"I suppose you don't have to do them very often, . . ." Roanna ventured, only to have her last hope dashed.

"They've really piled up. I was dreading having to spend the whole winter on them. But since you're here and want to help . . ."

"Oh . . . yes . . . I'd be glad to. . . ."

Jumping up, Colin grinned at her, an action which stripped years from him and gave her a startling glimpse of the boy this hard warrior chieftain had once been. "We can get started right away. Come on."

"Uh . . . I can't . . . my clothes . . ."

A dull flush suffused his lean cheeks. "I forgot. I'll have the serving women bring you something." He hesitated before explaining, "They won't be like your clothes. Our styles are different."

"I know."

It took a moment for him to understand. In the pleasure of seeing her again and realizing that he had an excuse to spend time with her, he had forgotten her family. Of course her Anglo-Saxon sister-in-law would have told her about local fashions, though none of the ladies in a Norman household would wear them. Frowning at the reminder of all that lay between them, he left the chamber quickly.

# Chapter Three

"WHAT MANNER OF MAN IS COLIN ALGERSON?" GUYON demanded, the very softness of his voice betraying his immense rage.

The priest hesitated. He was quite young, pale and quiet of nature, and not eager for confrontation with anyone, let alone a Norman warlord.

Staring at the hem of his brown serge robe, he murmured, "I have always found him honorable, sir. He keeps his word and fulfills all his duties nobly."

Guyon badly wanted to believe the priest. If what he said was true, Roanna was safe, at least for the moment. But how could he be sure? . . .

"If he meant to harm her," the woman standing a little to one side ventured, "surely he would not have sent a message offering to parlay."

41

The priest nodded, pleasantly surprised to discover that the Norman's wife was apparently as intelligent as she was beautiful.

Brenna's gray-green eyes were dark with worry. She had dressed hurriedly, not bothering to veil the silken mass of her midnight black hair. Her delicate features showed the strain of the last few days, but her slender body emanated feminine strength. Gently she touched a hand to her husband's sun-bronzed arm in reassurance.

The Norman towered over her. When he turned, his broad shoulders and massive torso blocked her briefly from the priest's sight. Instinctively, he shifted enough to see the tender look that lit the warlord's amber eyes and softened the hard planes of his face.

It was rumored that Guyon D'Arcy dearly loved his wife and that their devotion to each other had survived many trials in the turmoil of the Conquest. Seeing them together, the priest could well believe it.

Sensing his parents' worry, the little boy in Brenna's arms whimpered. He was only eight months old, but already strong and vigorous. Chubby legs kicked fretfully as he demanded attention.

With accustomed ease, Guyon took his son and soothed him ably. The Norman retainers gathered in the hall were used to the sight of their lord caring for his son in ways usually left to women. But the priest was not. His eyes widened as he beheld a side of the fierce warrior he would never have suspected.

When the child quieted, his father said softly, "If I followed my instincts, I would march on the Algerson stronghold at once."

Several of the knights, always ready for battle, nodded eagerly. But Brenna reminded them all of where such behavior would lead.

"The moment you were sighted, Roanna's life would be forfeit. To get her back safely, we must go slowly and cautiously."

The priest allowed himself a small sigh of relief when he realized the Norman was predisposed to accept his wife's counsel. So softly that only Guyon could hear her, Brenna murmured, "She will not be harmed, my love. I know it."

The words were far more confident than she truly felt, but her husband accepted them gratefully. Still holding Alain, he placed an arm around his wife's shoulders and drew her close. Silently, they offered comfort to each other.

Had the little family been able to see their missing member, they would have been far less concerned.

After a good night's sleep and an ample breakfast to which her restored appetite did full justice, Roanna sat in the corner of the great hall surrounded by sheafs of vellum, a pot of ink, and several new pens.

The clothes Colin had provided fit her far more loosely than Norman fashions, but she found the pleated tunic in deep blue and the richly embroidered white surcoat that went over it to be quite comfortable. It had been on the tip of her tongue to ask how he came to possess such garments when there was no lady in his house. An obligingly garrulous serving woman saved her the trouble.

"When his lordship's sister wed that Irishman last year, he lavished so many clothes on her she saw no

43

reason to take these. They've been packed away in the storage rooms ever since."

"Twasn't fit for anyone here to wear them," the servant explained matter-of-factly. "But for a lady such as yourself, they're perfect."

The woman's ready acceptance of Roanna was not matched by all Colin's people. From the men she had no trouble, since they would not venture more than a surreptitious glance when they thought she wasn't looking. But the women were a different matter.

Some treated her with dignified courtesy, a few were even friendly. Most, however, were clearly reserving judgment. From one of two of the younger, more comely girls there had even been angry glares whose origins Roanna understood quite well.

Colin was rarely out of her sight. He had shared breakfast with her, showed her around his home, answered her questions patiently, and only left her alone when she at last settled down with the ledgers. Even then his absence was brief. After a few hours, he was drawn irresistibly back to her side.

A slight frown furled her forehead as she looked up from the lists she was studying.

"I think you are paying too much for salt."

"Why is that?" Colin inquired mildly, more absorbed by her beauty than any household concerns.

"Look here." She pointed with the tip of her pen. "A year ago the price was half what it is now."

"A year ago there was no war in England. Since the invasion, merchants have felt justified in increasing all their prices on the grounds that there is added risk to them when they travel about seeing customers."

"That's what the spice merchant who came to our keep claimed," Roanna acknowledged. "But my sister-in-law would have none of it. She chafered him down to the standard prices, knowing full well few could afford to buy at all. While she was at it, she got enough to share with others who did not have her bargaining power."

She laughed softly, remembering the scene. "The merchant went away muttering that she had beggared him. But he came back a few months later with more goods to sell, so he couldn't have been too badly hurt."

Colin grinned at the story. But his silvery eyes were serious as he asked, "Can you haggle as well?"

Puzzled, Roanna nodded. "Most ladies are well trained to get the best for our coin. It is one of the duties expected of us."

A moment passed before he appeared to reach a decision. "There is a merchant due here today. If I show you the surplus goods we have to trade, would you deal with him?"

A slow flush suffused Roanna's high-boned cheeks. What he was asking was a task for his wife.

"Is there no one else? . . ."

Colin shrugged. "I did it myself last time, with the results you see." A teasing smile softened his hard mouth. "As in Normandy, men here are not trained in such things. I have no difficulty identifying the best iron for weapons or knowing which leather is suited to saddles. But when it comes to—"

"To more practical matters," Roanna interrupted caustically. She was sick to death of men's incessant preoccupation with fighting. "When it comes to keeping yourself and others fed and clothed, you end up being robbed."

If she had expected Colin to take offense, she was disappointed. He merely shrugged philosophically and pressed home his point. "So you will see the merchant for me?"

Unable to think of a graceful way out, Roanna accepted reluctantly. No matter how well she did, she knew some in the stronghold would find fault. But she was determined that Colin at least would not be disappointed. Sparing a moment's pity for the unsuspecting trader who had no idea what he was about to confront, she began to list the supplies needed for winter.

By afternoon, when the train of carts and mules passed through the main gate, she was ready. The merchant's arrival was greeted with great excitement. Children swarmed around the wagons, eagerly speculating on what might be inside each barrel and bundle. The women kept a close eye on them to make sure they didn't touch anything even as they listened avidly to the merchant's assurances that he had brought the finest quality of all the most desired goods.

When the trading for the great house was done, they would have their own chance to acquire what small luxuries they could afford to ease their lives. Only the men stood a little apart, betraying no great interest in what was going on, though they missed not a word.

When Colin greeted the merchant, the man

launched immediately into a paean of flattery well honed from much practice. But his host might have been deaf for all the notice he gave it. Cutting short the discourse, he brought the trader over to Roanna and introduced them.

"I have the honor to present the Lady Roanna, who will be dealing with you for me. My lady, this is Malcolm of Durham, Winchester, and various other places. He has a glib tongue and a sharp eye, but I trust you will have no difficulty with him."

Roanna was already sure of that. She recognized the man well from traders she had dealt with in Normandy. He was small and wiry, with a weather-beaten face and sharp black eyes she had no doubt had seen everything at least once.

Unlike some of his less wily compatriots, he had the sense to dress plainly. His fustian tunic and un-bleached shirt could be seen on almost any freeman. Somewhere securely hidden away he undoubtedly possessed a household that would arouse the envy of any wealthy burgher. But on the road he maintained a modest air which did not fool Roanna for a moment.

"Ah, my lady," the man intoned unctuously, "what a delightful surprise. I had no idea his lordship had married."

The object of his hastily proferred congratulations did not even have the grace to look embarrassed. As Roanna silently fumed, Colin said blandly, "Oh, her ladyship is not my wife. She is a hostage being held because of a dispute with her brother, Guyon D'Arcy."

Under other circumstances, the merchant's reaction would have been humorous. He turned ashen and his hands shook as he darted a disbelieving glance from one to the other. The hard glitter of Roanna's amber eyes convinced him.

"D-D'Arcy? . . ."

"You've heard of him?" Colin inquired impassively.

"Uh . . . yes . . . in fact, I was going to his keep next. . . ."

"Splendid. Then you can carry a letter from the Lady Roanna assuring her family of her well-being."

Such unexpected thoughtfulness melted Roanna's anger. She smiled gratefully, unaware of how her already remarkable beauty was thereby magnified.

Colin swallowed hard, fighting against the desire to cover those ripe, moist lips with his own and taste the hidden sweetness of her mouth. Taking his leave hastily, he did not see Roanna's gaze follow him with a poignant mixture of bewilderment and frustration.

To give the merchant credit, he recovered himself quickly. By the time she had ushered him over to a side of the bailey where the surplus goods were laid out, he had developed a strategy for dealing with her. Or so he thought.

"I am sure you are eager to dictate your letter, my lady. So if you will just leave me to decide what these goods are worth . . ."

"Hardly," Roanna snorted. "We might as well understand each other from the beginning. I have seen the prices you charged his lordship the last time you were here. They were far too high. If you have any thought of a repeat performance, you may turn your train around and depart right now."

The merchant's mouth dropped open. Hasty words of outrage formed on his tongue, only to be painfully swallowed. The look in Roanna's eyes was one her brother's men would easily have recognized. It was exceedingly bad judgment to challenge any D'Arcy in such a mood.

"Please . . . my lady . . . I assure you, I am an honest man. I ask nothing but fair trade for my goods."

"Then we shall get on famously," Roanna assured him drily. "I will begin by listing Lord Colin's needs for the winter, then you can show me what you have to meet them. That done, I am certain we will have no trouble arriving at a mutually agreeable exchange."

The merchant had no choice but to acquiesce. Glumly, he listened to her explain what would be bought, managing to hide his surprise when she read the list herself. Literacy was an invaluable asset in his business, but not one he cared to share with his customers.

"I would like to see the salt first," Roanna instructed, "since that is the largest requirement."

At the merchant's signal, an assistant opened a large sack. Roanna inspected it carefully. After tasting a pinch, she placed it in the palm of her hand with a swirl of water to make sure the grains were not of different weight. When they floated to the bottom at the same speed, she nodded.

The merchant, believing she was convinced of the

quality, smiled, only to have his satisfaction smashed when she said, "The sample from the top appears pure. I will take another from the bottom. While I am doing that, you may open ten more sacks to be likewise tested."

Blustering, the merchant complained, "There is no need!"

"Perhaps you are too honest to know that unscrupulous traders mix sand with salt to drive up their profits?" Roanna suggested, her tone making it clear she thought nothing of the kind.

Since this was exactly what the merchant had done, he could only curse his back luck at encountering so astute a customer. Gesturing to the assistant, he ordered the sack retied and had others brought from beneath a tarpaulin.

"This is the salt you want, my lady," he said resignedly.

Roanna did not agree until she had dug a hand through each sack and made certain that the contents were pure. Then she smiled sweetly. "Now, as to the other spices . . ."

There was no further attempt to show poor quality goods. The merchant brought out the finest seasonings and preservatives he possessed. Cloves, cinnamon, and nutmeg from the East passed before Roanna, along with mace, turmeric, and saffron. She made her selections judiciously before going on to consider the other foodstuffs the merchant carried.

"This wine has not aged long," she commented after taking a sip. The merchant nodded resignedly, only to be pleasantly gratified when she added, "However, I believe a few more months will see it smooth and dry." Considering the size of the household and the general preference for ale, she decided to buy a modest amount for holidays.

Bags of rice were inspected next. This new arrival from the East was being well received in England. It stored easily and was versatile in cooking. The merchant had both white and brown, and Roanna agreed that equal parts of both were most useful.

His supply of dried fruits was rather less than she had hoped, but the quality of apricots, raisins, currants, pears, and plums was excellent. Considering them essential to the maintenance of health during winter when there were no fresh fruits available, she was ready to buy all he had. But first they had to agree on the worth of the goods she had to trade.

Despite all the upheaval of the last year, Colin's vast sheep herd had produced an outstanding crop of wool. Luxuriously thick with a high oil content that would make for soft, sturdy cloth, it was worthy of gracing the looms of the most discerning weavers.

But the merchant claimed otherwise. "It is well enough, I suppose, to make rough clothing and blankets."

"His lordship does not pamper his peasants with cloth fit for kings," Roanna shot back. "But if you are not interested . . ."

"I did not say that!" the merchant interposed quickly. "Perhaps with proper treatment, it could be made acceptable."

"I do not doubt there are many weavers among the Walloons, Flems, and others who could work such magic."

"I might be able to find a buyer," he admitted reluctantly.

"I should think so, considering that the supply of English wool is greatly reduced due to the fighting and the looms of the Low Countries are going begging for lack of it. Now, what will you offer?"

An hour later, the merchant rubbed his face wearily. Seldom could he remember such a long, hard battle with any customer. The Lady Roanna was remorseless. She might trade wool herself, so well did she understand its value.

And when it came to the dried fish that was the estate's other major surplus product, she was no less knowledgeable. The barrels of cod, eel, salmon, and haddock that were prized on the continent brought their weight in trade goods.

As the afternoon drew to a close, the merchant had to be content with a fair profit, nothing more. Certain that she had gotten the best possible bargain, Roanna went off to write her letter. That proved far more difficult than the hours of chaffering.

She began with a heartfelt apology for her impulsiveness, which had caused the present predicament, then went on to assure her brother and sister-in-law that she was being looked after so well that they had no reason for the slightest concern. Ending with a plea for their forgiveness, she sent them her love.

Finishing the letter, Roanna left it unsealed. She

presumed Colin would want to make sure she had written nothing about the number of men-at-arms in his stronghold or its fortifications, information highly useful to her brother should he be driven to attack.

Going in search of him, she was quickly drawn to the training field, where dozens of men were hard at work refining their fighting skills. In deference to the warm summer day, they had stripped down to their loincloths to wrestle, practice archery and wield the immense battle swords on which their lives all too frequently depended.

The sight of nearly naked men grunting and straining, their powerful muscles and sinews rippling with their exertions, was nothing new to Roanna. She barely noticed them as she stopped at the edge of the field, shading her eyes to look for Colin.

The breath caught in her throat when she spied him. Towering above all the other men, his huge, supremely conditioned body glowed with the healthy sheen of sweat. Not an ounce of fat marred the perfection of his form. Yet he could hardly be called spare. His vast shoulders and chest looked more than capable of crushing any opponent. The hard ridge of sculpted muscle along his taut waist gave way to a flat abdomen beneath which the loincloth left no doubt as to the vigor of his masculinity. Long, sinewy legs were covered in the same golden fur that glistened on his chest and arms.

Roanna's brief glimpse of him in her bower had not prepared her for the piercing effect his body had on her. She was helpless to avert her eyes, even when

Colin caught sight of her and dropped out of the drill. As he walked swiftly toward her, her mouth went dry and tremors quaked through her.

So caught up was she in trying to control her startling response to him that she did not notice Colin was waging the same battle. His slate gray eyes were narrowed, revealing nothing, as they swept over her.

"Have you finished with the merchant?"

"Uh . . . yes, we're all done. I think you'll be pleased by the bargain . . . at least I hope you will be." Impatient with herself, Roanna struggled to ignore the remarkable sensations curling through her. Standing this close to him, she could feel the warmth of his bronzed skin and had to fight down the urge to reach out and touch him. Her hand jerked as she offered him the letter.

"I thought you would want to read this before it is sealed."

Colin glanced at the missive without taking it from her. His rugged features softened slightly as he asked, "Have you written something you should not have?"

"No, of course not!"

"Then there is no need for me to read it."

This further proof of his faith in her touched Roanna deeply. She stared up at him, trying to discover what it was about this man that affected her so powerfully. With his mane of coppery hair licked by the fires of the sun, and his quicksilver eyes, he was undeniably handsome. Even without such pleasing features, the lithe grace of his lean, heavily muscled body was enough to attract any woman.

But she had met many men in her nineteen years

who were almost as handsome and compelling. Not one had managed to penetrate the wall of her reserve. Colin did so effortlessly.

As she thought about it, Roanna realized there was no great mystery to her feelings. Despite the violent circumstances of their meeting, Colin had shown himself to be a man of both great strength and gentleness. Added to these qualities was an underlying sadness that she did not doubt stemmed from the pain of his people's defeat and his fierce determination to do all he could to help them even in the face of great adversity.

The combination of power and vulnerability was overwhelming. Roanna found herself longing to offer him both comfort and surrender. Having no true conception of her beauty or of the gentle strength of her nature, which was in every way a feminine match to Colin's own, she could only pray he might return some small measure of her interest.

In fact, she had no idea of the longings she set off in her captor. Remembering all too clearly the perfection of her unclothed body, he was now confronted by the knowledge that his desire for her went far beyond the physical. She spoke to every level of his being, and he was almost helpless to contain his response.

Forcing himself to remember the constraints of honor, Colin withdrew to find some hard, draining exercise followed by a dip in a pond fed by icy mountain streams. But not before inviting Roanna to share the evening meal with him in the great hall.

Dazed by the sheer impact of his nearness, she did not at first notice the serving girls on the edge of the field who had watched the entire exchange. Only when they laughed softly did she look up, straight into their knowing, slightly mocking eyes. Ladies, one murmured to the rest, were not so different after all.

Roanna's back straightened. She met their gaze calmly. Her head was high, her lovely features composed. She said nothing, but no words were needed.

After a moment, the serving girls looked away. Unspoken was the admission that there were indeed great differences between themselves and the proud, confident lady they confronted. The bond of their common womanhood did not erase the fact that only one of her station could fully understand and share their lord's arduous, demanding life.

When she returned to her bower, Roanna found fresh clothes laid out and hot water for a bath. She lay in the tub for a long time daydreaming, until her toes and fingers began to wrinkle and she was reminded of the passing hour. Rising, she toweled herself dry before vigorously brushing her hair until it shone like polished gold.

The lavender tunic she donned fit perfectly, as did the violet surcoat. A gasp broke from her as she realized the tunic sleeves and neckline were embroidered with pearls. No serving woman alone could have decided to bring her such opulent garments. They must be by Colin's instructions. Had he considered that she might feel a little out of place among his people and sent her the garments to give her confidence?

Telling herself not to read more into the gesture than was meant, she finished her preparations hurriedly.

There was no mirror in the room, so she could not see how the glowing colors of the garments complemented her coloring or how even their loose fit did not disguise the perfection of her body.

The hall was already crowded when she arrived. Men and women milled about, exchanging greetings and the gossip of the day as they waited for their lord. Following local custom, they would occupy separate tables with each group free to discuss its own pursuits.

Roanna presumed she was to sit with the other woman, but as soon as Colin arrived he indicated otherwise. Taking her arm lightly, he led her to the high table he shared with his most trusted retainers.

The large, burly warriors eyed her cautiously. It had been a long time since they had had a lady in their midst. Their lord's manner toward her was all that was needed to keep them on their best behavior. But in fact, Roanna was hardly aware of their presence. All her senses were absorbed by the man seated beside her.

His hair glowed like flames in the light of torches surrounding the hall. A clean, fresh smell mingled with his manly scent. He was dressed more formally than she had yet seen him. Above the buckskin trousers that emphasized the sinewy muscles of his thighs, he wore a shirt of finely spun wool dyed hunter's green. Across his massive chest, an intricately carved gold chain proclaimed his status as a warrior chieftain. Roanna's gaze was drawn irresistibly to the mythical beast in the center of the chain, whose challenging stare at once taunted and coaxed her.

"I trust you are hungry, my lady," Colin said softly as he studied her no less intently.

"What? Oh, yes . . ."

"I thought you would be after working so hard today."

"But I didn't . . . That is, it wasn't especially difficult."

"The bargain you wrested from the merchant says otherwise. Thanks to you, we have all we need and more for a comfortable winter."

Modestly, Roanna tried to convince him that it was the exceptional quality of the estate's produce that had won the bargain. But Colin would have none of it. He insisted the credit was all her own and showed his appreciation by serving her himself when the platters of food were brought round.

She possessed a healthy appetite, but his idea of what she could eat far surpassed her own. She had to dissuade him from piling her trencher of bread with all manner of poultry, fish, ham, and vegetables. The wine he kept pouring into her goblet proved as good as what she hoped her new purchase would become, and she enjoyed it thoroughly.

The talk throughout supper was of estate matters. Colin gently drew her into the conversation as he and his retainers talked of the need to winnow the livestock before winter, secure the peasants' huts against the storms that were bound to come, and dam the nearby river lest it flood again.

When she proved knowledgeable about all these matters, the men began for the first time to speak to her directly. Several asked questions about the Norman way of handling such tasks, but there was nothing in their manner to suggest they thought the conqueror's approaches might be better than theirs.

On the contrary, Roanna found in them the same deeply rooted pride her sister-in-law always showed, an inherent confidence that made it possible for them to accept the ways of others when they proved more successful without losing any of their own dignity.

Ruefully, she considered the immense task King William had set himself when he decided to absorb these people into his sphere of power. Though the Conquest appeared to be going all in favor of the invader, she suspected it was the native English who would eventually triumph.

Certainly much would have to change before both races accepted each other, but it seemed likely that when the dust settled it would be the Normans who adapted more than those they claimed to have vanquished.

Still there was a tacit acknowledgment on the part of Colin and his men that in certain areas the Normans were more advanced. As Roanna listened, it became clear that the Algerson thegns and the higher ranking housecarls who held responsibility directly from Colin were training to fight from horseback in the manner that had so savagely defeated them at Hastings.

The Anglo-Saxons traditionally used horses only to travel, not for combat. They were unprepared for the cavalry charge of William and his knights, which turned the tide of battle and assured the success of the invasion. Next time they went against Normans, Colin and his men would be prepared to fight just as effectively.

Curiosity aroused, Roanna wondered if he had been at Hastings. She knew that despite the English defeat and the death of King Harold, some of the force had survived. Finding no acceptable way to raise the question, she thought she would have to be content with speculation. But that did not prove to be the case.

When the last dishes were cleared away, the hall grew quiet. A white-bearded old man who had shared the high table moved a stool to the center of the room. A little boy approached with a lute, which he carried reverently in his small hands.

Accepting the instrument, the bard sat down. In the flickering glow of the torches, he appeared to throw off the weight of his years. Vitality emanated from him as his fingers lovingly caressed the strings.

A ripple of liquid light sang through the hall as the last whispered conversations died away.

Satisfied with the sound, the bard began a traditional ballad extolling the virtues of fallen heroes. The final verses honored those who had perished at Hastings. As was usual, he had tailored the song to his audience. Men of the Algerson forces who had perished in the fray were praised in words which brought tears to the eyes of the women and caused the men to swallow hastily.

Nor were those who fought and lived forgotten. Roanna learned that at the height of the battle Colin had led his men into the thick of fighting in a last, desperate effort to save their king. Grievously wounded by a Norman ax blow across the chest, he had fallen to the ground unconscious and near death.

So severe was his injury that the advancing Normans presumed him killed and left him alone. In the final moments of the battle, as the slaughter of the English reached its peak, several of his retainers managed to carry their lord from the field. Their loyalty and courage were praised, but so was the immense strength and fortitude Colin showed. Against all odds he had managed to regain consciousness and lead his men on a forced march home to secure their lands against the advancing enemy.

Roanna was no more immune to such painful memories than anyone else in the hall. Her eyes were damp as the song faded away. More than ever, she felt a stranger among those who had suffered so greatly at the hands of her people.

# Chapter Four

BUT BY THE NEXT DAY MUCH OF THE UNEASE SHE HAD felt in the hall had passed. Colin invited her to go hunting with him. Moreover, he paid her the compliment of asking her along not on a genteel hunt with falcons or a romp after deer but on a serious search for a wild boar. The animal, an oversized male with razor-sharp tusks, had killed several of the peasants' sheep and injured a child. Even for armed men on horseback, he was a formidable quarry.

Roanna agreed eagerly. Besides the sheer pleasure of being with Colin, she looked forward to the hunt itself. Several times she had asked her brother to take her along on such an expedition, but he had always refused, citing the dangers. Since he did not often place restrictions on her, she could not resent his concern too much. But she was glad Colin seemed to have greater faith in her strength and ability.

Still, he did feel constrained to caution her as they left the stronghold. "Stay in the center of the riders and let your horse have her head. She's a good distance runner with sound wind."

Roanna nodded, patting the mare's neck affectionately. She had expected a good mount, if only so she would not hold the hunt back. But the sleek chestnut was something special. She had great spirit, yet was well behaved. Only the slightest touch was needed to guide her.

It occurred to Roanna that on such a horse she could make a bid for freedom, but she dismissed the thought at once. Besides the sense of reluctance that filled her at the idea of leaving Colin, she knew full well that he would be able to ride her down without effort.

Past the fields surrounding the Algerson stronghold, the land was thickly forested. So dense were the trees and so thick the foliage that little sunlight penetrated. The damp, murky darkness made Roanna apprehensive. She did not really believe that spirits dwelt in such places, but one could never be sure.

Far into the forest, they were surrounded by the fecund scents of burgeoning life. Birds fluttered overhead as small ground animals darted through the underbrush. On every fallen log, moss and lichens grew in rich abundance.

Where the trees briefly thinned, patches of wildflowers and berries welcomed the sun. The steady plop-plop of water silvering down the hillsides to collect in lily-padded ponds was one of the few sounds to punctuate the muffled stillness.

Riding beside Colin, she took comfort from his nearness. He wore only the usual trousers and a leather jerkin that left his powerful arms and much of his massive chest bare. So tall was he that several times he had to stoop to clear branches the other men passed under easily.

The stallion moved beneath him with agile grace. They were so perfectly suited to each other as to seem a single being, the epitome of strength and virility. Yet the forelock of coppery hair that fell across his brow gave him an oddly endearing quality Roanna could not resist. It was fortunate that her mount was so well trained and did not need her guidance, for her attention was firmly occupied elsewhere.

An hour into the hunt, a series of low grunts from just ahead brought them up short. Peering through the forest gloom, they could make out the shape of an immense boar rooting around a fallen log.

Catching their scent, the animal raised its head. Small, yellowish eyes glared at them. Snorting, it shook itself hard as cloven feet pawed the ground.

The horses shied nervously. Few wild animals would stand and fight mounted men, but the boar was an exception. Its lethal tusks could rip out the throat of a stallion, sending its rider crashing to the ground to be similarly dispatched. Even when confronted by several hunters, such contests did not always end with the boar's death.

Roanna held her breath as Colin signaled his men to keep back. Dropping the stallion's reins, he slid easily from the saddle. The boar, surprised by this tactic, backed up slightly. Fangs glowed in the pale light.

Keeping a careful eye on the animal, Colin drew a spear from his saddle. It was the only weapon capable of killing with a single blow. Arrows or even a war sword had difficulty penetrating the hide that was tougher than any leather. But the lance also required extreme agility and perfect aim. Few men would attempt to use it in such a deadly confrontation.

Roanna had to bite her lip to keep from crying out a warning that would have been as distracting as it was useless. Her knuckles were white against the reins as Colin and the boar began warily to circle each other.

The animal was cannier than most of its species. It did not charge at once but waited patiently, sniffing out its opponent's weaknesses. Several times he lurched forward in mock attack that could have caught Colin off balance and left him open to the ripping tusks. But he was not fooled. When the boar at last launched itself into the air, he was ready.

Colin held his ground through a heart-stopping eternity, up to the very instant when the immense animal was almost upon him. Only then did he twist lithely to the side, the spear held rock-steady and his large body braced to take the boar's full weight.

The animal's front paws were lifted to grip and tear, its underbelly exposed. Colin moved forward on one foot, just enough to drive the lance home. A hideous shriek rent the forest air, shaking the very branches of the trees. Blood spurted over his arms and chest. Ignoring it, he held on grimly. Before it hit the ground, the boar was dead.

The men roared their approval. Few things pleased them more than such evidence of their lord's prowess. It reaffirmed the wisdom of their service to him and reassured them that whatever strange changes might be stalking their land, they were still right to follow him.

Only Roanna remained mounted as the rest of the company surged around the fallen beast, exclaiming on its fierce size and praising Colin's courage and skill.

He accepted their approbation patiently until his gaze focused on the white-faced girl. Leaving his men, he stepped quickly to her side. Gently, he pried her cold fingers loose from the reins and held her small hands in his own.

"Are you all right?"

Roanna nodded tautly. Her voice was little more than a whisper. "I thought you would be hurt. . . ."

Something flickered in the silvery depths of Colin's eyes. His hold on her hands tightened. One calloused finger stroked the inside of her smooth palm.

"There are those, my lady," he murmured, "who would say you should wish to see an enemy hurt."

A quiver of warmth coursed through Roanna. Helpless to tear her gaze from him, she could only whisper, "Are we enemies?"

Colin had no answer, or at least none he cared to give. He was silent as they began the trip home. The boar was tied to the back of an extra horse brought along for that purpose. Dead it appeared every bit as huge and impressive as it had alive. There would be great rejoicing when the peasants learned they no longer had to fear its attacks.

No part of it would be wasted. After it had been bled and scalded, the bristles would be scraped away for use as brushes. The hide would find service in the leather and chain mail armor that protected all the men-at-arms. From the sinew would come lashings and bindings for arrows. The tusks and hooves would be carved into ornaments. Sausages would be made from the intestines, hams and roasts from the meat.

But above all the memory of its killing would remain to be told and retold whenever the people felt the urge to acclaim their lord. Colin was still a young man, but there were already a multitude of such stories about him, which his clan was pleased to relate.

About to top the last rise before the stronghold, his keen eyes caught the faint movement in the brush ahead of them. Reining in, the men-at-arms kept their hands on their weapons as their lord called an order to whoever it was to come out at once. There was a moment's hesitation, then a low rustling as a small, fearful group of men, women, and children crept from their hiding places.

There were perhaps a dozen of them, all dirty, ragged, and clearly showing the effects of long hunger. Some clutched pitiful bundles, others seemed to have nothing but what was on their backs.

One of the men moved forward hesitantly, his eyes fearfully downcast. "Your pardon, my lord, we do not mean to come on your land uninvited. But we have fled the Normans since early spring when they burned our homes and killed most of those in our village. Our food is gone, our women and children cry out for shelter. We have nowhere to go."

"What was your village?" Colin demanded, his face hard.

The man named a hamlet near the coast. As he did so, a small sound of recognition escaped Roanna. She had heard her brother speak of the place, complaining bitterly that the Norman warlord to whom it was given had no care for the people and loved killing above all else. The mute evidence of children almost skeletal in their thinness, women so weak as to hardly be able to stand, and men on the last precipice of desperation left no doubt in her mind as to the horrors they had endured.

"That was a holding of the Cormac clan," Colin said. "What happened to them?"

"The lord and his sons died at Hastings, sir. His lady and the daughters fell into the hands of the Normans. I know not their fate."

Perhaps not, but it was all to easy to imagine. Roanna could not escape the obvious comparison with her own treatment as Colin's captive. Her face was ashen as she listened to him quietly instruct the man to lead his people to the stronghold.

"You will find rest and food there." Cutting short their heartfelt expressions of gratitude, he added, "If you prove willing, you may swear loyalty to me and join my people. The Normans do not come here, but if they do be assured their greeting will be different from what they have met elsewhere. You will be expected to fight."

Determination flared in eyes that a moment before were flat and dull. "Only give us the chance, my lord! We will serve you well."

Colin nodded, waiting until the refugees fell in behind them. He set a slow pace the rest of the way to
the stronghold, but even so the bedraggled group
would not have managed to keep up had not the
women and children been allowed to ride. Roanna
nestled a tiny girl in her arms, vividly aware of the
child's fragility. Though the day was warm, she took
the precaution of wrapping her cloak around her and
was rewarded by a tiny sigh of contentment as the
small survivor nestled closer.

The people who rushed out to meet them as they
passed through the gate seemed little surprised by the
refugees. Others of their kind had come before and
been taken in. Their lord turned no one away in this
time of need. They were quickly absorbed into the
milling crowd rejoicing at the successful hunt.

Lifted from her saddle by Colin, Roanna would
have preferred to seek the privacy of her bower. Once
again she felt the burden of her race acutely. But his
firm arm forced her to stand with him as he shared his
people's pleasure.

She was unaware of the longing that lit her face as
she looked up at the tall, powerful man beside her.
But her absorption did not go unnoticed by some in
the crowd, who glanced at each other knowingly.

After the celebration of the kill, matters turned more
serious. Roanna was caught up in the household
preparations for winter. While she did not push herself
forward, she did make it clear she wanted to help.
After some initial hesitation, most of the women
accepted her.

Despite all the sorrow of the last year, they were a

fundamentally kind and generous people. If their lord wished to treat her as an honored guest rather than a hostage, they were willing to do the same. The skill she showed and her capacity for hard, steady work quickly won over most of those who were at all reluctant to accept her.

Before long, she was busy with a multitude of tasks. At mid-week, Colin found her inspecting a vat before pouring in the mix of water and hops that would produce the heady ale everyone favored. He stood for a moment staring at her before she was aware of his presence. When she straightened at last, her face slightly flushed and her hair in disarray, he had to force himself to remember what he had come to tell her.

"I have heard from your brother. I thought you would want to know what he said."

Roanna nodded stiffly. It was bad enough suddenly to find Colin looking at her with a very intent gleam in his eye without also being reminded of her status in his household. The thought that Guyon might have agreed to release the hapless cousin filled her with dread.

Her breath left her in a rush as Colin said, "There is no possibility yet of an exchange. We have merely agreed to talk."

Did she detect a note of relief in his voice? If so, it was swiftly concealed. Critically, he observed, "Your brother seems unconcerned about any fear you may feel. Otherwise, he surely would not have left you here."

Bristling at this criticism of he who had always been

70

dearest to her in all the world, Roanna snapped, "My brother knows he can count on me to be strong." She did not add that she understood why he was seizing the chance for negotiations. Unlike many of his fellow Normans, Guyon did not consider the surviving Anglo-Saxon nobility to be enemies. Rather he hoped for an accord that would allow both groups to live together in peace and when necessary, even defend each other from common foes.

Grudgingly, Colin admitted, "Your letter must have reassured him."

"As it was meant to. You have said I am safe so long as your cousin remains unharmed, and I see no reason not to believe you."

He could not quite suppress his pleasure at this evidence of her trust. His harsh features relaxed somewhat as a different kind of tension grew within his hard, lean body. Almost without his being aware of it, he took a step toward her.

"Roanna . . ."

This was the time to make some lightly jesting comment that would break the mood. But she was helpless to do so. Instead, she could only stare up at him, her entire being caught by the silvery depths of his eyes and the heady promise of his nearness.

When his large, calloused hands reached out to touch her gently, she made no effort to pull back. Her body slipped as naturally into his embrace as though it was the one place she was most meant to be.

Several times in Normandy, Roanna had allowed herself to be kissed by young lords eager to win her favor. She had done so not out of any yearning for their touch, but in simple curiosity. Despite their undoubted expertise, she had come away still baffled by what compelled men and women to behave in such a fashion.

Now in a single instant the mystery began to unravel. The first touch of Colin's lips against her own sent fire spiraling through her body. All pretense to modesty vanished before the overwhelming need to know more of what he was clearly willing to teach her.

The gentle pressure of his mouth was enough to make hers open willingly. Enveloped in the warmth of his powerful arms, she trembled as strong, knowing hands slid down her back to draw her even closer. A fierce surge of pleasure tore through her as she felt Colin's huge body quiver in response. Joyful at the realization that he was not immune to her, Roanna welcomed the first tentative thrust of his tongue with unbridled eagerness.

A low groan broke from him as his restraint snapped. Avidly he took the full sweetness she offered, savoring her to the utmost. Pressed so closely together that not a breath of air could move between them, they luxuriated in their exploration of one another.

Roanna found quickly that she loved the taste and scent of him. The clean, slightly musky aroma of his skin sent ripples of delight coursing through her even as the flavor of his tongue and mouth drew her like nectar.

All thought of anything beyond the quiet, sun-dappled hut vanished. There was no world beyond his embrace, no consideration of anything but Colin and the extraordinary sensations he was making her feel.

Just as the spiraling waves of pleasure threatened to erupt beyond all control, he drew back. His breath was ragged and a dull flush shone on his high-boned cheeks.

"I didn't mean . . . Roanna, you intoxicate me. . . ."

No force on earth could suppress the giggle of purely feminine delight that slipped from her at this admission. Heady with the burgeoning sense of her womanly power, she moved against him temptingly.

"D-don't . . ." Colin grated.

The strong arms that had held her so tenderly a moment before were now pushing her firmly away.

"You don't realize what you're doing," he muttered thickly.

On the contrary, she knew exactly what she was about. In Colin she found exactly the combination of male strength and gentleness allied to intense sexual attraction that she had always sought. The heady combination was more than she could resist, nor could she think of any good reason to attempt to do so.

Dimly in the back of her mind she remembered the deep well of pain and rage that lay between his people and hers. But she pushed that thought aside as determinedly as she tried to move back into his arms.

Colin thwarted her efforts remorselessly. He could not hope to hide the full state of his arousal, but not for the world would he give in to it. Honor and pride, so essential to his very life, demanded that he resist.

His only refuge lay in mockery. Cuttingly he said, "What would your brother make of this scene, my lady? Surely he would find it difficult to accuse me of violating you when you are so clearly heedless of your own behavior."

Roanna flushed painfully. She pulled away from him as though burned, blinking rapidly to hide the sheen of tears that turned her amber eyes to glistening gems. But the effort was not in time to keep Colin from seeing how badly he had hurt her. Remorse filled him, even as he told himself he had no choice.

With her slender throat clenched so tightly as to make speech almost impossible, Roanna just managed to murmur, "You have a strange sense of propriety, my lord, considering what passed between us when I was ill. But rest assured, I shall not risk offending you again."

Briskly she turned from him. Her head was held high as she added, "I really should thank you for reminding me of my position here. Until you hear from my brother, I will remain in my quarters."

Before Colin could make any response, she hurried away, her graceful stride taking her quickly from his sight.

A moment later a young boy passing the hut was startled to hear a low string of virulent oaths accompanied by the solid thump of a large fist being pounded against the wall in sheer frustration.

Through the remainder of that day and the next, Roanna stayed in her bower. Her absence was noted by several women who brought her food and inquired with genuine concern about her well-being. Touched by such thoughtfulness, she nonetheless remained determined not to be misled again.

Colin's cruelty had forcibly reminded her of the gulf between them. The contented sense of belonging she had felt for a too brief time was now exposed as no more than an illusion.

Alone in her quarters, Roanna grieved for the loss of something that she sensed she would never find again in her life. She withdrew into herself just as she had during childhood when her brother's frequent travels made it impossible for him always to offer the comfort and reassurance she needed in their turbulent world. In the solitude of her soul, she found strength, but also profound loneliness.

Matters were no better outside. Colin's regret had blossomed swiftly into outright misery. He berated himself as an unfeeling cur. Never before had he been at a loss in dealing with any woman. Holding them in genuine affection and regard as he did, he had become used to having those sentiments returned. The women he had known intimately had understood the game of love as well as he did, and played it with equal relish.

After years of enjoyable if superficial experience, he suddenly found himself plunged into a situation he could not control. His feelings for Roanna touched a core of his being no one else had even glimpsed. The overwhelming desire she provoked was at once exhilarating and frightening.

He was tempted to take the safest route and keep the greatest possible distance between them, but two days of that was enough to task his endurance to the utmost. Telling himself he was merely worried about her, he made his way gingerly to her bower.

Roanna was preparing for bed. She wore a soft, almost sheer gown of pale blue that emphasized the glowing beauty of her skin. Seated on a bench near the bed, she ran a comb of carved oak through her hair, heedless of the silken purity of its lustrous strands.

Much of her stubborn hurt had faded. But there remained a pensive sadness that all unknowingly made her appear even more poignantly lovely. When Colin knocked, she presumed it was a serving woman and only just remembered to cover herself with a cloak before opening the door. His sudden appearance, as though materializing directly from her thoughts, took her aback.

"Oh, it's you . . . I thought . . ."

Taking note of her garb, Colin hesitated. "You are about to retire. I can speak with you tomorrow."

"No! That is, I am not at all sleepy. If you would like to talk now, I would prefer it."

After brooding about him for two days, she was not about to let him walk away. Still it took all her persuasion to convince him that she did not consider his presence an intrusion and that she could stay awake long enough to hear what he had to say.

Politely offering him the bench, she perched on the side of the bed. All her concentration was required not to think of the circumstances that prevailed when they were last together in the chamber.

The forest green tunic Colin wore in no way hid the

sculpted strength of his body. She had all she could do not to drink in the broad sweep of his shoulders and chest, the rippling muscles of his arms, the long tapering line of his waist and hips ending in sinewy legs. It amazed her that so large a man could move so gracefully and act, when he chose, with such gentleness.

Longing to heal the rift between them, she gave no thought to how she appeared to Colin. The fading light turned her hair to spun gold and cast delicate shadows across the hollows of her face and throat. Clad only in the fragile gown and cloak, she was as beguiling a picture as any man could wish for. Their seclusion in the bower strained his self-control to the limit.

Swallowing hard, he murmured, "There is no reason for you to remain in here. I know you are upset about what happened, but you must believe that I did not mean to hurt you. In fact, I only spoke as I did to protect you from harm."

Leaning forward on the bench, he stared at the big hands clasped between his knees as he added, "What I did was clumsy, but well meant."

Roanna, having had a chance to think over the events in the hut, could not help but recognize the truth of his words. She had acted impetuously without consideration of the probable results. Any man she had ever met, other than Colin and her brother, would not have hesitated to take full advantage of the situation.

The memory of her wantonness made her blush. Anxious that he not think such behavior was normal for her, she said, "It is I who must apologize. My actions were . . . out of character. . . ."

That was the closest she would come to expressing any regret. The joyful awakening he had sparked within her was too precious to be denied for any reason. If he chose to think badly of her, she would just have to bear it.

But Colin, far from condemning her, was even more enchanted. At last he had found a woman whose courage and intelligence equaled her beauty. Had she been of his own people he would have lost no time winning and wedding her. But she was part of that hated race whose very name spurred anger in the heart of every Englishman. Staring at her in the velvety light of the fading day, he struggled to remember that he must not think of her in any other way.

Yet he could not suppress his pleasure when she appeared in the bailey the following morning. As she crossed the edge of the training field, their eyes met and held. A surge of happiness rose within him at her quick smile followed by shyly lowered eyes.

Hours later he would remember that smile and curse himself for forgetting the difference between friends and foes.

# Chapter Five

"HIS BODY WAS SEEN BY MANY, MY LORD. THERE IS no doubt he is dead."

The freeman spoke with quiet assurance. He knew the words he brought were greatly unwelcome, but he understood his duty and would not shirk it.

A low murmur ran through the hall. The sudden arrival of the messenger had brought retainers and their womenfolk to hear what he had to say. Colin would have preferred to see him in private, but he did not get the chance. Barely had the man slid from his saddle when he blurted out his news.

The laggard cousin was dead in the Norman keep. His body had been seen by Anglo-Saxon servants, who quickly spread the word to the nearest freeman farmer they knew could be trusted. The man had ridden hard to bring the news to the Algerson stronghold.

Rage burned through Colin, not because of his cousin, whom honesty forced him to admit was a scant loss, but because of the untenable position suddenly facing him. How could any man, even a Norman, callously throw away the life of a woman such as Roanna?

That her life was forfeit could not be doubted. By every understanding of the role of hostages, he had the right to inflict on her precisely the degree of punishment suffered by his cousin. His people would certainly expect him to do so.

When the guards approached Roanna in the weaving hut she greeted them without apprehension. She had no premonition of danger. When they took her by the arms, gruffly informing her that she was wanted in the great hall, alarm darted through her. But not until she saw the openly hostile stares of some of the men and women gathered around Colin did she begin to feel genuine fear.

"We should have known better," muttered a grizzled warrior. "Normans have no honor. They'll betray anyone."

He said it loud enough to be heard by the crowd, who nodded in agreement. Roanna flushed at the insult, but remained prudently silent as she was led to the front of the vast room where Colin waited.

The urge to shake off the guards and demand to know what was going on almost overcame her. Only the implacable, brooding look in Colin's eyes stopped her.

He stood with his legs planted slightly apart and his arms crossed over his massive chest. So large and solid was he that he looked like a huge rock no force could ever topple. She was hard pressed to reconcile this with the gentle, considerate man she knew.

"My cousin is dead at your brother's hands," he announced abruptly. "All guarantees of your safety are ended."

Roanna whitened in shock. Her stomach lurched sickeningly. Painfully aware of the condemning glares from every side of the hall, she only just managed to hide her horror.

"I do not believe you. My brother is a man of honor who has never betrayed his word. Your charge is false."

A gasp rippled through the gathered men and women. Surely such effrontery would be dealt with in the harshest possible way? They leaned forward, eager to see what their lord would do.

The color had left Colin's cheeks as abruptly as it did Roanna's. Grim-faced, they stared at each other. Treacherous admiration rose within him as he considered her extraordinary courage. Here was a woman any king or prince would be proud to call his own.

He could think of no man who would dare to confront him so resolutely, let alone a woman whose more vulnerable body made her an easy target for the most brutal revenge. For all the concern Roanna revealed, she might have been standing in her brother's keep surrounded by loyal knights pledged to protect her.

Realizing at last the vivid interest of their audience, Colin moved swiftly to ease the tense situation.

"You have heard what has happened and you see that the Lady Roanna is still among us to pay for her brother's crime. When the matter of punishment is decided, you will be informed. Until then, return to your tasks."

There was a brief mutter of discontent from those most anxious to see blood shed, but many gathered in the hall found themselves remembering how much the Lady Roanna had helped them and how smoothly she had adapted to their ways. Faced with the prospect of seeing her suffer, they were not eager to linger.

It took only the slightest prodding from the men-at-arms to clear the hall before they too discreetly vanished. Colin and Roanna were left alone in the vast, echoing chamber, confronting each other across a space of several feet that might have been miles.

For a long moment, she studied him in silence. The days they had spent together had revealed so much that she could only marvel at her earlier misconceptions about him.

The man she once thought of as a marauding barbarian was in fact the epitome of everything she had ever hoped to find in a lover, friend, and husband.

The silvery eyes that at first glimpse seemed to glitter with deadly intent were actually the windows to a highly complex and intelligent mind. The rugged features that had appeared the skilled but unfinished product of a master sculptor revealed rare strength and resolve. Even the huge, infinitely masculine body that so stirred her possessed, upon more careful scrutiny, a certain vulnerability that made her long to reach out to him.

But the gulf between them was still too great, and growing larger by the moment. Unless she acted quickly, they might well be lost to each other. Even if, as she suspected, he returned her interest, his cousin's death made it even less possible for them to observe the usual proprieties between a man and woman. Some other way had to be found.

The half-formed plans that had occupied her thoughts over the last few days abruptly coalesced into firm intent. He was the only man to master her heart; she would not give him up without a struggle.

Quietly, Roanna asked, "Do you intend to kill me?"

The blunt question so calmly voiced stunned Colin. There were depths to this woman he had only begun to glimpse. Hiding his horror at the mere thought of what she dared to express, he hedged, "I have the right."

"Only if my brother has done as you charge. I know he has not."

"You cannot know that. You were not there."

Roanna remained stubbornly insistent. Though her skin was ashen and her knees trembled, she appeared utterly confident. "I do not have to see what happened to know the truth. My brother is a man of honor. Moreover, he would not willingly endanger me for any reason."

The certainty with which she spoke of her brother

angered Colin. Though he had never met the man, he thought him unworthy of such esteem. Further, he found himself unaccountably jealous of what was clearly no more than a normal brother–sister relationship.

Angrily, he reminded her, "You could have been freed days ago if he had been willing to release my cousin. Instead, he left you here and killed him."

Even this did not shake Roanna's confidence. "He left me here because he wanted an opportunity to negotiate with you, not just about your cousin but about all manner of mutual concerns."

Quietly, she added, "If you were interested only in your cousin's release, why did you agree to talk? The exchange could have been made without you and my brother ever meeting."

A gleam of respect shone in Colin's silvery eyes. It was impossible to put anything over on her. He was foolish even to try.

"It is true your brother and I face certain common problems. This seemed a good opportunity to discuss them."

"Understanding that, you still believe he would throw away both my life and the chance of an accord with you simply to punish a drunken poacher?"

"Men do not always act rationally," he reminded her, believing he spoke from personal experience since his behavior of the last few days had been anything but rational.

"The only time my brother has behaved with less than perfect reasonableness is around his wife, whom

84

he loves to distraction." She could not resist the impulse to add, "Brenna is English, as you may know, yet their devotion to each other surpasses all other considerations. They have not allowed the sorrow of Hastings to dim their happiness."

Challenged by her words, Colin growled, "You speak lightly of Hastings, without knowing anything of it beyond the gloating stories of Normans."

"I know far more than that," Roanna insisted. "Both my brother and sister-in-law were there, and they have told me of it."

"Your sister-in-law?" Colin could not hide his dismay at the thought of a woman on that blood-strewn battlefield.

"She went there seeking her husband after they were separated before the invasion. Perhaps some day I will tell you their story . . . if I have a chance to do so." Summoning all her courage, Roanna reminded him, "You still have not said if you mean to take my life."

The question was deliberately provoking. She was daring him to confront feelings that were still new and unexpected enough to be threatening. Colin found it difficult to meet her eyes. Never before in his life had he shied from a challenge. But in this case, with this woman, he found himself curiously unwilling to accept the truth.

"My people expect me to exact revenge."

Roanna paled a bit more, but did not give way. She continued to face him determinedly, her slender body held straight and firm, her features composed. Only the slight tremor of her rose-hued mouth betrayed her trepidation. Deep inside, she understood the time had come for a final, desperate gamble.

"Then if I am to die, I have a favor to ask first."

The pretense had gone far enough. Colin could not bear for her truly to believe he meant to harm her. About to assure her she had nothing to fear, he was abruptly and shockingly forestalled.

"I do not wish to die a virgin."

The cavernous spaces of the great hall must somehow be distorting sounds. For a moment it had sounded like she said . . .

"Did you hear me?"

"No," his voice grated sharply even on his own ears. "I don't think so."

Roanna sighed. It was going to be even harder than she had thought. But not all the embarrassment in the world would make her turn back now.

"Surely you understand how I feel," she ventured softly. "I do not wish to leave this life without experiencing what is reputed to be one of its greatest joys."

Colin could feel the heat rising in his face, matched by the sudden acceleration of his heartbeat. Her frankness stunned him as much as the burgeoning possibility that the desires which had tormented him since their first meeting might not be his alone.

"Do you truly understand what you are saying?" he demanded, grimly pleased that he managed to keep his tone harsh when everything inside him was exploding with exhilaration.

Drawing on a legacy of courage stretching back

generations, Roanna managed to meet his eyes. If he wanted it spelled out, so be it.

"I am saying that I would like you to make love to me."

The words out, their full impact struck her. She was violating every moral teaching of her upbringing because of this man who had so inextricably entered her heart and mind. To have him also in her body, she was risking all. If he scorned her, everything vital in her would shrivel and die.

"I have shocked you," she blurted hurriedly. "I can see that. But it doesn't change anything. There is no point in saying more."

With the last vestiges of her pride, she managed to walk calmly from the hall. Not even the perplexed stares of the people who saw she was unguarded made her hesitate as she concentrated solely on reaching the privacy of her chamber. If Colin did not come to her . . . No, she would not think of that. She would think only of how it would be when they were at last together, free of all that had so far kept them apart.

The serving woman hesitated when Roanna asked for hot water to bathe, but despite what the woman knew about the sudden deadly turn of events, she could think of no reason to deny the request. Especially when the young girl had long since earned her affectionate regard.

When some of the other servants grumbled at the task, she reminded them of how hard the Lady Roanna had worked to help them. The prompting was enough. Complaints ceased as buckets of steaming water were poured into the wooden tub set in the center of the bower.

With hands that trembled, Roanna pulled off her clothes. She had no idea how much time, or how little, she might have, but her own impatience made it impossible to delay.

Pinning her hair up, she rapidly soaped her slender form, lingering for a moment on the gentle swell of her breasts as she thought of Colin's touch there. Her niples hardened reflexively. Breathing deeply to still the rapid beat of her heart, she dried herself swiftly on a soft length of wool.

Before she slipped a thin silk gown over her head, she considered herself critically. For the first time she wished she conformed more closely to the traditional standard of beauty.

Her hair was far too golden and lustrous to match the silver gilt tresses celebrated by troubadours and love-stricken young men. Her skin, warmed by the sun and touched by a smattering of freckles, bore no resemblance to the alabaster purity every lady was supposed to possess. Her eyes were too large and the wrong color, she thought regretfully. And her full mouth did not look at all like the small, pale lips poets sang of.

Above all, her body distressed her. Though a lifetime of healthful exercise had kept her slim, she had not the slightest chance of being mistaken for one of the wand-like creatures praised as the height of female grace.

Her breasts were too large, her waist too sharply indented, and her hips too rounded. There was nothing insubstantial about her. Nothing that evoked the spiritual thoughts held to be the only truly worthwhile consideration of man. Instead she was vibrant with the promise of sensual delights.

Would Colin find her wanting? Would he be displeased by her earthy curves and the hungry demand of her body she could not conceal?

Consolation came with the thought that he had already seen her unclothed. Surely if he did not desire her, he would never have kissed her as he had or allowed her to leave the hall without firmly rejecting her outrageous request.

Honesty forced her to admit she hadn't really given him a chance to say no. Perhaps he was even now shaking his head over her extraordinary immodesty before going off to his own bed, not necessarily alone.

Anger brought an added glow to her high-boned cheeks. She had seen the appreciative looks of certain serving girls following him as he trained with his men or worked around the stronghold. There was no doubt he was a man of healthy appetites and, she suspected, considerable skill. The girls' fond smiles were enough to confirm that. Perhaps one of them was being invited into his bed at that very moment. . . .

Jumping up, Roanna paced back and forth across the small chamber. Unexperienced though she was, she would fight any woman for Colin Algerson. But how to get the chance? She could hardly go in search of him and make her intentions obvious to all. Instincts old as time warned that she had gone as far as she possibly could. Colin might be angered or flattered by her startling request, but if anything more was to happen between them, he had to take the lead. For both their sakes, the next move had to be his.

Admitting this, the thought that he might take another woman to slake the desire she was certain she had seen in his silvery eyes enraged her. Her pacing grew more anxious as the moment passed.

Outside the bower, Colin paused. He had nurtured the half-hearted hope that she would forget the whole crazy idea and go to sleep. But the light he saw burning through the narrow window and the shadow cast by a slim figure moving back and forth told him she had not.

Sighing, he girded himself for what was easily the most difficult task of his life. Men had been canonized for less, he thought grimly, as he knocked on the heavy wooden door.

Not waiting for Roanna to answer, he opened it and slipped inside. His people were curious enough without learning of this meeting. Not until the bolt was slipped into place behind him did he turn to confront the girl who had stopped stock-still at his entry.

Such was her nervousness that it was just as well Roanna had no idea of how she looked. Her pacing had restored her hair from its anxiously combed perfection to its usual tumult of glistening waves. The glow of the braziers behind her shone through her thin gown, turning it almost transparent.

Colin was painfully aware of the dark, inviting crests of her full breasts, the tiny span of her waist, and the enticing thrust of her hips and thighs shadowed by a golden triangle.

Swallowing hard, he reminded himself that he was a chieftain and a warrior. It was unthinkable that a woman should make him lose control. Determinedly ignoring the urgent pulsing of his loins, he forced himself to recall why he had come.

"Roanna," he began gently, "I cannot have you thinking that I intend to do you harm. If my cousin was killed, some punishment will have to be exacted, but you will not be involved."

A surge of deep pleasure ran through her. He was everything she had believed and then some, even if he was a tiny bit gullible.

Daring greatly, she took a step toward him. The time for pretense was gone. However he reacted, he had to know the truth.

"I never thought you would harm me, Colin. Although you believe you have the right, perhaps even the obligation, you are far too gentle a man to hurt someone weaker."

All the color fled from his features, only to come rushing back as he began to suspect the meaning of her words. "But then, why did? . . ."

Another small step further narrowed the distance between them. He became aware of the scent of her skin, lilac mingling with spice. His senses swam dizzily as he grappled with her astonishing revelation.

"There is so much hatred to separate us," Roanna said softly, "and so little to bring us together. Yet I find I cannot bear the thought of being apart from you. I don't understand what is happening to me, but I do

91

know that in these few days since we met you have become as necessary to me as air or water. I do not want to lose you."

The admission made, Roanna fell silent. Her eyes lowered, missing the vast wave of love and tenderness that swept over Colin. As she waited, hardly daring to breathe, he took the last few steps needed to bring him to her side.

Suddenly overwhelmed by the immensity of what she was doing, Roanna looked up fearfully. "Do not mock me."

A short laugh broke from Colin. It was himself he mocked for his total inability to master the situation. His hard mouth touched hers tenderly as he murmured, "I can do nothing but cherish you."

There was so much she wanted to say; that he should not think badly of her boldness, that she did not expect any commitment from him. But the words died in her throat as Colin bent toward her.

The world became a place of shimmering flame and rippling sensation. Unlike the first time he had kissed her, this time he held nothing back. All the vast need he at last admitted to was poured into his caress. He wanted nothing so much as to immerse himself in the sight, scent, and touch of what seemed the other half of himself for which he had searched all unknowingly throughout his life.

Roanna trembled in the massive arms that held her so protectively. The warm stroking of his tongue inside her mouth roused her to almost unbearable pleasure. The rampant yearning of his body communicated itself unmistakably. Huge hands slipped down her back to cup the firm curve of her buttocks, urging her against the proof of his desire.

Tension unlike any she had ever known uncurled in her loins. Her thighs burned and above them, in the secret place of her womanhood, she felt herself grow hot and moist. Surprise spiraled through her. There were forces in her she had never before suspected, which were only now awakening to full, demanding life.

With her body clasped intimately to his, Colin waged a last, futile battle with himself. Every particle of conscience he possessed told him he must put her from him. Every primitive drive essential to the sustenance of life told him that if he did so, he would perish. Never, not even in the fury of battle when death was a constant specter at his shoulder, had he been so single-mindedly determined to survive. Without her, all honor, pride, and purpose dwindled to insignificance.

But not even his desperate need could prevent him from assuring that she understood his feelings. Huskily, he murmured, "Roanna, if we had met at any other time, I would have done everything in my power to court you properly and win the approval of your family. You would have become my wife with full observance of all the proprieties. But we both know that is not possible." Echoing her thoughts of a short time before, he said, "We must find another way for I love you far too much to face life without you."

Joy turned Roanna radiant. Golden flecks shone in her thick-lashed eyes. A becoming flush warmed her cheeks as her arms came up to caress the silken fire of his hair. Wonder trembled through her. "Then show me, Colin. Please."

The man wasn't born who could resist such entreating. Lifting her gently, he crossed the room in swift strides. With infinite tenderness, he laid her on the large bed covered by a down-filled mattress and soft blankets. His touch never left her as he slipped down beside her.

His hands gently smoothed her hair as he nestled her into the curve of his arms. After long, tender moments, he asked huskily, "Do you understand what happens between a man and woman when they love?"

Roanna nodded hesitantly. She knew she was far better informed than most unmarried women of her class. She had grown up surrounded by kind, sensible guardians who saw no reason to make a mystery of anything so fundamental as sex. But she was just now discovering that knowing about something was not the same as doing it.

A shiver of inadequacy ran through her. Colin was undoubtedly accustomed to experienced, skillful women. What if he thought her clumsy or boring?

The man who held her so tenderly did not miss the trembling of her body, nor did he misjudge its source. A smile touched his hard mouth as he considered how much more confident she would be by morning.

"Good," he murmured softly, "then you know there is nothing to fear. What will happen between us is natural and beautiful, I promise you that. Now I want you to promise me something in return."

Wide-eyed, Roanna stared up at him. He was so

close she could see the molten glints of his eyes, the shadowy planes and angles of his face giving way to the firm line of his mouth and jaw. Longing to reach out and stroke the faint scar above one eyebrow, she murmured, "Promise what?"

"That from this moment, you will consider yourself my wife in every way and as such you will withhold nothing from me. If anything displeases or frightens you, you will tell me at once. Later we will fully share the joys of lovemaking, but this time your pleasure is far more important than mine. I want this to be perfect for you."

Roanna opened her mouth to protest, to tell him she cared far more for his satisfaction. But the words were stopped by lips hard and demanding against her own.

"Promise."

The word echoed in her mind as big hands cupped her breasts, the thumbs rubbing with sensual roughness against her nipples. Shivers of rapture undulated through her.

Helpless, she nodded.

# Chapter Six

NOTHING IN ROANNA'S IMAGININGS HAD PREPARED her for the heaven Colin took her to.

He did not, as she expected, remove her clothes at once and lay her on her back. Rather he seemed determined to prolong the slow buildup of desire until she teetered on the sharp edge between pain and pleasure.

For long moments, he did no more than kiss and caress her gently. His warm, searching mouth explored the delicate line of her jaw before slipping up to nibble lightly on her ear lobe. Unerringly he found the ultrasensitive pulse points of her throat and savored each. Only then did he at last honor her wordless plea and bring his mouth to hers.

She learned the feel of his probing tongue and the taste of him, the way his rougher skin teased the softness of her cheeks, the lean strength of his fingers that stroked all around the curve of her breasts while refusing to return to the thrusting nipples that throbbed for his touch.

Through the thin fabric of her gown, she could feel the straining hardness of his manhood. Men in such a state, she believed, were impatient to satisfy their desire. But Colin was clearly in no such hurry. He laughed throatily at the little purrs coming from her as he slowly slipped the gown from her shoulders. When it rested on the peaks of her breasts, he tilted her head back and smiled tenderly.

"You are so beautiful, my love. Like a dream come to life."

To him the words seemed inadequate. They said so little of what he truly felt about the loveliness of her body and spirit. But to Roanna, they were exactly the reassurance she needed at that moment.

Nor did he stop there. As each portion of her body was slowly revealed, it was gently, tantalizingly savored until she thought she would go mad from the delicacy of his touch. Still fully clothed, Colin bent over her reverently. Never before in his life had he so delighted in a woman. Not even the burning ache of his fully erect penis could hurry him to completion. Oblivious to the discomfort that was increasing with each moment, he indulged in a full, unbridled exploration of her.

Roanna moaned brokenly as her small hands pulled at his tunic. She desperately needed to feel his flesh against her own. The warm wetness of his tongue circling her nipples made her arch wildly. When he at last pulled the straining peaks within his mouth to suckle them gently, she writhed beneath him, the smooth softness of her thighs instinctively parting.

Colin's hand slid down across the silken curve of her belly. His fingers tangled in the honeyed curls, stroking the slight mound before slipping gently between the satiny folds of her womanhood. A groan of delight tore from him as he found her warmly moist.

Rising slightly, he quickly stripped off his clothes. They fell forgotten beside the bed as their bodies lovingly entwined.

Despite the red haze of rapture engulfing her, Roanna was not content to be only the recipient of pleasure. Her hands roamed over him at will, discovering the bulging muscles of his shoulders and back, the taut line of his waist and hips, the hard contours of his buttocks.

Nor was the rest of her body still. Her breasts, brushing against the velvety steel of his chest, relished each sinewy contour. A tiny gasp escaped her as she encountered the long, straining hardness lying hot against her. Tentatively she moved her leg, touching him with the inner softness of her thigh.

An agonized gasp tore from Colin. He had at all cost to prevent her from arousing him further. One more brush of her flesh against him and he would have no choice but to enter her swiftly.

Determined to prevent that, he slid lower in the bed, Roanna murmured in protest, until she realized what he intended. The murmur turned to a gasp of shock.

Gently but inexorably Colin forced her legs wide

apart. Big hands squeezed her buttocks as he lifted them high enough to slide a pillow beneath her.

Some remnant of modesty made her realize that she was now fully exposed to his gaze. She tried to draw her legs together, but Colin would not allow it. Holding her open, he explored the silken cleft of her womanhood with his eyes and hand.

When she was twisting frantically on the bed, soft mews tearing from her, he allowed his finger to circle the tiny entrance to her lingeringly before slipping carefully inside. Her passage was gratifyingly wet, but also small and tight, and he could easily feel her maidenhead.

He had hoped that with the vigorous life she led, the barrier would be thin and fragile. But instead it firmly resisted the slight pressure he applied.

The reminder of her vulnerability to pain was sufficient to restore his hard-pressed control. Slipping an arm beneath her hips, he held her firmly. The downy curls were brushed aside as he found the hidden bud glistening with her desire. Carefully, he touched the calloused tip of his finger to it, pressing gently in a slow, circular motion.

Roanna bit down hard on her lip to stifle a scream, found that she could not and was forced to let it out. The sound exalted Colin. Her sensuality thrilled him. Achingly aware of how much trust she must place in him to respond so unrestrainedly, he moved to taste her intimately.

Roanna's head jerked up, stunned surprise darkening her amber eyes. "Oh, no! Don't . . . !"

"Oh, yes!" Colin laughed. He held her immobile as she struggled.

In the small part of her mind still capable of thought, Roanna was shocked that he would want to touch her like that. With all the superstitions she knew men harbored about menstrual blood and other womanly mysteries, she had thought her private places would be felt only by his manhood. Now realizing what he intended, she was terrified that he might find her taste or smell displeasing. Far too innocent to guess how exciting Colin considered both, she could only twist futilely in his hold.

"Y-you said you would not do anything . . . if I-I asked you not to. . . ."

For a brief moment conscience warred with certain knowledge. He *had* promised her. . . . But on the other hand, she could not begin to suspect how he could make her feel.

"Roanna, trust me. You'll find this very . . . pleasant. . . ."

*Pleasant?* Surely he must know how far beyond simple pleasure he had already taken her? Her body felt about to explode into a thousand shimmering fragments. The sensation both awed and frightened her. Once more she tried to close her legs.

Colin hesitated, but only for an instant. Carefully yet with resolute intent, he bent her to his will. His strength was so overwhelming that there was no possibility she could escape. Her eyes glistened briefly with frustration, but the tears vanished as waves of ecstasy undulated through her.

Her knees were bent, her small, perfectly formed

feet resting over his shoulders. His arms were stretched between her limbs, holding her in exactly the position he wanted, his hands grasping her buttocks. Implacably he lifted her into his caress.

At the first touch of his tongue against her, Roanna cried out. Surely she could not survive this. Her body was turning to molten flame. She was an incandescent being swept by an ever increasing firestorm of rapture. The muscles of her abdomen clenched spasmodically. Her back arched, her head tossing widely.

That tiny, hidden part of her that she had been only distantly aware of was swelling into radiant life. The soft tissues beneath it tightened with exquisitely building tension that could be freed only by his touch. But Colin withheld it. He savored her everywhere else, but not until she was almost delirious with need did he bring her to release.

As gently as he had with her nipples, he first licked and tasted her before drawing her into his mouth. His teeth raked carefully at the soft, palpitating bud as his tongue flicked over her relentlessly.

Roanna's hands grasped his massive shoulders in desperation. Nothing mattered except to somehow hold onto him as the world quaked through long, powerful shudders that built and built until at last the pressure could no longer be sustained. The explosion shattered her very sense of herself. She was hurtled far from consciousness to a realm where there was no thought, reason, or restraint. Only absolute, blinding ecstasy that left her at once utterly satisfied and drained.

It was almost too great an effort to open her eyes,

but when she did so she was rewarded by the sight of Colin smiling down at her with infinite tenderness. He looked highly pleased with both himself and her.

"I suppose it would be ungentlemanly to say I told you so."

"I might manage to forgive you," Roanna murmured breathlessly. She had traveled such a great distance that she could hardly believe she was back in the quiet room with the man who had taken her to such ecstasy. The expression in his eyes made her throat tighten. It was so . . . loving. . . .

Sitting up slightly so that she could see him more clearly, she smiled shyly. "I'm beginning to understand what all the fuss is about."

"Just beginning?" he whispered, his lips moving against her throat.

"Well . . . I might need a few more lessons."

He was relieved to hear it. After the intense orgasm she had just experienced, she might have wanted only to sleep. If that were the case, he would be left in acute distress. But instead she seemed to more than eager to continue. Silently thanking God for sending him such an incredible woman, Colin drew her closer.

Roanna's eyes widened in surprise. Not crediting what she had felt against her thigh, she reached a hand down hesitantly. The long, thick hardness it encountered amazed her.

"Oh! You're still . . . I mean, you didn't . . ." Flustered, she broke off. Her mind told her she was behaving with incredible immodesty and should remove her hand at once. Some other, far stronger voice told her the time for modesty was long passed. She kept her hand where it was.

Colin's huge body shook with joy at her touch. Gently, reassuringly, he moved his own hand over hers, showing her how best to please him. She caught on instantly, and was delighted by the results. Fascinated at being able to stir him so, she was disappointed when Colin abruptly moved away from her.

No vestige of prudery remained to prevent her from protesting, "I don't want to stop. . . . Please . . ."

"We aren't stopping," he assured her huskily. "But I want to be inside you now." Roanna's instinctive skill made his need urgent. His self-control was on the verge of shattering.

"Oh . . ." The words shivered through her. Of course, he would want that. And suddenly she found that she did too, very much.

The moment she had heard girls speak of with so much dread passed in such gentle beauty that Roanna could scarcely believe it. Lying above her, Colin carefully opened and stretched her passage before moving to take her fully. He caught her tiny cry, far more of pleasure than of pain, in his mouth as he thrust slowly and cautiously within her. The barrier so weakened by his gentle touch and by the ecstasy he had already given her broke easily.

With his weight supported by his arms and legs, Roanna was free to move beneath him. She caught his pace quickly, her hips rising and falling with each exquisite stroke.

The full possession of her body was so enticing that

Colin knew he could not endure much longer. To his delight, he found he did not have to. The hot, moist velvet sheathing him began to contract in long, slow undulations.

Groaning with pleasure, Colin took one rosy nipple into his mouth, suckling it with the same rhythm of his manhood moving within her. Not even the ecstasy Roanna had experienced a few minutes before had prepared her for the explosion of joy that tore through her now, made all the more intense by the knowledge that this time Colin was with her. Together they found the furthest limits of rapture before drifting slowly back to earth.

"Yes," she murmured a long time later when she was at last able to speak. "I finally understand why this is so popular."

"I'm delighted to hear it," Colin teased. "Otherwise, I wouldn't be sure you had enjoyed yourself."

Blushing, she took a playful swat at him. "You look rather content yourself."

"Far more than that." Bantering gave way to loving sincerity. "You are the woman I have longed for all my life, but had almost given up all hope of ever finding."

Tears of happiness turned Roanna's eyes to shimmering topazes. Utterly satisfied, she snuggled against him. They drifted off to sleep entwined in each other's arms.

After such exertion, they might have expected to slumber through the night. But their bodies had other ideas. The moon was still high in the sky when hunger of a different but no less compelling sort woke them.

Giggling like children, they scampered into their

clothes and made their way to the kitchen occupying a long wooden building next to the great hall. The watch guards who noted their progress hand in hand across the bailey kept their expressions rigorously blank. If their lord had decided to avenge his cousin in some way which left his hostage looking languorously radiant, that was entirely his affair.

Back in Roanna's chamber, they happily devoured slices of chicken and mutton, bread baked with honey and chopped nuts, and fragrant cheeses washed down by wine. Throughout the meal they talked of what most interested them, each other.

"Why haven't you married?" Roanna asked, finally daring to voice the question that had bothered her for days. How had such a magnificent man who was clearly aware of his duty to his people managed to escape the bonds of matrimony? Or had he?

"I was married," Colin explained gently, "ten years ago when I was eighteen. My wife's name was Catherine. She was the daughter of one of my father's closest allies. It was his last wish that we wed."

"What happened to her?" Roanna murmured, fighting down her resentment at the thought of him belonging to any other woman.

"She died in childbed about a year later. The child died with her. I blamed myself because she was so young, only fifteen, and she hadn't wanted the marriage, hadn't wanted to be a wife in any way. Afterward, when I was able to put at least some of the grief behind me, I resolved to learn two things: how to bring a woman to the pleasure men take for granted but which I was never able to give to my wife, and how to heal so that I would never again have to watch someone's life drain away while I stood by helpless."

Deeply moved by his revelation, Roanna reached out to gently stroke his cheek. "You learned both most thoroughly. For you have saved my life *and* shown me ecstasy beyond anything I could have imagined."

Colin drank in the comfort she offered like a man parched by the unrelenting sun. He had never spoken of his wife since her death, burying his guilt deep within him even as it spurred him to become the man he now was. But the gentle balm Roanna gave allowed him to see the past in proper perspective. Whatever he should or should not have done, it was over. This was the present bright with the promise of everything he had ever longed for. He marveled at his immense good fortune as he gently gathered her into his arms.

"What about you? How did you reach the elderly age of nineteen without being at least betrothed?"

Roanna laughed softly against his bare chest. Once back inside they had not hesitated to strip off their clothes. She was finding the sight of him naked in the firelight like a bronzed god to be highly distracting.

"You can thank—or blame—my brother for that. He has been reluctant to inflict me on any poor male."

Colin frowned. Such possessiveness went against the way he thought a brother should feel. "Why is that?"

The faint thread of harshness in his voice made Roanna smile. She who had chaffed at any restrictions on her freedom now found she enjoyed his protectiveness.

"Because he has seen too many women given in marriages that made them unhappy. He always hoped I would wed someday, but only to someone I love, as he has done."

Mollified, Colin silently admitted that perhaps her brother wasn't so bad after all, for a Norman. He was even willing to consider that there might be some other explanation for his cousin's death than the one he had already heard. But whether there was or not no longer really mattered. He was resolved that there had to be peace between their families.

Exhilarated by their discovery of one another, they had no further need for sleep. When the food was gone, they settled back into bed as naturally as though they had done so every night of their lives.

Roanna managed a half-hearted squeal of protest that quickly gave way to delighted laughter as Colin trailed ruby drops of wine between her breasts before industriously licking them away. By the time he reached her nipples, she was already dissolving into the now familiar mist of desire.

Gently pushing her breasts together, he flicked his tongue across both as his huge body settled carefully over hers. In the midst of his intense arousal, he still managed to mutter thickly, "Tell me if you are sore inside and I will not enter you."

She wasn't. The only pain she felt was the spiraling need for him. All shyness gone, she took his mouth with her own, her darting tongue assuring him there was no need for restraint.

Having determined for himself that she was ready to receive him, Colin went into her swiftly. This time he wanted to remain within her as long as possible. Slipping his arms beneath her, he lifted her until she was almost sitting against the pillows. His own body shifted slightly so that they faced each other, his hands free to caress her at will. All the while, his organ remained within her, pressing just a few inches inside her womanhood.

Smiling at her surprise, Colin kissed her lingeringly as his fingers tugged gently at her nipples. He rocked slowly back and forth, savoring the sensation of building pressure. With only the tip of his manhood inside her, the long, hard shaft rubbed against her most vulnerable point.

"I can't stand this . . . !"

"Yes, you can," he assured her with supremely male confidence. "We're only beginning."

Incredibly they were. Through long, exquisite minutes, Colin moved with her, exciting her with slow, languorous strokes that brought her to the edge of release.

Facing him, she stroked and kissed his massive chest, marveling at how the flat male nipples tautened at her touch. Her lips traced the long, ragged scar from his left shoulder across the breadth of his torso.

His own hands were busy caressing the soft inner flesh of her arms with a light, teaching touch before moving round to rhythmically caress her breasts. And all the while he watched her, the silvery eyes warm with loving passion.

"So beautiful," Colin gasped as their pleasure neared its peak. "Everything I have ever desired."

Grasping her waist, he pulled her down on the bed.

He wanted to be deep inside her when he came, driven by the most primitive desire to fill her womb. Roanna was infinitely soft and yielding beneath him, her slender body arched in rapture, as together they scaled the heights of ecstasy. Her joyous cries mingled with his own as they joined in exquisite union.

Sleep proved irresistible afterward, despite both their wish to stay awake and savor each other. They passed the remainder of the night nestled together, Roanna's golden head cradled on Colin's huge chest, his arms holding her lovingly.

The man-at-arms who rushed to their door shortly after dawn had to pound frantically for long moments before he was finally heard.

# Chapter Seven

"NORMANS, MY LORD! A WAR PARTY, COMING OVER the ridge at full gallop!"

Colin was out of bed instantly. Not even the blinding ecstasy of the last few hours could dull instincts honed since childhood.

"How many?" he demanded as he threw on his clothes. Roanna huddled under the covers, her face ashen, still dazed by sleep but all too aware of what the man-at-arms was saying.

Scrupulously avoiding looking at her, the warrior responded, "Fifty, at least, carrying the D'Arcy banner. They are in full armor and their weapons are already drawn. This is no parlay."

Clearly not, Colin thought grimly. He cursed the abysmal luck that had brought Roanna's brother down on him at such a time. Just when there was so much he wanted to say to her, so much to arrange, he had to go face her irate kinsman instead.

Seconds later, dressed and armed, he turned to her. "Stay here. Don't leave the bower."

Roanna opened her mouth to protest. She was useless there, whereas outside her presence might be enough to prevent what she feared was coming. About to speak, she hesitated. The man before her was not the gently passionate lover of the night before. Instead, he was every inch the implacable warrior chieftain, accustomed to absolute obedience.

It did not occur to Colin that she might object. In the everyday course of events, he was willing to accept some give and take, but when life and death hung in the balance he expected his will to be law. Without giving her the chance to say a word, he strode from the room, the man-at-arms hurrying after him.

Left alone, Roanna dressed hurriedly. It was a mark of her deep love for Colin that she gave serious consideration to obeying him, if only for a moment, before her horror at what might happen drove her to leave the bower. She could not huddle inside while the two men she loved, albeit in totally different ways, shed each other's blood.

The stronghold bustled with orderly, purposeful activity. Women who moments before had been preparing food, washing clothes, or seeing to all manner of other chores had broken off their tasks to collect the children and usher them inside the great hall. That done, they took their places near the palisade, where they would help supply weapons to the men and tend the wounded.

111

The gates were already secured, but not before livestock grazing just outside was hastily herded in and penned near the center of the compound. Boys too young to fight but too old to gather with the children were set to guard the cows, pigs, sheep, and horses.

There was very little talk. Everyone was well drilled in what needed to be done and went about it swiftly. Faces were grim, but Roanna saw no sign of panic. These people were resolutely determined to protect their homes, or die in the effort.

Colin stood on the palisade wall surrounded by his most trusted thegns and housecarls, watching the Normans approach. Taller and bigger than all the other men and further set off by his pelt of coppery hair shining in the sunlight, he made an obvious target. But he showed not the slightest concern for his own safety as he gave crisp orders for the deployment of their forces. Roanna's heart beat painfully as she prayed the fighting he anticipated could be avoided.

Ignoring the startled look of several men-at-arms, she climbed up a ladder perched along the high wooden wall to get a better view. It wasn't difficult to spot her brother. Like Colin, he was an unusually large man who towered head and shoulders over even the big, brawny knights who accompanied him. Riding at the front of his men, he brought the war party to within several hundred yards of the stockade, just out of mutual target range.

As the hot summer sun rose in the cobalt sky, Guyon pulled off his battle helmet. Hair as golden as Roanna's shone brightly. Even at that distance, she could she how tired and worried he looked. To reach the Algerson lands so quickly, he must have ridden hard through the night. Once more, Roanna berated herself for causing so much trouble.

Her throat tightened as she considered the thoughts which must have passed through her brother's mind in the last few hours, only to be quickly followed by a blush when she considered what he would say when he learned how she had in fact spent the night.

That he had to be told she did not doubt for an instant. Her new relationship with Colin was the best weapon she had to ensure that the two men would not fight. Guyon would have mercilessly slain any man who dared to seduce his sister, but when he realized that the shoe was on the other foot, so to speak, he would have no grounds for challenging Colin.

On the contrary, he would have the best possible reason to want the whole incident to end peacefully.

The urge to call out to him was almost irresistible, but she fought it down, knowing that were she to do so Colin would be greatly angered. For the moment at least, she had to defer to the men.

Not that they were handling the situation very well. Guyon's voice carried clearly on the slight breeze.

"Algerson, I demand you produce the Lady Roanna at once! Prove her safety or we attack!"

Only rigorous discipline hid Colin's slight smile of admiration. This D'Arcy was much like his sister. Both plunged head first. But unlike Roanna, he had a few things to learn about persuasion. Colin intended to teach him.

"You *demand*, Norman? Then I do not hear you. When you stand on Algerson land, you *ask!*"

Roanna began to move quietly along the wall to where the two men confronted each other. The way things were going, she figured she had very little time to waste.

"Your cousin died of his own folly," Guyon called back. "My sister will not suffer for it. If you have harmed her, I will burn your stronghold to the ground and slay everyone within it!"

This last part was a lie. Guyon would kill any man in battle without a second thought, but he would never harm women and children. If he was forced to attack, his men had strict orders not to touch them. But he thought it best to appear as ruthless as possible.

Within the stronghold, his threat was believed. Other Normans behaved in exactly the fashion Guyon described. Since Hastings, they had rampaged across the land, raping and pillaging wherever they went. Only those lucky enough to be protected by powerful lords such as Colin had any measure of safety.

His words had exactly the opposite effect from what he hoped. Already firm resistance stiffened further. It was time the arrogant Norman dogs learned the worth of true Englishmen.

"You are fifty, Norman," Colin sneered. "We are hundreds. I will send your body back to your wife with my condolences!"

That was enough for Roanna. They could hurl insults at each other all day as far as she was concerned, but when they started talking seriously about killing it was time to intervene.

Her sudden appearance at Colin's side shocked both men. "I told you to stay inside," he growled even as his eyes wandered over her lovingly. Having left her only minutes before, he was astonished to discover that she was even more beautiful than any memory his mind could retrain. It was all he could do not to sweep her into his embrace in front of everyone.

"She appears unharmed," her brother's lieutenant murmured. Like all the men, he nurtured genuine affection and respect for the Lady Roanna. Much as he hated to miss a good fight, he was relieved by her apparent well-being.

After his initial surprise, Guyon could only shake his head ruefully. Trust Roanna to triumph over any danger. Not only was she safe, but she showed not the slightest fear of Colin Algerson.

The look on the Englishman's face brought him up short. His mouth tightened ominously as dangerous sparks flared in his amber eyes. Guyon was no stranger to the passionate regard he saw on Colin's rugged features. He knew he himself had looked at his wife many times in just that way, and he understood quite well what it signified. If his sister's captor had dared to . . .

Guyon's stallion shied nervously. He could feel the sudden tension in his master. Big hooves pawed the air.

"Algerson, I would speak with you under flag of truce! Do you come out or will you allow us to enter?"

Roanna's small hand touched Colin's arm in a gesture that told her brother even more. "Let him come in, please! So that we may all talk. It is the only way to settle this."

Colin was willing enough to comply. Things were

going even better than he had hoped. It took only a short time for the terms of parlay to be arranged. Half a dozen thegns went out to the Normans to serve as hostages for the safety of Guyon and the five knights he led into the compound.

Barely had the Normans dismounted when Roanna was in her brother's arms. They embraced warmly. "Are you well?" Guyon asked softly when he at last stepped back to study her. His tawny eyes missed nothing of her flushed face, swollen lips, and luminescent gaze.

Roanna nodded shakily. "I am so sorry. This is all my fault."

"Nothing matters except that you are safe," he assured her sincerely. His throat tightened painfully. Roanna would always hold a special part of his heart. He could never condemn her for anything she might do. But if anyone had hurt her, he would drench the ground in blood.

The watchful eyes of Colin Algerson reminded the Norman of where he was. Silently he studied the man who had dared to steal his sister from within the shadow of his own keep.

The two men assessed each other warily. Honesty forced them to admit that had they met under different circumstances, they would have been disposed to like each other at first sight. Both exuded strength and intelligence, as well as the calm self-confidence that marked them as leaders. They might have been friends, but contrary fate had decreed otherwise.

"We will speak inside," Colin said, gesturing toward

the great hall. Briefly he considered sending Roanna back to the bower where she would be spared any arguments that might ensue. The stubborn set of her chin warned him she would not accept such a suggestion kindly.

Once inside, the two men wasted no time getting down to business. As Roanna and their most trusted retainers listened, Guyon said, "Your cousin bribed one of his guards to bring him wine. While drunk, he stumbled and fell against the stone wall of his cell. He was found the next morning, dead of a head wound. The guard has been punished and I have brought the body for you to see. If you look at it fairly, you will know I speak the truth."

Colin didn't need to examine his cousin's remains to believe what the Norman claimed was at least possible. Such behavior followed the pattern of a misspent life. It was ironic that the dead man had by his end unintentionally achieved great good. The barriers that had made any shared future with Roanna seem impossible were now gone forever. It only remained to convince both her brother and their two peoples that she belonged at his side.

"I suspect," Guyon continued when he was not immediately challenged, "that you were told he was executed. Considering all that has happened in this land, it seems inevitable that we believe the worst of each other."

Colin's eyebrows rose fractionally. He had not expected such reasonableness. "I may have been hasty in my judgment," he admitted softly.

"I thought you might be," Guyon muttered. With just a touch of skepticism, he added, "Yet you refrained from harming my sister. Very commendable."

Roanna shifted uneasily. She did not like the hard glint in her brother's eyes, which tended to see too much anyway.

Very softly, he went on, "I would wager there are few ladies who could come through such an experience untouched and be returned safely to their families. You *do* intend to return her?"

Colin smiled slightly. He had no compunction about where the conversation was inevitably headed. In fact, he and the Norman were understanding each other perfectly. It saved quite a bit of time.

Standing tall and straight, his legs braced slightly apart, he said matter-of-factly, "You may wish to reconsider the question of her return, since you are quite wrong about her being untouched. Your sister is no longer virgin."

Roanna's horrified gasp did not quite drown out the low, feral growl that broke from Guyon. His amber gaze turned to molten fire. A dull flush suffused his face as he took a step toward the fierce warrior who had dared to violate his sister. A massive fist lashed out, smashing into Colin's stomach.

Though he was prepared for the blow, it drove the breath from him. He swayed, but did not fall. Nor did he retaliate. As his men unsheathed their weapons, surrounding the Normans, he ordered, "Stand down! That was deserved."

Ruefully rubbing his middle, he added, "But don't

expect me to permit another. You and I are going to have to strike a truce if we are to be brothers-in-law."

Still flushed and angry, Guyon shook his head in disbelief. "You English cur! Do you really expect me to force my sister into marriage with you out of some perverse sense of honor? I would never condemn her to live with a man who took advantage of her helplessness."

"It wasn't like that!" Blushing fiercely, Roanna glared at both men. She was outraged at Colin's abruptness and appalled by her brother's reaction. But she was not about to let such a charge go unchallenged.

Before she could say another word, Colin curtly dismissed his men from the hall. They had served their purpose and he saw no reason for them to be privy to revelations of such an intimate nature. Guyon, already suspecting what he might be about to hear, did likewise.

Not until the three were alone did Roanna say quietly, "Colin did not take advantage of me in any way. On the contrary, I took advantage of what I knew to be our mutual desire for each other." Her head rose proudly. "I know many would say I behaved immorally. But I do not regret it for a moment."

Colin gazed at her in loving admiration. The words had cost her dear. She was pale and her shoulders trembled. Swiftly he moved to her side, not touching her but still close enough to offer reassurance.

"Direct your anger to me, Norman," he advised tightly. "Roanna has done nothing wrong."

Guyon stared at the pair, swept by contrary emotions. He was infinitely glad his sister had not suffered even as he felt some slight regret that she had left the shelter of innocence for the responsibilities of womanhood. The protective way the Englishman stood over her and her instinctive move closer to him forced him to give serious attention to her outrageous statement.

Gruffly, he demanded, "Was this truly as you say?"

Meeting her brother's gaze unflinchingly, Roanna nodded. "It was."

A long sigh escaped Guyon. He looked from one to the other slowly. Reluctantly, he felt compelled to ask, "Have you given any thought to all the problems you've created?"

Colin drew Roanna nearer. She nestled against his side, safe and content. Firmly, he said, "Together we can overcome any difficulties."

"What if I do not give my permission for you to remain together?" Guyon demanded. "How will you overcome that?"

It was, in the final analysis, the ultimate question. And only Roanna could answer it. Both men waited anxiously for her response.

"You know that my love and respect for you have no limits. But I cannot leave Colin. We will live together with or without your blessing."

She had feared her words would anger Guyon, but instead they seemed to reassure him. His own experience with his wife had taught him that such profound love could triumph over the worst dangers. A slight smile, the first in many days, curved his hard mouth.

"Before we come to that, let us at least discuss the alternatives."

Roanna nodded mutely, hardly daring to believe her brother was at all willing to consider the only other real possibility. Seated at the table between the two men, she glanced from one to the other anxiously as Guyon launched into what rapidly became a full-fledged interrogation.

Patiently, without the slightest hint of rancor, Colin replied to pointed inquiries about his upbringing, training, position, wealth, and preferences on a host of issues from the philosophical to the personal. At no time did he show the least irritation. His every response was marked by reason and candor. Some of Roanna's tension eased as she realized more forcibly than ever the extraordinary depth of his strength, wisdom, and courage.

Even Guyon was reluctantly impressed. He had sat down prepared to find numerous objections to the marriage. Instead after several long, wearying hours he was left with none. Ruefully he was forced to admit that while his sister's behavior was shockingly improper, it was at least understandable. Colin was everything he would have wanted for her in a husband.

When he at last ran out of questions, Colin did not hesitate to take advantage of the silence. Seizing the initiative, he suggested that they be married at once and that the ceremony be held at the Algerson stronghold, since Guyon's keep was still too small and rough to house many guests. That many would wish to attend was not in doubt. The joining of two such powerful and hitherto opposing families was an event not to be missed.

"Our supplies are more than ample. Would next week be acceptable?"

If Guyon was to quash their hopes, it had to be now. Roanna held her breath through the seemingly endless moments before her brother muttered, "So soon?"

Masking his immense relief, Colin flatly reminded him, "Several months from now we might regret delaying."

The point was well taken. If Roanna had already conceived, both men wanted to squelch the gossip that might result.

Guyon hesitated only once more. Reaching across the table, he took his blushing sister's hand in his own. Their eyes held. "Are you absolutely certain this is what you want?" he asked softly.

With greater assurance than she had ever felt in her life, Roanna nodded. No shadow of doubt remained as she confirmed, "This is right, brother. Believe me."

A moment more Guyon looked at them both, sitting so close together. He saw Colin's tender regard, saw the gentle smile that curved his lips as she returned his look. They spoke to each other without words, in a way Guyon knew quite well. Reassured, he allowed himself to be convinced.

But having decided to support the marriage, he was at a loss as to what to do next. Vaguely he knew there must be decisions made about the dowry, guests invited, a priest chosen to officiate, and so on. Nothing in his experience had prepared him to take charge of such an event. Not did the bridal couple have any clear idea of the preparations. They were far too caught up in each other to be more than vaguely aware of the rest of the world.

It was left to Brenna to see to it that all the proprieties were observed, if only belatedly.

She arrived promptly in response to her husband's startling message and lost no time assessing the situation for herself. Roanna was obviously happy, she radiated the supreme contentment of a woman who has found what she most wants in all of life. One look at Colin made it clear that her sister-in-law had chosen wisely. Though he and Guyon did not appear at all alike except for their unusually large size and strength, they shared certain traits obvious to the women who adored them.

The tender protectiveness Colin showered on his betrothed, coupled with his appreciation of her intelligence and character, boded well for their married happiness. It only remained to see them safely wed.

Barely had she arrived when cooks were bustling about preparing foods for the bridal feast, tailors were stitching new garments, servants were scrubbing all the buildings within the stronghold and laying fresh rushes on all the floors, even the grizzled thegns and housecarls were getting their beards trimmed and polishing their armor.

Nor were the Norman retainers immune. Guyon had actually heard two of his knights arguing over who had the best gift for the couple, while the servants

Brenna hastily summoned from their keep had set up their own kitchen to prepare the Norman delicacies they were sure the feast could not do without.

He was at a loss to understand how any place as essentially male as an armed stockade could have been transformed so swiftly into a feminine domain. Colin shared his confoundment. Though the two men were still wary of each other, they found common ground in their need to escape, if only briefly, the whirl of female activity surrounding them.

They spent a pleasant afternoon hunting, returning late to the stronghold with a dozen deer and several braces of pheasant for the feast table. More important- ly, they came away impressed by each other's abilities and more at ease than they had yet been.

Yet just as they were congratulating themselves on having at least the beginnings of an accord, they struck an impasse neither could surmount. It began after supper when Guyon raised the matter of the dowry.

Roanna had never given much thought to her marriage portion, but as she listened to her brother list its contents, she was frankly amazed. Because she helped to keep the estate accounts, she knew the extent of Guyon's wealth. Despite their lack of inheri- tance, he had acquired great riches in service to their overlord. Since William's victory, his properties had increased even further. But what he was proposing to relinquish as her dowry was still a startlingly large amount.

Colin listened patiently. Not until the Norman was done did he say, "That is very generous. But I cannot accept it."

There was a moment of stunned silence before Guyon demanded tautly, "Why not?"

Colin sighed inwardly. He prayed for the words that would make them understand. "I know you hold lands in Normandy as well as here, but my people would never believe Roanna's dowry came exclusively from there. They would suspect you were making use of properties granted to you by William, properties which in the eyes of many were stolen from loyal Anglo-Saxon families. That is unacceptable."

"Are you seriously suggesting I let her come to you without property when you know full well a woman's worth is measured by her marriage portion?"

"Not by me," Colin said flatly. "I want Roanna only for herself."

The two women glanced at each other worriedly. No bride could take exceptions at such sentiments, yet neither could she ignore the importance of a proper dowry. Soothingly, Brenna offered the solution she thought obvious, but which had apparently not occurred to either man.

"Why don't you deed the contents of the dowry to their children?" she suggested to her irate husband. "Surely, Colin's people could not object to that?"

It was so simple that they were both embarrassed at not having thought of it themselves. Gruffly, they agreed. But with the dowry settled, the matter of the priest proved thornier.

To the Normans, any proper marriage was celebrated by the church. Without its blessing, a woman was not wife but whore, and any children were considered bastards.

To the Anglo-Saxons, it was not so straightforward. Granted some marriages were sanctified, but there was also the time-honored tradition of the "handfast" wife recognized by secular law.

Not for a moment did Colin believe Roanna should be content with this more ambiguous arrangement. But he was also vividly aware of the anger his people felt toward the church because the Pope had approved the invasion. Since the conquerors came marching under a papal banner, the faith had been in great disrepute. Even native-born priests were reluctant to show their faces outside Norman territory.

Several possibilities were considered and rejected until Brenna remembered that an old priest who had served in the household of the late King Harold resided at a nearby abbey. Because of his connection to their martyred sovereign, it was likely Colin's people would accept him without demur. An escort was hastily dispatched to bring him to the stronghold.

That night, Roanna slept poorly, tormented by the emptiness of her bed and the needs of her awakened body. She paced the floor nervously, unaware that not very far away Colin was in the same predicament. Returning from an icy dip in the spring that had done little to calm his ardor, he counted off the hours until he could make her his forever.

# Chapter Eight

"I'VE NEVER SEEN ANYTHING SO LOVELY," ROANNA gasped. The bridal raiment laid out on her bed took her breath away.

A magnificent tunic of golden silk embroidered with traditional emblems exactly caught the color of her lustrous hair. The bliaut to be worn over it was of amber damask, that rarest of all fabrics imported from the East. A belt of intricately braided gold thread lay beside it. Nearby was a silk veil so finely spun as to be transparent and the jeweled circlet that would hold it in place.

Had the preparations for her wedding been going on for months, she would still have been surprised by such magnificent garb. As it was, she could not begin to imagine how the seamstresses had contrived to create the stunning garments so quickly.

Brenna laughed at her astonishment. "It took a bit of doing," she admitted modestly. "I brought some lengths of fabric with me and found others here. Once I explained to the sewing women what was wanted, they went to work with a will." She smiled faintly. "I think it was quite a challenge to them."

Roanna nodded understandingly. Besides the haste with which they had to finish, there was also the difficulty posed by combining two such different styles of fashion. Never before would she have thought of wearing the pleated tunic of Anglo-Saxon design with a Norman surcoat. But in this case, it worked perfectly. Her bridal garb was not merely beautiful, it was also a declaration of her hope that within her marriage the two peoples would be united.

As the servants removed her bath, Roanna poured a small quantity of cream made from attar of roses into her palm and began rubbing it into her skin. The rough stone of sand and pumice she had used while washing had smoothed away any suggestion of roughness. From head to toe, she was warm, honeyed satin.

A faint blush stained her cheeks as she thought of Colin's skilled hands running over her. Turning quickly, she pulled the linen chemise over her head to conceal her hardened nipples.

Her hair, washed in an infusion of marigold and rosemary, fell in a tangle to her waist. Seating her sister-in-law on the bench, Brenna patiently toweled and combed it. As she did so, she kept up a running commentary on nothing in particular, which had the desired effect of distracting and calming the bride.

Though she had not been able to eat anything that

morning, Roanna did accept a mug of tea made from valerian. She knew the herb would further soothe her nervousness.

Despite the tension growing in her with each passing moment, she saw a certain humor in the situation. She was going to a husband she knew far better than she could ever have hoped, to a wedding night that would hold much pleasure but certainly no shock. Yet she felt as anxious as an untried virgin confronted by a stranger.

By the time Brenna dropped the golden tunic over her head and smoothed it into place, Roanna was trembling. Her face was pale except for the unnatural brilliance of her tawny eyes and the lushness of her ripe mouth bitten by small, white teeth. Her hands were cold and her fingers stiff, so much so that she could not fit her circlet in place.

Brenna took it from her gently, easing it over her hair and veil as she said, "It's quite natural to be a little scared. But surely you know there is no cause?"

Roanna nodded numbly. Sounds were beginning to reach her from outside the bower. She heard the eager laughter of men and women gathering for the nuptials, the excited shouts of children who could not remember such a great event ever before occurring in their lives, the first tentative notes of flutes and harps beginning what promised to be many songs.

Aromas from the cooking fires made her stomach turn over queasily. She doubted she would be able to eat anything. It seemed beyond her even to move, yet somehow with Brenna's help she found herself at the door.

"Try to relax," her sister-in-law murmured. "This will all be over before you know it and then you and Colin will be alone."

Roanna held on to that thought resolutely. Over and over she reminded herself that she was marrying the man she loved, that this day was the culmination of all her most romantic hopes and dreams, that she was a fool to be even the least bit anxious.

The litany worked to some small degree. Greeting her brother, she was able to smile with some semblance of ease. Guyon was not fooled, but he admired the effort. He took her hand tenderly.

"I have only seen one other bride as beautiful, and I was fortunate enough to claim her as my own. Colin is a lucky man."

Roanna accepted the compliment automatically, without realizing the truth of it. She was unusually lovely under any circumstances, but the outfit she wore highlighted the startling perfection of her face and form.

Standing still, she was a golden goddess who could inspire awe in any man. When she moved, the woman was revealed in all her lithesome grace. Not even the most disciplined thegns or knights could be impervious to such beauty.

Guyon was all too aware of the ardent looks cast her way as they crossed the courtyard. He was glad for her sake that she did not notice them. Her composure could not take the strain.

Because of the balmy weather, the festivities were to be held outdoors. Carpenters had kept busy for days building tables and benches to hold the several hundred guests.

In addition to all those who lived in the stronghold, many others from the surrounding countryside were in attendance. None wished to miss seeing their lord wed. Guyon had prudently left a large number of his retainers to defend the keep in the unlikely event of trouble, but the Norman contingent still added dozens to the total.

No one came empty-handed. Numerous hams, roasts, cheeses, and breads were brought as gifts. Along with barrels of wine and ale, they contributed to the already more than ample supply prepared for the feast. Far from the danger of anyone going away hungry, it was doubtful the guests would be able to budge when they were done eating.

Roanna's appearance brought a roar of approval from the crowd. Her beauty was lavishly praised and good wishes were shouted unstintingly. The press of guests eager to get close to her slowed their progress, but eventually the bridal party arrived before the small, open-air bower erected for the ceremony.

Beneath a canopy of fresh-cut oak boughs whose pagan significance he carefully ignored, the priest stood waiting.

At fifty-five, Father Elferth's slender frame and serene demeanor made him look at once far younger than his years and ageless. His fine-boned features were framed by thick dark hair freshly washed and brushed. He wore the simple fustian robes of his calling with a wooden cross his only ornament. The violence and grief of the months since Hastings had stooped his shoulders slightly and etched deep lines around his aquiline nose and kindly mouth. But they had in no way impaired his appreciation of what was about to occur.

Glad though she was to see the priest, Roanna gave him only the briefest glance. All her attention was held by the man waiting at his side. Her heart began to beat erratically as Colin's gaze met hers. Never had he looked so compellingly virile or so unexpectedly threatening.

The deep blue tunic he wore stretched tautly across his massive shoulders and torso. It fell to his knees, meeting the tops of boots made from the finest leather. In deference to the weather, the sleeves were short. Roanna caught a glimpse of the wide gold bands at his wrists which with the bejeweled chain draped over his heavily muscled chest were the symbols of his rank.

The coppery pelt of his hair was brushed smoothly back and held in place by a leather thong tied round his broad forehead. In the bright sunlight, the harsh planes and angles of his face stood out in high relief. His mouth was set in a narrow, almost grim line. The quicksilver glimmer of his eyes held hers relentlessly. He appeared rock hard and utterly implacable. She could read nothing in his look except determination. The lack of any gentler sentiment made her tremble.

Guyon felt the tremor and glanced down at her anxiously. Colin's manner did not distress him, understanding as he did what a strain it was for a man to stand so close to a woman he desired without touching her. But he guessed Roanna might interpret it differently. Regretting that there was no opportunity to reassure her, he gently placed her hand in Colin's.

At the first touch of his skin against hers, Roanna started. The coldness of her fingers made his feel burning hot. She dared a further glance at him, only to be met once again by his inscrutable gaze. Her eyes fell, not to rise again even as the priest began to speak.

Father Elferth had seen the bride's nervousness and sought to ease it. His voice was deliberately slow and gentle, though loud enough to be heard by all the guests.

"We gather here today to witness and sanctify the joining of this man and woman into the blessed state of matrimony. No higher earthly union is so solemn and holy a covenant. It symbolizes the spiritual union of Christ and his Church and as such it is inviolate. In this time of pain and turmoil, it is also a special reminder of God's love and His concern for us."

Covering their hands with his own, he prayed that the favor of the Lord would shine upon them, that they would always be a source of mutual comfort and support, and that, if it was the Creator's will, they would be blessed by children.

Turning to the cross set above the altar, he blessed the wine and bread that were the living symbols of belief. As Roanna and Colin knelt before him to receive communion, the ancient Latin litany drifted over them, calling the faithful to everlasting life.

Having been so long without this ritual, many others wished to partake. Father Elferth had wisely brought several young priests with him who spread out among the crowd. After the briefest hesitation, men and women pressed forward to receive the salty wafers. Few eyes were dry as the grief-stricken memories of recent months slowly gave way to the hope of salvation.

"Before God and man," Father Elferth said at last, "I charge you all to recognize the sanctity of this union. May this man and woman be united forever as one flesh, one spirit, one will." Smiling gently at Roanna and Colin, he concluded, "In the name of Christ our Lord, I pronounce you man and wife."

The hushed silence erupted in joyful acclaim. Guests surged forward, each anxious to be the first to offer congratulations. In the melee, the bridal couple would easily have been separated were it not for the steely arm Colin kept wrapped around Roanna's waist. Locked firmly to his side, she could hardly breathe. Her smile was frozen as she responded unconsciously to the rush of tributes.

In a departure from custom permitted only at weddings and the fertility festivals of early spring, the men and women were seated together. As the newly wed couple took their place at the high table, servants rushed to fill mugs and begin serving the seemingly endless supply of food. The first of innumerable toasts began, each more florid than the last.

Roanna was careful only to touch her cup to her lips and was relieved to see that Colin did the same. With the conclusion of the ceremony, he unbent a bit. Some of the tension eased from his rugged features as he joined her in accepting the company's good wishes. There was even a glimpse of laughter in the silvery eyes as acrobats and jesters darted about and song-sters offered tunes which became increasingly bawdy as the afternoon wore on.

Though she had been prepared for a long feast, Roanna had underestimated the effect of such pro-longed celebrations. She accepted little food and ate even less, yet she still felt filled to bursting. The small amount of wine she sipped sent her senses spinning. The constant clamor of shouts, laughter, randy jokes, and the like made her head pound.

Long before the light began to fade and torches were lit against the darkness, the small of her back ached. She understood that it was necessary for a chieftain of Colin's standing to observe his marriage with proper expansiveness. But she could only wish it was all over and done with.

With the coming of dark, Father Elferth discreetly excused himself and his young priests. Their depar-ture was the signal for a new phase of the festivities. The Christian rituals had been observed; it was time for the pagan to have its due.

Brenna had warned her of what would take place, so she was not unduly shocked by the sudden appear-ance of a figure robed and hooded in white, horns upon his head, and a red cord wound round his waist.

The Norman guests, likewise prepared, had drunk enough to view the spectacle as no more than an interesting local custom. Only later would a few among them wonder where the line was drawn be-tween ancient gods and the devil. For the rest, their loyalty to Guyon would be too great for them to voice any such doubts.

Roanna swallowed hard as the figure approached. So forbidding was its appearance that the raucous merriment died away in an instant. Even the musicians set down their instruments, their jaunty tunes replaced by a low, sinuous chant from the shadows.

Were it not for Colin's firm grip on her arm, Roanna doubted she could have stood. He led her to the open space before the tables where the figure had stopped. They exchanged a few words in a language she could not understand.

At a signal from the hooded one, several young girls stepped forward. Their hair lay loose about their backs. Their feet were bare. They wore thin white gowns that hid little of the beauty of their forms.

Flowers were laid around the bridal couple. Burning herbs perfumed the air. The hushed crowd leaned forward, anxious to miss nothing of this rite performed only at the marriage of great warriors.

A silver chalice was brought forward and handed to Roanna. Glancing into it, she felt a rush of relief when she saw nothing more than wine. Holding the cup before her, she faced Colin. Silently, they both drank from it.

The ceremonial dagger he had worn strapped to his waist was withdrawn from its scabbard. In the flickering firelight of the torches, it gleamed menacingly. Roanna had to call on all her courage to stand motionless.

In the instant before his arm lifted, she thought she saw a tiny smile quirk his hard mouth. It reassured her just enough to keep her still as the lethal blade plunged. Straight into the chalice.

The crowd roared its approval. As the deep red wine closed round the dagger, engulfing it, raucous comments left no doubt as to the meaning of the ritual. Roanna's face was hot and her hands shook when a smiling young girl took the chalice from her. The blade was carefully dried on a white linen cloth before being presented to her. She was given to understand that it was now her property.

Silence fell again as the hooded one removed the red cord from around his body. Roanna stiffened as Colin took her hands. The chanting increased as they were bound firmly together. Ancient prayers were recited over them.

Though the words were unknown to her, she sensed the sentiments were not all that different from those expressed by Father Elferth. Far from the satanic rites she had vaguely feared, they were simply being wed again before the spirits of fire, air, earth, and water.

Comforted by Colin's nearness, Roanna did not shirk when the hooded one at last untied the cord.

The white-robed girls were instantly at her side. Before she could take a step, she was hustled away toward the private quarters she would henceforth share with her husband.

Colin's chamber was somewhat larger than those provided for guests, but furnished in much the same way. Copper braziers provided enough light to see clearly. A large bed covered by a down-filled mattress took up most of one wall. Across from it stood a table flanked by benches where Roanna guessed he sometimes held private meetings with his most important retainers. Carved chests held clothes and ornaments. A shield and several swords were propped against one. The floor was strewn with fresh rushes sprinkled with sweet-smelling herbs.

Roanna had attended several nuptial beddings in Normandy and understood their purpose. But she was thankful to be spared such exposure. It was enough to be stripped naked by the girls, her body sincerely admired in terms that made her blush. Resignedly, she allowed herself to be guided to the bed.

The blankets were pulled back, revealing a coverlet of smooth white linen. Lying down, Roanna told herself that the sooner they were done the sooner Colin would come. She lay quietly as the girls anointed her with a light, pleasantly scented oil from the tips of her toes to the gently rounded curve of her shoulders.

Beneath their ministrations, Roanna sighed softly. She must be even tireder than she had thought. It was growing difficult to keep her eyes open. They fluttered shut as her skin grew warm and flushed. She was unaware of the oil's sensual effects as it permeated her body, nor did she hear the low moan that broke from her.

The girls glanced at each other, satisfied. One of the youngest giggled, only to be instantly hushed. Preparing the bride was a sacred ritual handed down from the days of the mother goddess. There was no place for levity in actions meant to make intercourse both easy and pleasant no matter how inexperienced a woman might be or how clumsy her husband. Gathering up the discarded clothes, they withdrew discreetly.

Outside, Colin watched them go with relief. If it had been left up to him, he would gladly have dispensed with this part of the ceremony. Confident of both his own ability and his bride's response, he knew it was not necessary. But ancient traditions demanded respect. With the ritual's completion, however, he need wait no longer.

There was a masculine equivalent of the preparations Roanna had just undergone, but that Colin firmly refused. He had been almost painfully aroused since first laying eyes on her at the beginning of the day. The skilled priestesses charged with assuring his potency were not only unwanted but unnecessary. Certain that their disappointment could be readily assuaged elsewhere, he rose to join his bride.

The ribald jokes and eager offers of assistance faded quickly behind him. Reaching his quarters, he stepped swiftly inside, shutting the door firmly on any prying eyes. The sight that greeted him made his breath catch in his throat and sent a tremor racing through his huge body.

Roanna lay on her back, her honeyed skin glowing in the lamplight. Her slender arms were raised above her head. A dreamy smile curved her lush mouth. As her amber gaze focused on him, her eyes darkened. In the deep shadows around the bed, he looked like a huge, savage warrior intent on plunder. A flicker of fear darted through her, only to be banished by the overwhelming desire to give everything he demanded.

"Colin . . ."

He stood for a moment relishing the ardent beauty

of his wife before crossing the room swiftly. Dropping on the bed beside her, he reached out a trembling hand to touch the smooth perfection of her body. His calloused fingers closed round her nipple, gently bringing it to a hard, yearning peak.

"Hmmm, . . ." Roanna murmured breathlessly, "please . . . keep touching me. . . ." Arching under his hand, she sought more of the exquisite sensations rushing through her.

Colin was delighted to comply. Easing himself fully over her, he stroked and caressed the silken length of her until she was quivering with need. Only then did he step away from the bed long enough to strip off his own clothes.

Roanna welcomed him back with open arms. What few inhibitions might have remained after their earlier lovemaking were banished by the ointment that drove out all restraint and opened the way for unhindered fulfillment.

As his mouth wandered over her, his tongue flicking from the satin firmness of her breasts down along the flat plane of her belly to the hidden treasure of her womanhood, Colin absorbed some of the salve into himself. His caresses became slightly rougher, though no less pleasurable. Drawing her even closer, he moved to possess her fully.

The smooth thrust of his manhood within her made Roanna groan with delight. She moved against him eagerly, thwarting his efforts to prolong their pleasure. The shattering burst of ecstasy hurled them both far from consciousness. Colin cried her name into her mouth as together they hurtled toward the stars.

With any other woman, he would have been astounded to find himself still hard after such release. But with Roanna, he was not at all surprised. His need for her was endless, as hers was for him.

Holding her firmly to him, Colin rolled over on his back. Roanna straightened above him, her high-pointed breasts beckoning his hands. He gently squeezed and stroked them as they began another, slower ascent heavenward.

Even then they were not satiated. Long after all effects of the ointment had worn off, they continued to love unrestrainedly. Not an inch of Roanna's body went untouched even as she learned to know Colin as thoroughly. Together they sought the furthest reaches of ecstasy, not stopping until sleep at last claimed them both.

Much later, when she ruefully soaked away a certain lingering soreness, Roanna would reflect on the wages of such erotic excess. But just then she knew only that she lay with the man who made her heart and soul complete, and that she had everything in life she could ever wish.

No shadow darkened her happiness, no premonition hinted at the mortal danger already gathering just beyond the confines of their love-dazzled world.

# Chapter Nine

"WE'LL EXPECT YOU WHEN WE SEE YOU," BRENNA advised lightly. For good measure, she added, "Don't hurry back."

Roanna and Colin were willing enough to accept her advice. Married three days, they were still far too absorbed in each other to need anyone else's company. The preparations for winter were well ahead of schedule, the stronghold lay secure in the combined protection of both English and Norman forces. There was nothing to keep them from fully enjoying the balmy summer afternoon.

Hand in hand they wandered across a field bright with wildflowers. Colin bent to pluck a daisy, teasing it beneath Roanna's chin. Laughing, she made to pull away, only to be stopped by his gentle but firm grip.

Pulling her to him, Colin tilted her head back. His lips brushed hers tenderly. "I love you, my wife."

Would she ever grow used to his touch? Roanna wondered dazedly. Her throat tightened as she met his smile with her own. "And I love you, my husband." A teasing gleam entered her amber eyes. "Were we not within sight of the stronghold, I would show you how much."

Without another word, Colin scooped her into his arms and set off toward a nearby glen.

"Where are we going?" Roanna demanded, trying without success to sound stern.

"To a secluded spot I know," her husband informed her roguishly.

"The last time I wandered too far from home," she reminded him, "I was carried off by an arrogant, fearsome lord."

"What a coincidence," Colin growled, his lips nuzzling her throat. "I can guarantee the same thing is about to happen again."

Not quite the same, Roanna thought with just a touch of pardonable smugness. This time there was no terror or remorse, no dread of pain or dishonor. Only joyful anticipation and the certainty of love.

With new-found docility, she yielded. It was no great hardship to be laid on fragrant grass, stripped of her clothes, and slowly, relentlessly caressed to exquisite ecstasy. Nor did she regret the long, languorous hours of the afternoon during which she greedily explored her husband's lean, hard form with skillful hands and mouth.

Afterward, Colin fell asleep while Roanna nestled contentedly in his arms. Her body was pleasantly tired, but her mind was too full of happiness to rest. Staring up at the bright blue sky dusted with fluffy clouds, she gave silent thanks for the joy that had come to her. Her life before meeting Colin seemed no more than a dream, from which she had at last awakened.

Far off in the back of her mind, she was aware that this blissful interlude could not last. Protected by the loyalty of his people and the support of her brother and sister-in-law, she was insulated from the problems of the world. But harsh reality would inevitably intrude. The country was still too torn by hatred and violence to allow lovers any great degree of peace.

Instinctively, she was storing away each precious moment as a source of strength against the darker days she could reluctantly foresee.

Determined to shake off her somber mood, Roanna brushed a feather-light kiss across her sleeping husband's lean cheek before going off in search of some distraction. A glimpse of irises blooming beside the stream drew her in that direction.

Humming softly to herself, she filled her arms with the flowers. They would bring a welcome note of color to the guest chamber Brenna and Guyon were sharing, as well as to her own and Colin's bower. One particularly lovely blossom was just beyond her grasp. Stepping around moss-draped rocks, she reached for it carefully.

The flower was in her hand when she saw the still form lying half-hidden by the underbrush. The man lay on his stomach, his arms and legs spread in the

attitude of falling. He was roughly dressed in the garb
of a peasant. A brown serge tunic covered him to his
knees. Stained and torn hose sheathed his legs down
to wooden clogs, one of which was missing.

Though she could not see his face, the firm muscu-
larity of his body suggested he was a young man. That
was substantiated by the sight of thick brown hair
heavily matted with blood.

Dropping the bouquet, Roanna moved forward,
intent on determining whether the man was alive and,
if so, offering what help she could. She was at his side
before she remembered that Colin was only a short
distance away. If he found she had approached a
stranger by herself, even one so grievously hurt, he
would be angered.

Picking up the skirt of her tunic, which was her only
covering, she darted back to him. An urgent hand on
his shoulder shook him awake.

"Roanna. . . ." The sight of her strained features
and wide eyes banished his sleepy smile. Instantly
alert, he sat up. "What is it? Has something happened?"

"There's a man, in the underbrush. I don't know if
he's alive or not."

Colin was on his feet before she finished speaking.
He dressed swiftly. "Show me."

They reached the spot by the stream within minutes. Motioning her back, Colin glanced round cautiously. A body meant assailants, who still might be
nearby. His hand was on the dagger strapped to his
side as he turned the still form over.

Roanna had been right to think the man young. His

face, ashen from loss of blood, revealed him to be little more than a boy. Besides the wound at the back of his head, he showed numerous other injuries. Wherever he came from, he could not have gotten very far in such condition. But despite his grave condition, he was still alive. Kneeling down beside Colin, Roanna was able to find a slight heartbeat.

"We must get him back inside," she murmured, "whoever he is. . . ."

Her husband's face was grim. "I know him. He lives on one of the farms in my holding."

Shock turned Roanna's eyes to darkened pools. Violence of any form was almost unheard of within the Algerson lands. Colin ruled justly but firmly. He did not allow his people to injure one another. Whoever had done this was an outsider.

Stunned by his revelation, she said nothing more as Colin easily hoisted the young man over his shoulders and started back toward the stronghold. The flowers lay forgotten on the bank as Roanna hurried after him.

Guyon was crossing the bailey as they entered. He came quickly to their side. Glancing from one to the other to make sure they were all right, he asked quietly, "Are there any others?"

Colin shook his head. His eyes met Guyon's in the silent way of men who have come to understand each other. "Not in the same area. Perhaps elsewhere."

Standing between them, Roanna could see the sudden tightening of her brother's face. For the first time since finding the injured man, she began to consider the implications of her discovery.

It was likely, given where she had found him, that he was heading for the stronghold when his injuries overcame him. His desperate effort suggested he was trying to get word of some peril to those best able to defend against it.

Colin laid the man down gently in a corner of the great hall. "Take care of him," he instructed the old woman who had helped bring Roanna through her relapse. "If he regains consciousness and can talk, make careful note of all he says."

Drawing Roanna a slight distance away, he added, "I'm not sure yet exactly what this means, but it can't be anything good. Gather the women together and begin preparations in case we are attacked. In the meantime, I will ride to the farm he comes from to try to discover what happened."

It was on the tip of her tongue to ask him not to seek out danger, but she bit back the words. His duty as chieftain demanded he go. Moreover, she knew full well that Colin was not a man to hide behind strong walls while his people were threatened. He would find the enemy and, if at all possible, slay him before further damage could be done.

Understanding all this, she was still taken aback to see her brother mounted and ready to ride with him. When she questioned him, Guyon merely shrugged. "I need the exercise."

The grim hardness of his eyes belied his easy words. Nor did his knights look as though they anticipated an amiable outing. Wearing full armor including battle helmets, they appeared every bit as implacable as the thegns and housecarls who rode beside Colin.

With surprising ease, the two groups formed up into a single unit. Roanna stared up at her husband, sitting so tall and resolute on his great stallion. His features softened momentarily as he met her gaze. No words passed between them, but they were not needed. With difficulty, he tore his eyes from her. His shouted order to move out sent the war party forward in a flurry of pounding hooves and flashing steel.

The day passed slowly. Having had so much practice in the last few months, the women completed their preparations swiftly. A large contingent of men-at-arms had been left to guard the stronghold. They took up their places along the outer palisade, alert for any sign of movement beyond the clearing.

None came as the sun rose higher in the sky and the day grew hot. Roanna and Brenna offered each other what comfort they could, but the hours stretched out with excruciating slowness. Neither woman would give voice to the fears that were uppermost in both their minds as they waited for their husbands to return.

Several miles to the east, Colin reined in above a small settlement. His worst expectations were confirmed by the sight of spiraling smoke. A rough-hewn hall that had served the farmer and his family was engulfed in flames. Off to one side, a barn burned fiercely. Livestock lay wantonly slain in their pens. Bodies of men, women, and children were scattered across the grounds.

Despite the immense destruction they had already wrought, the attackers were not yet finished. Oblivious to the war party on the ridge, several dozen men were carrying off booty and breaking open casks of ale.

Others were amusing themselves with three terror-stricken young girls stripped naked and tied spread-eagle near the corpses of their kin.

The faces of Colin and his men were white with fury as they surveyed the hideous scene. But their revulsion, great though it was, was surpassed by that of the Normans.

To Guyon and his knights, the pillagers were all too recognizable. Their armor and weapons marked them as countrymen. The orgy of violence and death was being carried out by men they had crossed the Channel with and fought beside at Hastings. They had marched under the same banner, served the same leader, and pledged themselves to the same cause. Yet they were separated by an immense gulf marked by savagery on one side and honor on the other.

When the Algerson battle cry filled the air, English and Norman alike surged forward as one with no thought but to wreak vengeance in the name of their common humanity.

The fighting was swift and ferocious. Weakened though they were by drink and rapine, the raiders were still formidable foes. From childhood they had been trained to one task, killing. They performed it with relentless efficiency.

Several of Colin's party fell beneath their swords, but many more of the attackers perished as the thegns and housecarls made excellent use of their newly honed skills. They fought from horseback as ably as any Norman. Guyon and his knights backed them fully. They accounted for their own share of the enemy while taking scant losses.

The hot summer air was heavy with the stink of blood long before the last foe fell beneath Colin's sword. Dismounting swiftly, he rapped out sharp orders to his men.

"Find the wounded and keep as many as possible alive for questioning. Alaric, set a watch. We will stay here tonight. Send a messenger back to the stronghold to tell the Lady Roanna and her sister of our safety, but say nothing of what we found here. Guyon, will you put your men to erecting a shelter?" He gestured toward the three young girls still alive despite their sufferings and the battle that had raged around them. "They will need it."

Colin took several of the older warriors who had wives and daughters of their own to help him untie and care for the victims. There was little that could be done for them beyond warm blankets and reassurance that their ordeal was over. The men's faces were grim as they gently covered the girls's abused bodies and settled them beneath the hastily constructed lean-to.

The knights kept their distance. The sight of any men clearly terrified the girls; they did not need to be confronted by replicas of their attackers.

Helping to sort out the wounded, Guyon paused beside one of the mangled corpses. There was something familiar about the dead man. It took a moment to recognize the significance of the blazoned shield lying beside him.

Joining his brother-in-law, Colin glanced down disinterestedly at the body. He was concerned only with those of the enemy who still lived and could be made to talk.

But seeing Guyon's concern, he asked, "What's wrong?"

"I know him. He is the younger brother of Frances DeBourgnon, one of William's most ambitious supporters. They both fought at Hastings and were in London with the King, last I heard."

"Why would the brother be here?"

Guyon hesitated, but only for an instant. "DeBourgnon was waiting to be granted an estate. If he got it, he would be likely to bring his brother along to help him take possession of his new lands."

Colin's head jerked back, his gaze fierce. "You mean *my* lands?"

"It looks that way." Seeking to explain, not excuse, Guyon said, "To William any holding still in the possession of native lords is a potential threat to his security. He knows that a successful invasion is not the same as a conquest. To consolidate his rule, he must put his followers in power throughout the kingdom. DeBourgnon probably came out here expecting an easy takeover. With most of the Anglo-Saxon nobility destroyed at Hastings, few families have been able to hold out."

"Couldn't he have simply come on his own?"

"It's possible," Guyon admitted. "Many of those who sailed with William are hotheaded and too impatient to wait for anything. But if he had the King's authority, he would go to any lengths to take what he considers his."

The two men stared at each other in dawning recognition. Being an experienced campaigner, De-Bourgnon would be likely to delegate the smaller settlements to his brother while he . . .

"Alaric!"

The startled warrior came running at his master's command. "My lord?"

"Get the men mounted. We ride for the stronghold at once."

Behind him, buckling on his battle helmet, a grim-faced Guyon muttered, "And pray God we are in time."

The young man peering into the heat haze blinked rapidly. He was hot, thirsty, and bored. Moreover, he had not yet gotten over his disappointment at having been left behind at the stronghold. Perhaps his imagination was playing tricks on him.

No, there was definitely movement in the trees just beyond the clearing. He leaned forward, trying to get a better view. A flash of light bouncing off steel froze him for just a moment before he gathered himself enough to bellow a warning.

Below in the great hall where she was helping to care for the injured man, Roanna jumped to her feet. Running outside, she found the stronghold in an uproar. Men-at-arms who moments before had been drifting close to sleep were suddenly upright and tense. Tight-faced thegns were barking out orders. The battle-hardened housecarls who in Colin's absence ruled over all were already on the palisade, making a quick assessment of the enemy.

Climbing up next to one of them, Roanna asked, "What is it?"

"Normans, my lady," the man grated, "gathering to attack." He raised his hand, summoning a man-at-arms. "Take her ladyship back to the hall and stay with her."

"That is not necessary," she assured him quickly. "You need not take men from the fighting to watch over me. I will see to my own safety."

The housecarl looked unconvinced. His courage was beyond question, but he did not want to consider the penalty should Lord Colin return and find his lady injured. About to argue with her, he was prevented by the sudden emergence of a line of knights taking up position at the rim of the clearing.

Their high shields extending from knee to shoulder obscured much of their forms, but the dull glint of chain mail was still visible, as were the conical helmets whose pronged nose pieces gave their wearers the look of carrion birds. Powerful war horses also protected at their most vulnerable points by widths of iron rings sewn to toughened leather pawed the ground eagerly.

Behind them, a detachment of archers on foot hurried into position. But it was on the man in front that Roanna's attention focused. Rarely had she seen such ornate armor. The metal hauberk that protected his torso was made not from links of chain, as was customary, but from overlapping strips of metal the fashioning of which must have driven some poor armorer to despair. His helmet was topped by a brilliant red plume that matched the crest emblazoned on his elaborately carved shield. The same emblem flew from the banner carried by his squire.

Aware that the worst thing she could possibly do at that moment was to further distract the housecarl who had to muster the stronghold's defense, Roanna hurried back downstairs. She found Brenna still in the great hall, although standing close enough to the door to get a glimpse of what was going on outside.

Briefly, Roanna explained what was happening. No long discussion was needed for the two women to understand that attack was imminent. With a minimum of words, they calmed the children who were also sheltered in the hall, set them to work preparing bandages and splints for the wounded who were sure to come, and started servants filling buckets with water from the two wells within the courtyard.

The water was soon needed. In an effort to weaken the defenses, the Norman bowman shot flaming arrows into the stronghold. Most gutted out against the palisade. But a few reached the vulnerable thatch roofs of the great hall and outer buildings and had to be swiftly drenched.

It was left to the women and servants to guard against a conflagration as the men-at-arms concentrated on readying vats of boiling tar and oil. No effort was made to return the volley after volley of arrows. At that distance, not even the most skilled archer would be likely to penetrate the Normans' armor. Wisely, the housecarl in charge chose to reserve their resources until they could do the most good.

They did not have long to wait. Stirring impatiently on his charger, the Norman lord gave the signal to bring up the catapult. Loaded with stones, it was laboriously maneuvered into position directly opposite the main gate of the stronghold. Straining men released the taut lines holding it in place. Their aim was slightly off. The barrage struck the wall to the side of the gate, sending up splinters of wood but otherwise doing little damage.

So well constructed was the palisade that subsequent attempts had only slight effect. The repeated efforts, however, wore everyone's nerves to a fine edge.

"If only it would stop," Brenna murmured tightly, covering her ears with her hands.

Roanna surprised her by disagreeing. "We won't really be in trouble until they realize they can't break through the wall that way and try something else." She didn't add that she knew full well what the next tactic would be and dreaded it.

All too soon the impatient lord recognized that the catapult could not hold stones heavy enough to smash through the palisade. He shouted an order that sent his men scurrying to gather dry grass, wood, and anything else that would burn. Soaked in oil and set afire, the blazing missile struck the center of the gate.

Fire spread instantly as logs dried by the long summer days caught flame. Heedless of their own safety, Roanna and Brenna were among those who rushed to put it out. As they frantically filled buckets of water, the Normans began their advance.

Under protection of their shields, they were able to move ever closer to the stronghold's perimeter. The English archers picked off many, but still more kept coming. All too soon, the Normans reached the base of the wall.

The housecarl shouted a command to the women to get back, but Roanna and Brenna ignored him. They joined the men pouring vats of tar and oil down on the enemy and tipping over the siege ladders that began to appear along the palisade.

For a time the tide of battle was clearly in the defenders' favor. But as more and more burning arrows fell within the compound and the air grew thick with acrid smoke, two men recently admitted to Guyon's service made the decision to switch sides. They told themselves they were driven by horror of the satanic rites they had witnessed at the wedding. But in fact it was their disappointment at the lack of booty allowed by a lord anxious to keep peace with his people that made them welcome the chance to help loot so wealthy a stronghold.

Roanna's eyes teared, her face and clothes were streaked with soot. Pain gripped her lungs as she struggled to breathe. Terror flared through her as she glanced toward the gate, only to find it swinging open. Beside her, Brenna stumbled. Roanna just managed to catch her before she could fall. Together, they raced for safety within the inner bailey surrounding the hall where the stronghold's defense now centered.

With the wall breached, what had looked like certain victory began turning relentlessly toward defeat. The thegns and housecarls fought magnificently, but they could not withstand the overwhelming might of their foes who now held an irresistible advantage as they brutally slashed and stabbed their way toward the great hall at the center of the compound.

Realizing that only minutes might remain before this last defense was breached, Roanna's hand fastened on the dagger hidden in her bliaut. It was the ceremonial blade of her wedding day, but as sharp as any war sword. Grimly she pressed it into her sister-in-law's hand, rejecting Brenna's efforts to refuse it.

There was little chance that either of them would survive what was to come, but the instinctive protectiveness of her nature demanded that she do everything possible to help her brother's wife.

In the next instant, the two women were separated by the sudden surge of battle. Brenna vanished in the midst of screaming children and struggling fighters. Roanna was thrown in the opposite direction toward the back of the hall. Frantically, she glanced round for some weapon. If she was to die, she was grimly determined it would not be alone.

But the Norman who spied her crouched in a corner of the hall did not have death on his mind. At least not right away. Though the battle was far from over, he was so maddened by blood lust as to be easily distracted. Spurring his horse forward, he drove directly for her.

Roanna had a moment to recognize the ornately dressed lord who commanded the attack before she was trapped against the wall by the heaving sides of his mount. Sliding from the saddle, the Norman seized her brutally. The visor of his helmet was raised, giving her a clear view of his small, smoke-reddened eyes, grime-encrusted visage, and thick mouth. Her stomach heaved as his hard hands roamed over her at will, savoring the ripe softness of her body.

"God's blood, what a prize! My men can finish off those English dogs. You and I have other business, wench!"

Pulling her by the nape of her neck, he half carried, half dragged her into an alcove. Flung on the floor, Roanna lay momentarily stunned as DeBourgnon yanked off his helmet and sword belt. As she struggled to rise, his booted foot lashed out, catching her in the side.

"Stay still, bitch!" A vicious leer curved his wet mouth. "I advise you to do your best to please me. Otherwise, you'll spread your legs for every one of my men before this day is out!"

Roanna barely heard him. All her energies were concentrated on a desperate effort to get away. But her strength and speed could not match his. Before she could move again, he was on her.

The thin fabric of her surcoat and tunic gave way easily before his tearing hands. He grunted with pleasure as he bared her breasts, squeezing them brutally as he ground his hardness into her.

"You're too beautiful to belong to anyone but Algerson. All the better." DeBourgnon laughed thickly. "He must be lying dead out there by now. I wanted to fight him myself, but this is almost as good." He ripped the remainder of her clothes open and forced his legs between hers.

Dizziness engulfed Roanna. Burning tears slid down

her ashen cheeks. Her lungs labored futilely as she prayed for unconsciousness. The hard shaft of his manhood touched her thigh, forcing her to relinquish all hope.

In the next instant she was free. DeBourgnon was hurled from her, his face white with shock as he confronted the enraged giant looming over them.

"You wanted to fight," Colin growled.

Drenched in blood, his eyes glowing like molten steel, he looked as though he had stepped from the very bowels of hell. His hard features were drawn so tightly that they seemed no more than a mask symbolizing death. Each bulging muscle of his massive arms and chest moved like a living thing. Against the flickering flames, a dripping war sword flashed in his hand.

Frantically, the Norman glanced at the weapon he had so foolishly unbuckled. It lay beside Roanna, close to the remnants of her tunic she was dazedly gathering about her. Colin sneered, kicking the blade toward him.

"Pick it up. You will have a chance to defend yourself like a man before I skewer you like a pig."

DeBourgnon lost no time doing as he said. Rearmed, some of his swaggering confidence returned. "You can't win. My men will have taken your stronghold by now."

So quietly that it was a moment before his words sank in, Colin corrected him. "Your men are dead or dying. The victory is mine."

He moved forward slightly, the weapon balanced

easily in his huge hand. "A word of instruction, though it comes too late to benefit you. Never attack a stronghold when half its defenders are away. Because"—his heavily muscled arm lifted—"they are likely to return at the least opportune moment and"—the blade slashed downward—"catch you in a pincer from which there is"—DeBourgnon's weapon rose too late to block the blow; his scream ripped the air—"no escape."

Roanna averted her head swiftly. Colin had meant what he said about forcing the Norman to die like a pig. Razor-sharp steel pierced the gaudy armor just above his intestines. Blood and gore poured from him as he fell to the ground, writhing in agony.

Impervious to the hideous sight before him, Colin made no effort to end the other man's torment. His face was expressionless as he stepped over the living corpse shrieking in mindless horror.

Roanna collapsed into his arms, hiding her eyes. "I thought there was no chance. . . . H-he was going to . . ."

"I know," Colin muttered gruffly. Cradling her to him, he lifted her as easily as a child. His voice shook as he murmured, "It's all over now. You're safe, my love."

The truth of his words was evident moments later when he carried her into the main part of the hall. Groups of retainers and servants were working together to put out the remaining fires. A makeshift dispensary was already being set up to care for the wounded.

A few men and women were wandering dazedly,

but most were well in control of themselves. They went matter-of-factly about the business of dispatching those of the enemy still alive within their walls and separating their own dead for burial.

Roanna was deeply relieved to see that despite the ferocious fighting and the nearness of defeat, few of the stronghold's forces had actually been killed. Far more of the Normans had fallen once Colin and his men arrived to turn the tide of the battle.

Her relief deepened as she spied Brenna standing safe within the circle of her husband's arms. She looked bruised and disheveled, but otherwise unhurt. Beside her on the ground lay the body of a Norman attacker, the ceremonial dagger protruding from his throat.

The combined effects of terror and relief proved overwhelming. Roanna's thick lashes fluttered against her amber eyes as a tiny sigh escaped her. Nestling into the iron warmth of Colin's chest, she yielded to his care.

Gazing down at her, his silvery eyes darkened with profound worry. The victory was as ashes in his mouth as he was forced to recognize that it would not be long before another Norman tried to take his lands . . . and another . . . and another.

If he did manage to kill them all, he would only have established himself as a major threat to the new regime and invited an all-out assault that would drench his lands in blood.

For the first time in his life, Colin felt the keen edge of despair. The future that a few days before had appeared infinitely bright now seemed to promise only pain and death.

His proud head bent as his arms tightened spasmodically around all that he cherished most in the world. Silently he vowed to find some way to keep her safe, no matter what the cost.

# Chapter Ten

LONDON WAS NOT AT ALL AS ROANNA HAD EXPECTED. The city Brenna and Guyon had described as a prosperous, vital center of trade and commerce was instead a filthy, crowded, sullen blot on the landscape.

Glancing round at the morass of jostling men and women, straining horses, and creaking carts, she shook her head wearily. Everyone seemed in a great hurry to get somewhere, but their grim faces indicated they were less than certain what they would find when they arrived. A cloud of uncertainty hung over the city made all the worse by the somber grayness of the heat-laden sky.

With no rain in several weeks, the narrow streets stank from the accumulation of trash and waste. In the days of King Edward and during most of King Harold's brief reign, the capital was kept fairly clean. But now in the chaos of the new order even such fundamental services as collecting the bodies of the dead and disposing of stray animal carcasses had broken down. Roanna was appalled as much by what she smelled as what she saw.

The swift journey from the Algerson stronghold had tired her. Nights spent sleeping on the ground and rising after only a few hours to move on left her spent and aching. She was dirty, hungry, and distinctly out of sorts. But not for the world would she let Colin see her discomfort. Especially not when she was there on sufferance, against his better judgment, which had urged him to leave her at home.

Their "discussion" about that still rankled. Once the last remnants of the battle were cleared away and the traitors who had opened the gates were executed, it was quickly decided that Colin must present his case to William himself if he was to have any hope of retaining his lands.

"The King is a reasonable man," Guyon had claimed. "He knows he can't possibly replace all the native lords, nor does he wish to. As long as you can convince him of your loyalty, he will be likely to accept you."

"Even though I killed DeBourgnon?" Colin asked skeptically.

"Even so. William respects strength above all. In his eyes, you will only have proven your worthiness to rule by slaying the man he sent to replace you. Once he's assured you have no argument with him, he will give you no further trouble."

Colin was doubtful. Part of him wanted nothing to do with the new sovereign, but another, far wiser side warned that he could not wage a one-man crusade against the inevitable. At least not without destroying himself and all those dearest to him.

Pride was a hard taskmaster, but honor proved stronger. His obligations to his people demanded that he at least try to make peace with the Norman.

"Very well, I will go to London. And do my damnedest to convince William I am not his enemy." A slight smile softened the hard line of his mouth. "I don't envy you. You will have to guard both our lands while I am gone."

The calmness with which he said this was an eloquent indication of the new relationship between them. In the days since their two families had been joined by marriage, and in particular since they had fought side by side against DeBourgnon's forces, Colin had come round to accepting the fact that he could trust and rely on his brother-in-law without reserve. Guyon felt the same way. The differences separating their two peoples were forgotten as they prepared to present a united front against those who dared to oppose either of them.

More softly, Colin added, "Keep Roanna safe for me."

Guyon surprised him by grinning mischievously. He glanced toward his sister, who had abruptly broken off her conversation with Brenna and was glaring at them. Glad that it was not he who provoked her ire, her brother settled back to watch.

"Am I a child, to be left in another's care?"

Colin frowned, perplexed by the angry glints in her amber eyes and the sudden haughtiness of her manner.

"No, of course not. But I thought naturally you would prefer to remain here."

He didn't add that she was only just beginning to recover from the effects of near-rape. The bruises he saw each night on her honeyed skin filled him with rage he barely managed to conceal. Holding her in his arms as she drifted to sleep, he lay awake long hours wishing DeBourgnon was still alive so that he might kill him again and again.

"You were wrong. My place is at your side."

The flat certainty of this statement made Colin's eyebrows arch. "Your place," he reminded her firmly, "is for me to decide."

Before Roanna could reply, his sister-in-law interrupted. Gently, she said, "Guyon, why don't you tell Colin what happened when you tried to go off to London alone last year."

A low laugh escaped her husband. He smiled in rueful memory. "My sweet wife decided to accompany me. She hid in the baggage train of a merchant and then made her way on board my ship. I didn't discover her until it was too late to turn back." He shrugged resignedly. "I was angry enough at the time, but truth be told, I quickly became glad to have her with me."

Colin stared at them in astonishment. Brenna was a gentle, tractable woman deeply in love with her husband and disinclined to oppose him in any way. If she was capable of going off on her own, how much more likely Roanna would be to do the same.

166

"Well . . . perhaps, if you're really certain you want to come along. . . ."

"I am." Her anger faded as she reached out a hand to him. "Fifty years hence I may be willing to be parted from you for some short time, but right now I cannot bear even the thought."

Forgetting the other couple who watched them tolerantly, they gazed into each other's eyes with all the intentness of lovers enthralled by one another.

That, Roanna remembered ruefully, was their last peaceful moment for quite some time. Colin quickly became caught up in preparations for the journey. The most skilled and highly disciplined of his retainers were chosen to accompany them. They had the formidable appearance of a war party eased only by the presence of Roanna, several baggage carts, and a dozen somber servants not at all sure they wanted to make the journey but with no other choice.

As she took in the full extent of London's unruliness, she felt justified in having brought so much help. It would be an uphill battle to establish any sort of orderly household in the midst of such chaos. They were fortunate in having already secured lodgings. Alaric and several thegns had ridden ahead of the main party for just that purpose. The grizzled old warrior waited to greet them at the entrance to a rather dilapidated but good-sized residence.

"Welcome, my lord, my lady. I trust your journey was uneventful."

Colin nodded gruffly. He was in no mood for small talk. "Well enough. How are things in the city?"

Alaric shrugged. "About as you see." Signaling

grooms to take their horses, he walked inside with them where they could not be overheard by passers-by.

"The court, such as it is, is in turmoil. As near as I can determine, William's supporters are split in two groups. The more sensible seeks an accord with us so that he can reign peacefully. The other will not be satisfied until the last piece of English land is held by a Norman. Balanced between them is our audacious Conqueror. He needs the support of both, though how he expects to reconcile two such opposing views is beyond me."

"Don't underestimate him," Colin muttered. "He has already accomplished more than anyone would have thought possible."

Roanna half listened to them as she looked around her new home. What she saw did not inspire confidence. The former residence of an Anglo-Saxon noble fallen on hard times since the invasion, the three-story structure might once have been a gracious, well-appointed establishment. But months of neglect had taken their toll. The plaster walls were peeling, birds nested in the rafters, the floors were covered with waste-encrusted rushes that served no purpose other than to attract vermin, and what little furniture remained looked about to collapse.

Leaving the men to their talk, she hastily summoned the servants. The first priority was to get the kitchen in operation. Colin had brought some fifty retainers with him, all of whom would expect to be fed well and amply before the day was out.

Setting three of the strongest men to work scouring

the floor and walls, she soothed the irate cook and baker who claimed they could not function in such surroundings, ordered the food supplies to be off-loaded at once from the baggage carts, and began setting up her pantry. Later she would have to go to market, but first something had to be done about the sleeping arrangements.

The retainers would sleep on the lower floor adjacent to the kitchens. They had their own pallets and blankets, so that was no problem. But not even the most hardened warrior would cheerfully bed down in such filth. Giving thanks for the foresight that had caused her to bring along so many mops and buckets, she put more servants to work cleaning the men's quarters.

The main floor on a level with the street would serve as their hall. Colin had already taken possession there, along with his most trusted thegns and housecarls. Heedless of the disorder, they were deep in discussion and would not welcome any disturbance. Deciding that part of the house could wait, Roanna continued upstairs.

The rooms she would share with her husband were in somewhat better repair than she had hoped. Several shutters covering the small windows were askew, but they could be quickly put right. There were signs of damp rot in the walls, but since the weather was warm that was not an immediate problem. It was the probable infestation of vermin that worried her.

At both her brother's keep and Colin's stronghold, stringent measures were taken to keep down the ubiquitous fleas, lice, and rats. Rushes were changed frequently, tapestries and bed covers regularly beaten, wastes scrupulously removed, and foodstuffs kept in metal bins. Even so, constant vigilance was needed to prevent those carriers of disease and death from invading even the best-run household.

Spotting several small holes near the floorboards, she ordered them closed up at once. What little furniture remained was removed for burning. A harsh solution of lye and camphor was prepared to clean every surface before Roanna would allow her own goods to be brought in.

By afternoon, the air was considerably fresher and the house looked far brighter and cheerier. Even Colin, absorbed though he was in worldly matters, noticed the difference.

"You have done wonders," he told her sincerely as he prepared to leave for court. "I'll be back before dark. Don't see how hard you can work."

She agreed perfunctorily, well aware that men had no idea of what it took to make a house livable. The servants were already drooping with fatigue, and Roanna felt that her very bones ached. But far too much remained to be done for anyone to rest just yet.

Forcing her weary body back up on her palfrey, she set off for the London market with a suitable escort led by Alaric.

The small shops and stalls were densely packed together and crowded by all manner of produce and goods. Colorful banners fluttered in the slight breeze as the shouts of peddlers, oracles, healers, horse traders, and gaily dressed women offering more personal services added to the din.

To the casual eye, it looked as though little had changed since the invasion. But the prices were ten- and twentyfold what they had been, and the merchants were quick to ignore anyone who looked Anglo-Saxon in favor of the Norman conquerors.

Despite the richness of her garb, Roanna still had some difficulty getting served. Only the well-armed men behind her assured that the grain merchant whose shop she entered first gave her his full attention. At least until a plump, overdressed Norman matron decided she did not care to wait.

"Here, here, my good man. I have far better things to do than waste my time. If you prefer the patronage of"—the matron looked down her nose derisively— "natives, I will go elsewhere."

The flustered shop owner instantly broke off his discussion with Roanna. "Oh, no, my lady! My apologies, I assure you I had no intention to keep you waiting. Please, how may I serve you?"

Somewhat mollified, the matron sniffed. "Well, perhaps you do have some quality goods. . . ." With a doubtful look, she fingered a sample of bread before popping it into her ample mouth.

Only a slight flush betrayed Roanna's anger. Drawing herself up, she said firmly, "If you don't mind, I have not yet finished giving my order."

The matron swallowed abruptly. About to deliver a proper dressing down for such presumptuousness, she realized the disdainful young woman had addressed her in perfect Norman French. Unable to reconcile the Anglo-Saxon garb with such fluency, she stuttered, "W-why you aren't . . . that is . . . are you Norman?"

"What difference does it make? I was here first, therefore you will wait until my business is completed."

As though to emphasize her words, her watchful guard stepped closer. The large, grim-faced thegns had not missed a word of the exchange. Their hands on their weapons were enough to make the merchant wish he had chosen that day to remain abed.

Sputtering, the matron glanced from Roanna to the men-at-arms in disbelief. "Why I never. . . . How dare you! Have you no idea who I am?"

Amber eyes looked her over scornfully. "Your dress and manner proclaim you the wife of some landless knight, one of the multitude who have come here hoping to be given property. If your husband is as foolish as you, I doubt even the beneficence of King William will stretch far enough to grant your wish." Dismissively, she added, "Your upstart behavior displeases me. While I finish my business, you may wait elsewhere."

The matron turned alternately bright red and sickly gray. She was tempted to argue further, but Roanna's self-assurance stopped her. Few social gaffs were as serious as annoying a member of the aristocracy. Her chest heaving in indignation, she stalked off, still unsure as to whether she should stand and fight or thank God for having gotten off so lightly.

Behind her, Alaric and the men laughed, very pleased with the way their high-spirited mistress had handled the situation.

Ignoring both their amusement and the merchant's dismay, Roanna calmly completed her order. Since she had no idea how long they would be in the capital, she arranged to receive large quantities of flour and grain. In such tumultuous times, there were likely to be sudden shortages of staples.

The cost was outrageous, but Colin had fortunately anticipated the effects of war on the economy and had brought along a more than ample supply of gold. Any lingering hesitation the merchant might have felt evaporated when he saw the glint of her coin.

Saying a silent prayer of thanks that she had sensibly packed her own salt, spices, and herbs, Roanna was eager to complete the rest of her business. There were similar orders to be placed with the vendors of poultry, beef, and cheese.

Leaving the last shop, she was just beginning to relax when a sodden group of Norman knights stumbled from a nearby tavern. Her guard was instantly alert. Surrounded by the thegns, Roanna was in no danger of being harmed. But she was nonetheless subjected to the lewd comments of the knights who despite their state quickly noticed her extraordinary beauty.

"You there, wench! Wha'd'you want with those piss-ass Anglos? Come ov'r here an' we'll show wha' a real man's got!"

Roanna turned away, intending to ignore them. But her guard was not willing to overlook their explicit gestures and catcalls. Before she could make a move to prevent it, the fierce thegns drew their blades.

"Show *us* what you've got, Norman," one growled menacingly. "We'll be glad to hack it off for you!"

"Alaric, stop them! We don't want trouble."

Roanna's plea fell on deaf ears. The housecarl had no intention of letting such insults go unpunished. His own weapon was in his hand as he gently but firmly motioned her aside.

"This won't take long, my lady. We know you're anxious to get home."

"Alaric! I meant it! I want you to stop them!"

"I will, my lady, I will. But just not quite yet. . . ." Stepping forward with agility that belied his years, he joined the thegns.

Inebriated though they were, the Normans quickly realized their danger. Hastily drawing their own weapons, they spread out in a shaky line to meet their attackers. The crowd swiftly drew back until a large, open space was cleared before a row of stalls. Merchants rushed to remove the more breakable of their goods, but the rest of the men and women kept their attention focused firmly on the confrontation.

It turned out to not be much of a contest. When sober, the Normans were undoubtedly quite able fighters. But with their reflexes so dulled, they could do little to block the Anglo-Saxons, who struck remorselessly. Alaric drew the line at killing, but he permitted his men to wreak full vengeance up to that point. None of the knights escaped without severe wounds. Battered and bloodied, they fled ignominiously to the delighted shouts of the crowd, which left no doubt of its loyalties.

"There now, my lady," Alaric soothed as he sheathed his sword, "that didn't take long at all."

Roanna could not deny her satisfaction at the way the situation was handled. She was about to admit that it had been worth the wait when a sudden exclamation from the sidelines forestalled her.

"That was absolutely marvelous," declared a low, feminine voice. "If only there were more such men left in England!"

Turning, Roanna came face to face with a middle-aged but still quite comely woman of noble bearing. Apparently overcome by her own daring, the lady blushed becomingly.

"I beg your pardon, I should not have interfered. But after all that has happened . . . it was just so good to see an Englishwoman protected by such strong, able men."

Roanna was about to assure the lady that her approval was appreciated when she was suddenly brought up short by Alaric. In the space of moments, the grizzled housecarl had somehow acquired the look of a callow, bashful youth. He flushed painfully, his black eyes wide with dawning wonderment as he stared at the lady.

"Uh . . . it was nothing . . . really. Anyone would have done the same."

Turning the full force of her admiration on the hapless man, the lady said, "I beg to disagree, sir. You must not underrate yourself. Rarely have I seen such bravery or skill."

Roanna watched the exchange with fascination. The lady's veil covered a thick braid of chestnut hair lightly streaked with silver. Her large blue eyes were surrounded by tiny wrinkles, the legacy of a lifetime of frequent smiles. Her complexion was smooth, and her generous mouth framed perfect white teeth. The figure hidden by her tunic and surcoat veered toward matronly, but there was nothing displeasing in the ample curve of her breasts and hips. Alaric evidently did not think so, for he was hard pressed to tear his gaze from her.

Nor did the lady seem any less fascinated by him. Long moments passed as they stared at each other. Only a slight movement by Roanna broke their preoccupation.

"Forgive me," the lady murmured at bit breathlessly. "You must think me very rude not to have introduced myself. I am Lady Margaret Yateson, from Norfolk."

"I am pleased to meet you," Roanna said kindly, identifying herself. "Thank you for your praise of my guards. I agree that it is well deserved."

She hesitated for a moment, unwilling to intrude on the privacy of one who was still a stranger. But the unusual circumstances of their meeting forced her to speak.

"I can't help noticing that you seem to be alone here. After what has just happened, I appreciate more than ever the value of an escort. Perhaps we could conduct you somewhere?"

"Oh, no," Lady Margaret broke in, clearly embarrassed by the offer. "I really did not mean to intrude."

"But you have not," Roanna assured her hastily. Something in the woman's manner suggested she was suddenly uncomfortable with the situation and would try to take her leave. Alaric's interest alone was enough to make Roanna want to prevent that, but she was also curious herself about why a lady of quality should be wandering about the market unguarded.

Swiftly, she went on, "I have only just arrived in London and being without the company of women, I am anxious to make new friends. You would be welcome to sup with us."

"That is very kind, but . . ."

"The kindness would be yours." A bit shyly, Roanna added, "You see, I am but newly married. This is the first time I have set up a household. I have so many questions, but there is no one to answer them."

"Oh! Well, in that case. . . ." Assured that her presence would not be a burden, Lady Margaret was more inclined to accept. There was only one more problem to overcome. "I will need to send a message to my friends so they do not become concerned about me."

"Certainly. One of my men will take it."

"Uh . . . no . . . that is very kind, but there are always children around the market eager to run errands." As though to prove her point, Lady Margaret swiftly summoned an urchin. She spoke to him very softly, but Roanna could not help but overhear the directions. He would find her friends, Lady Margaret said, "by the river, under the bridge."

Well aware of the acute housing shortage in the city and its impact on anyone who did not have ample coin to buy shelter, Roanna immediately understood why her new acquaintance had not wanted her to send one of her own men. The thought that any lady should be ashamed of circumstances foisted on her by a cruel twist of fate dissolved the reticence that would normally have kept her silent.

"Lady Margaret, I do not mean to intrude upon your privacy. But I am not ignorant of the problems confronting many in this time of turmoil. The residence my husband has secured for us is not luxurious, but it is large. You and your friends would be welcome as our guests."

All the color fled from their new acquaintance's face as she protested. "Oh, no! That is very kind, but we couldn't."

"Of course, you could," Alaric insisted. He, too, had grasped the meaning of Lady Margaret's unease and was horrified that a gentlewoman should be so impoverished. "As her ladyship has explained, she is but one lone woman struggling to set up a household without any prior experience. Surely any help you and your friends could give would be a godsend."

Roanna raised her eyebrows slightly at what she regarded as a rather exaggerated view of her ineptitude. But she was willing to overlook his presumptuousness if it convinced Lady Margaret to give in. For good measure, she added her own plea.

"I would be most grateful. Truthfully, I have nowhere else to turn."

The older woman hesitated a moment longer before at last accepting the sudden upturn in her fortunes. "I would be delighted to assist you," she said softly, "and I am sure my friends will be as well."

A glimpse of what must have once been a vibrant nature showed as she added, "Why between us your house may quite well become the best-organized, most precisely run, and relentlessly immaculate residence in all of London. And then your poor husband will undoubtedly rue the day you came to market!"

Roanna joined her laughter. She did not as a rule make friends easily, but she already guessed that Lady Margaret would prove the exception. Arm in arm, the women left the market with a bemused Alaric and the highly diverted thegns trailing after them.

# Chapter Eleven

"WHO ARE ALL THOSE WOMEN?" COLIN ASKED AS HE entered the bed chamber. Returning late from the court, he had wearily climbed the stairs to the family quarters expecting to find only Roanna and a few servants. Instead he encountered half a dozen ladies, who greeted him politely before hurrying about their business.

Putting down the linen she had just folded, Roanna motioned to the two girls who were helping her. Bobbing swift curtsies, they slipped from the room. Not until they were safely in the passageway did they giggle to each other about why their recently wed lady was so anxious to be alone with her lord.

Standing on tiptoe to brush a kiss against his lean cheek roughened by a day's growth of beard, she explained, "I met them today in the market. They are all from Norfolk, women of good birth and rank. Their husbands were either killed at Hastings or died later trying to resist the Normans. Their lands have been seized by marauders who did not even wait for the King's approval before taking what they wanted. They have come here in the hope of finding someone to present their case to William and obtain redress."

Colin grimaced. The women's painful story was only one of many he had heard that day. They had left him not only saddened but frustrated by the unfamiliar sense of acute powerlessness.

"Do you have any idea how many such women there are in England?" he demanded sharply. "Hundreds at least, if not thousands. The chances that they will ever regain even a fraction of their property are almost nonexistent."

"Surely that is no reason to ignore their plight?" Roanna objected, her eyes widening at his acerbic tone. She had expected him to unhesitatingly approve her actions. "They have almost no money and have been without proper food and shelter for weeks now. Was I supposed to turn away from them?"

Sighing, Colin lowered himself into a chair. He stretched his long legs out before glancing round the room. Dimly he noticed that it was swept clean and well appointed with their own furnishings brought from the Algerson stronghold. The large bed was already set up and covered with fresh linens. Vivid wall hangings softened the harsh plaster walls. Copper braziers filled with charcoal stood ready in case the night turned cool. A pitcher of steaming water sat on a small table. Next to it lay a basin, towels, and a small bar of soap.

Ignoring her question, he posed one of his own. "You didn't follow my instructions, did you? About not working too hard."

Pouring him a mug of ale, Roanna neatly turned the subject back to her new friends. "I had a great deal of help. All the women have ample experience in running households. In just the few hours they have been here, they've accomplished miracles."

Colin smiled wryly. He would get no rest until the matter was settled. "All right, if you insist on talking about our guests right now, we will. I counted six. Are there any more?"

"No . . . but some do have children with them."

"Where do you expect to put them all? Surely not downstairs in the men's quarters?"

"Of course not! I know you haven't had a chance to really look over the house, but it happens to be very large. There is plenty of room for them on this floor." Handing him the ale, Roanna added, "Besides, any place is better than where they were."

Hastily she sought to defuse any further objection he might have. "These women know a great deal more than I do about how to make the most of our supplies. They've already mentioned several ways to stretch the foodstuffs and organize the house so that it is less costly to run."

As she spoke, she stared at him closely. Granted, she could not claim to have known her husband long, but their acquaintance had been, to put it mildly, rather intense. She felt she knew him well and was certain his seeming reluctance to welcome the women was completely out of character. So much so, in fact, that she wondered if he wasn't using it to distract both himself and her from far graver matters.

For the first time since he entered the room, she noticed how exhausted he looked. Deep lines were etched into his face, his mouth was set grimly, and his huge, powerful body seemed drained of energy. His vulnerability shocked her.

Since his remorseless destruction of the Norman attackers, she had fallen into the unconscious habit of thinking he was too powerful and too resolute to be overcome by any danger no matter how immense. That belief provided great comfort to her at a time when she badly needed it. But it also did him a terrible disservice.

Kneeling down beside him, Roanna gently took his hand in hers. The calloused palm was rough against her skin. She caressed it tenderly as she gazed up at him with eyes dark with worry.

"What happened at court today?"

He shrugged and glanced away. "Nothing for you to be concerned about."

"Don't say that!" Roanna exclaimed, dismayed that he should treat her like some spineless fool who had to be sheltered from every problem. "I am your wife. I have a right to know what has so distressed you."

"Nothing," Colin repeated stubbornly. More softly, as though the words were dragged from him against his best intention, he added, ". . . and everything."

Roanna's hand tightened on his. "Tell me."

183

A moment more he hesitated before a low sigh escaped him. "It's difficult to explain exactly. Much that I saw and heard was helpful to us. It's unlikely that I will have any real trouble meeting with William, even if it does take a few days to arrange. What will happen then is anyone's guess, but at least I will have the chance to present my case. If I consider only our own situation, I should be optimistic. But there is so much else. . . ."

"Like the women in the market," Roanna murmured.

Colin nodded. "I was not prepared for the more insidious effects of the Conquest. Men I've known for years and have always looked up to are suddenly stripped of everything important to them. Not just property, but pride, confidence, initiative. . . ."

A harsh edge entered his voice as he added, "It's as though they're simply going through the motions of being alive. I think some of them really wish they had died at Hastings. At least then they would be fallen heroes instead of the guilty survivors they perceive themselves to be."

"Why would anyone regret surviving that battle?" Roanna asked, genuinely bewildered by a possibility that had never so much as occurred to her before. "Even the Normans agree that you all fought magnificently and did everything you could to win."

Colin reached out to gently touch the silken fall of her hair. It glowed golden against his bronzed skin. "I can't explain it to myself, much less to anyone else. But the point is, whatever we tried to do, or might have done, we failed. Now we have to come to terms with the fact that someone else was stronger, luckier, more determined. It doesn't really matter what gave the Normans their victory. What counts is that we have to live with the effects of it." A rueful smile curved his hard mouth. "Some of us are managing that better than others."

Silently Roanna gave thanks for the fact that he was one of those whose strength and courage were equal to the task. She did not doubt that his present weariness was only a temporary setback he would swiftly overcome, especially since she would give him all possible help.

Her head dropped into his lap. Filled with the desperate need to ease his burdens, she was thwarted by her own limits. Beyond encouraging him to talk out his worries within the comfort of a tranquil home, there seemed nothing she could do.

Colin gazed down at her lovingly. He could feel her strength flowing into him and marveled that she had so much to give. For the first time in his life, he understood what the union of a man and woman could truly mean. Father Elferth's prayer that they would be united in spirit seemed to be coming true.

Inevitably, this new, deeper realization of all their love meant had physical consequences. Fatigue vanished as desire surged through him. He longed to reach out for her, but the memory of what she had almost suffered at DeBourgnon's hands stopped him.

Roanna felt the tension in him and was bewildered by it. Since the attack on the stronghold, Colin had not touched her except to give comfort. She had told herself that the time and circumstances were not right for them to come together again physically. But the privacy they had lacked during the journey to London was no longer a problem. In the quiet room separate from the rest of the household, he had only to reach out to her.

When he did not, she felt unbearably bereft. Coldness washed through her. Her body stiffened as she fought down the urge to plead with him to tell her what was wrong. Only dread of the possible answer stopped her. Stiffening, she pulled away from him.

Colin mistook her anxiety for aversion. He dropped his hands instantly, making no effort to stop her as she stood up. The precious moment of unity evaporated. They were once again isolated in their separate worlds.

Stung by what she regarded as his indifference, Roanna had to call on all her courage to get through the rest of the day. Already exhausted by the journey and the task of setting up the household, her resources were further strained by the jovial mood prevailing during supper in the great hall.

In addition to their women guests, Colin had invited several of the men he met at court to share the meal with them. The chance to come together at the table of a powerful Anglo-Saxon lord just as in the old days was an unlooked-for opportunity to forget briefly the hardships of the last few months. Barely had the meal begun when it took on the air of a celebration.

Roanna had generously shared her wardrobe, with the result that Lady Margaret and her friends were all elegantly turned out. Vast relief at the sudden change in their fortunes brought a glow to faces that only a few hours before had been strained and careworn. After balancing for so long on the keen edge of pain and despair, they could not contain their joy at being once again surrounded by the familiar talismen of their own way of life.

Nothing could ever lessen the shadow of grief for those who were lost. But there was still room in their hearts for gladness as they took their places in the hall bright with torchlight and boisterous with the din of reassuringly male voices.

Nor were the men immune to the sudden appearance of women whose serene graciousness made the events of the last few months seem no more than a terrible dream. For a brief time, it was possible to throw off the weight of despair and luxuriate in the well-remembered but hitherto lost pleasures of congenial company, excellent food, and feminine admiration.

The shortage of furniture in the keep made it necessary for everyone to sit together. The ladies were quickly surrounded by appreciative gentlemen vying for their attention. Roanna could not help but smile as she watched Alaric maneuver to keep Lady Margaret at his side. But her smile faded when she glanced wistfully at Colin, only to find his eyes shuttered and his expression blank.

Though they sat side by side throughout the meal, they said hardly a word to each other. Roanna forced herself to pretend interest in the conversations going on around her. But try though she did, his nearness remained a constant distraction.

Seated as close together as they were, she could feel

the warmth of his body through her thin silk tunic and surcoat. Several times as they passed platters between them their fingers brushed. The contact robbed her of what little appetite she had. The food might have been tasteless for all the attention she was able to give it, and the wine she sipped seemed sour.

Acutely aware of how strange their behavior must appear, she was grateful for their guests' absorption in each other. Only Lady Margaret showed any sign of noticing that something was wrong. Her quizzical glance fell first on Roanna, then on Colin. For just a moment there was a glimmer of understanding in her bright blue eyes before simple courtesy compelled her to look away.

As the meal wore on, Roanna sensed a change. Soothed by ample food and drink, reassured by their familiar surroundings, and perhaps innocently provoked by the presence of the women, the men were slowly moving from nostalgic talk of the time before Hastings to tentative consideration of what had happened since then.

It was the battle itself that became the focal point of an increasingly spirited discussion. All the men had fought on that blood-drenched plain, and each had his own ideas about what had gone wrong.

"It was the forced march from London," one asserted. "By the time we found William the army was exhausted. A few days rest would have made all the difference."

"The reinforcements we were expecting from Northumbria would have turned the tide," claimed another. "But they never arrived."

A red-bearded lord shook his head vehemently. "We still had the Normans outnumbered *and we were* winning, until that false retreat they staged tricked us into giving up the high ground."

There were reluctant nods around the table. "King Harold, may he rest in peace, tried to stop that," Alaric remembered. "But the army wasn't sufficiently disciplined. Once the ranks broke, there was no calling it back."

"The Normans didn't have that problem. Whatever else they may be, they know how to fight as one."

"Still, if Harold hadn't been killed, it might have been different."

"Aye, it was when he fell that the battle was lost."

"What army can be expected to fight without its leader?"

"If William had died, the Normans would have been the ones to lose."

"It was just the luck of the draw that Harold was cut down."

"Who could have figured a Norman archer would be skilled enough to hit him from that distance?"

"No one could have prevented it."

"That's right, no one."

Instinctively, the men glanced toward Colin. He had remained silent throughout the discussion, but they presumed he would agree with them. Instead, he shook his head firmly.

"The battle was lost before Harold fell. With the Normans fighting from horseback and us on foot, our only chance was to hold the high ground and make them come to us."

His silvery eyes clouded over as he recalled the scene. "The rain that had fallen over the last few days made the going slick. The horses wouldn't have been able to keep their balance. It would have been a matter of picking them off man by man. But instead some of us gave up the advantage to follow the feigned retreat. That lack of discipline and the failure to obey even the King's direct orders destroyed us."

So softly that the men had to lean forward to hear him, he added, "Don't look to chance for the cause of our defeat. It lies in ourselves. We were a loose coalition fighting under a leader some of us did not want. The Normans were completely unified and unshakably disciplined. Moreover, we clung to the old methods of warfare that had always worked for us while the Normans made great advances."

"It's easy to find fault after the fact," the red-bearded lord protested, "but you sound as though you think we deserved to lose."

"To the degree that we were unprepared to protect ourselves, our families, and our lands, that is true."

His somber judgment settled slowly over the table. The women glanced at each other anxiously, unsure how the men would react. But they need not have worried. Having achieved his aim in puncturing the cloud of rationalization and excuse, Colin moved quickly to bolster the shaken company.

"None of which is to say it is too late for us to learn from our mistakes. Certainly we have lost much. But if we conduct ourselves properly, we also stand to gain."

"How so?" Alaric asked softly. He had never before

heard his lord speak so ruthlessly and could only wonder where it would all lead.

Leaning back in his chair, Colin twirled the wine cup between his fingers absently before he said, "William's position is precarious. He has sufficient men to keep us at bay, but not enough to take over the country completely and remake it in the image of Normandy. Without our cooperation, he will have to spend the rest of his life fighting to hold on to what he won at Hastings, and in the end he will be defeated anyway because he will never have the time to implement policies and truly rule."

"Are you seriously suggesting," growled Redbeard, "that we should help William?"

"Why not? We share the same quandary. If we continue to resist him, we condemn ourselves and our families to a life of perpetual fighting. But if we accept him and work with him, we will have the chance to create our own future instead of merely having it imposed on us."

Gently, he concluded, "What it comes down to is whether we are to be the conquered victims of a bloodthirsty tyrant or the loyal subjects of a just sovereign."

"*Just!* What makes you think William is prepared to treat us fairly?"

"Are you so foolish as to trust him?"

"Why would he ever see us as anything but enemies?"

"Because," Colin explained calmly, "William believes above all that it is his destiny to be King of

England. To achieve that, he risked the considerable wealth and power he held as Duke of Normandy, as well as his very life. But without our loyalty, his victory is empty. Therefore, I believe he will go to considerable lengths to effect an accord with us."

Long moments stretched by as the lords considered this. Some clearly wanted to believe Colin was right. Others fought against relinquishing the dream of continued resistance and an eventual return to the old ways. It was left to red-beard to express what seemed to be the consensus.

"Then God be with you, if you intend to act on that belief. For if you are wrong, the suffering of the past months will seem as nothing compared to what you will have to endure."

Roanna clasped her hands tightly in her lap where their trembling could not be seen. Red-beard's hope seemed more in keeping with a curse.

If Colin shared her thought, he did not show it. His manner betrayed no doubt as he said quietly, "But if I am right, all those who choose to follow me will share the benefits."

It was clearly an invitation that held intrinsic attractions to the sorrow-ridden men around the table. They could have no hope of a better future without a leader to guide them to it. Colin possessed all the requirements of strength, intelligence, and most importantly, the vision of what might be. Moreover, they sensed he was an honorable man who would not simply use them to achieve his own aims.

No such decision could be taken without due consideration, but already there were signs of how the men might respond. Their earlier vehemence gave way to thoughtfulness. The meal ended quietly, each going off to consider his own position.

Roanna watched them leave with mixed feelings. Part of her resented the burdens she did not doubt they would shortly place on Colin. But the other, wiser part accepted the inevitable. She could not pick and choose from among his attributes. It was the whole man she loved, and he was clearly called to the service of his people in their time of need.

But it was her own needs that occupied her thoughts as she made her way upstairs. Having sent her maids to their beds long before, Roanna was alone as she slipped out of her tunic and surcoat and laid them neatly away. With the night so warm, she left the few sleeping robes she had brought in the chest and selected only a thin wrap to wear as she combed out her hair.

The polished metal mirror perched on a table reflected back a vision of loveliness. A radiant tumult of golden silk framed the slender line of her throat and delicate shoulders. Her thick lashes cast shadows on the high cheekbones brushed by a faint touch of rose. The amber eyes they shielded were turned inward upon the landscape of her own thoughts. The ripe curve of her mouth was even softer than usual, giving her a poignant air of vulnerability.

Her slender body but lightly covered by the robe was unconsciously tensed. Each sound from the corridor reverberated through her. Long moments passed, but still Colin did not come.

Plaiting her hair in two loose braids, Roanna rose

with a sigh. She blew out the candles and climbed into bed disconsolately, shivering at the wide expanse of empty mattress. The long, arduous day had left her exhausted. Her limbs and back ached, but it was the pain deep inside her that kept sleep away.

Lying on her side away from the door, she stared into the darkness. Images of Colin rose to torment her. They had such a brief time together before the attack on the stronghold, yet every moment of it stood out in sharp detail.

She did not even have to close her eyes to recall the look, sound, touch of him on the night they first made love when his tender passion and consummate skill brought her to blinding recognition of her full womanhood. Nor had she forgotten an instant of the blissful time they spent together before their marriage as all the world faded to insignificance before the sheer, overwhelming joy they found in being together.

Their wedding and the incandescent hours that followed remained as clearly etched in her mind as though they had just occurred. But after that there was only darkness.

Her terror during the attack and her revulsion at DeBourgnon's brutal handling of her had long since faded to only a faint echo of what they had been. It was Colin's behavior since then that tormented her with each breath she drew.

No woman could have asked for a kinder, more considerate husband. He had cared for her himself, washing the soot and grime from her body and rubbing a soothing salve into the bruises left by the near-rape. It was his hands that wrapped her in a warm blanket and his arms that held her as she drifted into healing sleep. But through it all, she had sensed a remoteness about him, as though he was forcibly restraining himself from giving vent to his true feelings.

And now, after the long days of their journey to London and especially since their brief encounter before supper, she greatly feared that they might never recapture their earlier happiness with each other.

A single, glistening tear slid down her cheek. Roanna brushed it away impatiently. She was not one to give in to self-pity. Refusing to indulge her melancholy thoughts any further, she was about to light the brace of candles beside the bed and fetch something useful to do when the sound of footsteps in the corridor stopped her.

Colin entered the room quietly, apparently expecting her to be asleep. After the relative brightness of the torchlit corridor, it took his eyes a moment to adjust to the darkness. When they did, he was startled to find his wife sitting up in bed regarding him with steady eyes that betrayed nothing of her thoughts.

"You must be very tired," he murmured. "Why aren't you asleep?"

"I was waiting for you." This was the truth, although she had only just realized it. Instinctively, she had not wanted to let another night pass without learning whether or not her fears were justified.

Colin did not seem pleased by this announcement. He frowned slightly as he sat down on the edge of the bed to pull off his boots. "That wasn't necessary. I know you need to rest."

"There are other things I need more." She had not expected to state the case so bluntly, but now that the words were out she was glad.

Colin, however, heard her through the filter of his own concerns. He thought she was referring to the present uncertainty of their lives, to the dangers that would face them if William refused to acknowledge his suzerainty of his own lands. Certainly it was the right of women to expect a secure home.

His eyes were bleak as he said, "I am sorry. If I had suspected what was going to happen, our marriage would not have taken place."

Roanna swallowed painfully. His words seemed to confirm her deepest fears. Colin regretted their marriage, wished it had never happened. How was she to blame him when every time he looked at her he must be reminded of the suffering others of her race had brought down upon his people? If her love alone was not enough to overcome his abhorrence of all she represented, there was nothing more she could do.

Wordlessly she turned from him, burying her head in the pillows. Her tears fell soundlessly into darkness that held not a glimmer of light or hope.

# Chapter Twelve

"I'M NOT SURE HOW LONG WE WILL BE, ALARIC, SO why don't you escort Lady Margaret to the market and then see her safely home?" Colin smiled as he made the suggestion, well aware of how eagerly his housecarl would accept it.

"Well, if you think that's best. . . ." The older man hesitated, but only for a moment. He was a bit embarrassed at having his desires so plainly known, yet nothing could detract from the pleasure of spending a day alone with the lady who made him feel like a young and eager boy on the verge of first love.

They went off together happily, not seeing how swiftly Colin's smile faded the moment their backs were turned.

Roanna stood beside him silently. Much as she

enjoyed Lady Margaret's company, she was glad he had sent the pair away. The strain of hiding her feelings from such astute eyes was becoming intolerable. At least inside the court she would be surrounded by people who were far too occupied with their own concerns to notice hers.

Leaving the rest of their escort with instructions to wait, they proceeded through the gate set in the high wooden wall guarding the new royal residence. At first glance, William's headquarters were singularly unimposing. A rough-hewn round tower on top of a hastily erected mound commanded a view of the murky Thames and the southeastern portion of the city. It was large enough to house only William and his closest retainers. The rest of the Conqueror's court made do with tents scattered about the bailey, or when that proved too crowded sought shelter in the nearby taverns and inns.

Off in the distance about half a mile upriver stood what had been the royal home in the time of Edward and, very briefly, Harold. It was a far larger and more gracious structure, but lacked the security William considered essential.

Until he could construct the great White Tower for which his architects were already drawing up plans, he would make do with shelter that was, if not elegant, at least easily protected.

Roanna did not consider his caution misplaced. The citizens of London were notorious for their willingness to rise up and make trouble on the slightest pretext. And they were only the most visible danger in a country finely balanced on a knife's edge between war and peace. If hotter heads than Colin's prevailed among the remaining Anglo-Saxon lords, William would need every bit of his military advantage to keep his newly won kingdom.

Still she couldn't help but wish that he had spared a moment's thought for those who had to make their way through the crude bailey to reach him. Dust stirred up by countless feet and hooves clogged the air. The stench of uncollected garbage and overloaded latrines made her nose wrinkle. She had to step carefully to avoid the piles of manure which in a well-run household would have been gathered for fertilizer almost before they hit the ground.

Shaking her head, she wondered what the Duchess —or was it now Queen?—Matilda would say if she could see such squalor. William's ducal manor in Normandy, presided over by his wife, was a model of cleanliness and comfort. But no such feminine influence yet existed in his new domains. The few Norman women who had so far arrived were not of sufficient rank to dare to advise him. As for the others of her sex Roanna glimpsed around the stronghold, they were clearly bent on providing services that had nothing to do with cozy domestic concerns.

Turning a blind eye to the prostitutes who were, after all, an expected feature of such an encampment, she followed Colin up the steep wooden stairs to the tower. The entrance to the great hall was unguarded, but not because of any carelessness. No guard was needed when everyone inside was armed to the hilt and ready to pounce at the slightest sign of trouble.

Roanna's back stiffened as she saw the instant

belligerence Colin's presence provoked. Several of the knights nearest them actually reached for their swords, while others were content merely to step forward threateningly.

Only her husband's firm hand on her arm kept her moving forward. Glancing up, she was relieved that he seemed unaffected by the hostile display. His slate gray eyes revealed only confident assurance. The hard planes and angles of his face were set impassively. But for the gleaming chain mail stretched across his powerful torso and arms, and the war sword buckled to his side, he might have been in his own keep.

Though he showed not the slightest hint of anger, his manner alone was enough to cause the knights to hesitate. Not even their vastly superior numbers were enough to make them risk challenging so powerful a warrior, who, it was already rumored, just might have William's favor.

Despite the muttered speculation about why he was there, no effort was made to stop them. Still Roanna did not breathe comfortably until they were through the great hall into the anteroom which led to the new King's private quarters.

The room was crowded, but they were instantly spotted by the man awaiting their arrival. Odo, Bishop of Bayeaux, newly made Earl of Kent, and half-brother to William, was a startling figure. His ecclesiastic robes were rigorously correct, yet the scarlet velvet embroidered in lush gold thread and the massive cross embedded with precious stones looked utterly out of place on a man so evidently born for the battlefield rather than the pulpit.

Not that the apparent contradiction between his character and his calling seemed to trouble Odo. At thirty, he was renowned as the ruthless facilitator of his half-brother's policies. His abilities were manifold, extending from the skilled manipulation of legal doctrine to the deadly wielding of a studded mace at Hastings, where he accounted for more than his fair share of the slaughter while technically honoring his church's prohibition against her servants carrying swords.

Since being appointed to the bishopric at the scandalously young age of nineteen, Odo had never permitted his holy orders to interfere with his pursuit of either power or pleasure. He was known to favor an accord with the Anglo-Saxons for the simple reason that further warfare would threaten the wealth he hoped to accumulate. Said to be far readier to destroy an enemy or tumble a wench than to say a mass, he had nonetheless impressed Roanna as a man who, once having decided where his interests lay, could be trusted to follow through. As such, she was glad to see him.

The bishop shared her delight. Odo's small black eyes set beneath bushy brows glowed as he looked her over appreciatively before reluctantly turning his attention to Colin.

"My Lord Algerson, you are most welcome, as is your lady. Roanna, my dear, you look glorious as ever. I trust you have been well?"

"Exceedingly, sir. And you?"

"Much better now that you are here." Dropping his voice confidentially, he added, "Never have I seen a drearier court. We are starving for even a morsel of beauty and here you provide a banquet."

Colin's eyes widened slightly at such blatant flattery, but he made no objection. No man, even one as bold as Odo, would advertise his intended seductions in the very presence of an armed and clearly watchful husband.

Nor did Roanna mistake his compliments for anything more than what they were. The bishop, greedy and lustful though he might be, was the furthest thing from a fool. Even as he gave the appearance of flirting with her, he was adroitly steering both Algersons toward a secluded corner where they could all talk privately.

Her presence provided the necessary cover for what quickly developed into a serious discussion.

"Ordinarily, it would take several weeks for you to arrange a meeting with the King," Odo began, "his schedule being so hectic. But frankly I think William will be curious to meet the man who killed DeBourgnon. So I will present you to him this morning after he finishes with the council."

This was far better than Colin had hoped. Whatever William's reaction to the Norman's death, he wanted to get this first meeting over with as soon as possible. At least then he would know if there was any basis for accord.

Cautiously, he said, "I thank you for your assistance. There must be many here who don't want me to get anywhere near William."

"That is true," Odo confirmed. "It is an unfortunate

fact that we are suffering an excess of shortsighted fools."

The prelate's bushy eyebrows arched toward a tall, red-faced man standing near the door. "Take FitzStephen, for instance. He won't be content until every Anglo-Saxon lies dead and every inch of land is ruled by a Norman. It doesn't seem to occur to him that if we embark on such a course of wanton destruction, there will be no one left to tend the fields, reap the harvest, pay the taxes, or do any of those other mundane things necessary for a kingdom's survival. Moreover, FitzStephen and the others like him forget that William still has another realm to rule. Part of his time each year must be spent in Normandy. But he cannot leave here until he is confident of peace."

"Perhaps I can help instill that confidence," Colin suggested quietly. Meeting the bishop's gaze, he added, "For a price, of course."

Odo nodded philosophically. He lived in a world in which everything from eternal forgiveness of sins to the sexual use of another's body could be had for a price. Far from objecting to Colin's pragmatism, he applauded it. William, the bishop believed, would find this Anglo-Saxon chieftain a great improvement over the blustering hotheads who had all too much in common with the more belligerent faction of his own supporters.

A short time later, as the council filed out, the bishop ushered both Algersons into the royal chamber. For all its grand name, the room was in fact no more than an alcove partitioned off from the rest of the hall and sparsely furnished by a table cluttered with papers and several chairs.

William rose as they entered and came forward to meet them. He was little changed from the man Roanna remembered. From their mother, he and Odo had inherited certain shared characteristics. Both had straight black hair and penetrating onyx eyes, and both were tall, ruggedly built men with barrel chests and long, powerful arms and legs. But there the resemblance ended.

The bishop's blatantly sensual nature was in sharp contrast to his half-brother's marked self-restraint. All William's considerable intellect and energy was poured into the single goal of attaining and keeping power. At thirty-nine, he had no time or thought for other pursuits, no matter how pleasant they might be. Not even his love for his wife, Matilda, who was in every sense his helpmate and confidante, was allowed to distract him from what he clearly regarded as his life's purpose.

In another man, such single-mindedness might have been distasteful. But in William it was balanced by innate charm that made even the most skeptical feel easier about him.

The smile he beamed at Roanna lacked the teasing lustfulness of his half-brother's welcome. Rather it was a genuine expression of warmth and pleasure that evoked an instant response in kind.

Sweeping him a graceful curtsey, she said softly, "It is good to see you again, my lord. My brother sends his greetings and hopes that all continues to go well with you."

William nodded kindly. On closer inspection, she could see new lines cut deeply into his tanned features and shadows beneath his eyes that bespoke too many nights with little sleep. But his voice was firm as he said, "It does, although I miss Guyon's help. Is he pleased with his new lands?"

"Very much, sire. Your generosity touched us deeply."

"Not at all," the King protested. "All that your brother received was more than deserved. But now, let us speak of you. What's this about you marrying?" His gaze slipped to Colin as Odo stepped forward to make the introductions.

"Algerson . . ." William murmured thoughtfully after a moment. "That name is familiar."

"I do not doubt it, my lord," Colin said quietly, "since not too long ago you awarded my lands to another man."

The King's eyebrows arched in a mannerism he shared with his half-brother, but which on him looked less benign. Though he was several inches shorter than Colin and not as powerfully built, he exuded no less a sense of authority and confidence. Coldly, he demanded, "Indeed, and have you come to ask me to rescind that decision?"

"Not precisely. I have come to tell you that the man you sent is dead. DeBourgnon perished at my hand, as will anyone else who attempts to take what is mine. Therefore, in the interest of preventing further bloodshed, I ask you to simply confirm my right to the lands so that my people may live in peace with yours."

Roanna held her breath, afraid that William would

not take this advice well. Certainly he could not be accustomed to an Anglo-Saxon warlord flatly telling him what he should or should not do. But the King surprised her. He appeared at least willing to listen to what Colin had to suggest. The glance he shot at Odo indicated his wish to be alone with his unexpected guest.

"Come along, my dear," the bishop said, taking her arm. "I'll fill you in on all the latest gossip and you can tell me how that exquisite sister-in-law of yours is doing."

Resignedly, Roanna allowed herself to be led away. She understood that her husband and William had to speak privately, but that didn't stop her from worrying about what would be said. The reassuring smile Colin gave her only slightly eased her concern. She gave scant attention to the bishop's chatter as he guided her back into the antechamber.

With rare sensitivity, Odo quickly gave up the effort to distract her from her concern. When she was settled on a bench along one side of the room, he discreetly took his leave. She was left to gaze at the curtained partition concealing the royal chamber and wonder anxiously what was being decided within.

The slender, pale-skinned young man who appeared at her side had to cough several times before she noticed him. When she at last looked up, he smiled shyly.

"Hello, Roanna. It's been a long time. How have you been?"

Much of the tension fled from her delicate features, to be replaced by genuine pleasure. "Robert! It is you. I wasn't sure for a moment. You look so . . . impressive. . . ."

A boyish grin wreathed his long, narrow face as he glanced down at the richly made tunic, chain mail, and sword that had sparked her comment. Teasingly, he said, "Why, thank you! I can remember a time when you thought me quite the opposite."

Flushing slightly, Roanna made room for him on the bench. Gently, she insisted, "I always found you a valued friend, Robert. If I ever gave you any other impression, I am sorry."

Light blue eyes softened as he gazed at her, missing nothing of her radiant beauty or of the faint hint of tension evident in the set of her firm chin and the slight stiffness of her shoulders. "No, you never did. It was just that I wanted more." There was no rancor in his tone as he added, "At any rate, you are right about my looking different. I suppose the last few months have changed me quite a bit."

"Have you been here all that time?" Roanna asked, anxious to steer the conversation away from talk of the past.

Robert nodded. "I came in October with the Duke, I mean, the King. My father secured a place for me in the army, although at the time I don't imagine anyone thought I could be much use." His thin, sensitive mouth curved in a self-deprecating grin. "As you may remember, I was never all that good at fighting."

That was true. When she had last seen him in Normandy the year before, Robert d'Almaric was still conscientiously plugging away at his martial training, without much success. His lanky build and poor coordination worked against him, but more serious than either was his lack of aggressiveness. Robert never experienced the fierce blood lust that propelled his kinsmen into battle. His patient, reasonable nature predisposed him to far more peaceful pursuits. By the time he reached his eighteenth year, he was almost the despair of his warlord father, who could scarcely believe he had sired so unsuitable an heir.

Not until Robert suddenly, and from Roanna's point of view quite unexpectedly, asked for her hand in marriage did his father come round to thinking there might be some hope for the boy after all. If he had the sense to go after one of the most bedable girls at court, and an heiress to boot, perhaps he wasn't completely lacking in manly instincts.

To Roanna, the proposal was so unwelcome as to be almost a betrayal. She and Robert were friends. They shared many of the same interests and enjoyed each other's company, but never for an instant did he make her feel the slightest desire to be his wife.

Fortunately, Guyon understood her dismay. He had gently turned aside the proposal, but not even his considerable tact was enough to spare Robert from hurt. He left court for his father's estates, and Roanna did not see him again until he suddenly appeared at her side in the King's antechamber.

"You were good at many other things," she reminded him gently.

Robert's mouth tightened. "Perhaps, but they didn't count for much. I finally came round to accepting the fact that to get what he wants in life, a man has to be willing to fight for it."

Sadness darkened Roanna's eyes as she recognized a harshness in him that had never before been present. Whatever part she had played in bringing that about, she regretted it deeply. Meeting his gaze, she asked, "And have you gotten what you want?"

Robert glanced away, still more self-conscious around her than he liked to admit. "Some of it. I fought well at Hastings. William recognized that by granting me an estate. It isn't large, but it's enough to start. I'm no longer dependent on my father's wealth, although now he's willing to give me anything since I convinced him I'm really a man."

"You were always a man, Robert. There was never any doubt about that."

Slender shoulders shrugged dismissively. "Maybe not, but I prefer things the way they are now." Hesitating a moment, he added, "That's enough about me. What brings you here? I heard you were . . . married. . . ."

Roanna nodded. "I am here with my husband. He has come to speak with the King."

"Do I know him?"

"I doubt it. His name is Colin Algerson."

Robert's eyes widened. He could not quite hide his shock. "An Anglo-Saxon? What was your brother thinking of to allow such a union?"

Not even the memory of their friendship would cause Roanna to tolerate such prejudgment of her marriage. Stiffly, she said, "He was thinking of my happiness."

"Oh . . . well . . . I suppose if Guyon gave his approval, there must have been some good reason. It's just that . . ." Turning to face her, he suddenly took her hand in his. "I'm still very fond of you, Roanna. You must know that."

Uncomfortable with his touch but not eager to cause a scene, she let her hand stay in his as she said, "We have been friends for a long time. I hope we can remain so."

This was not precisely what Robert wanted to hear, but before he could press her they were interrupted by a low, feral drawl. "Very touching. I hope I haven't arrived at an inconvenient moment?"

Colin loomed over them. To the casual observer he looked perfectly calm and unruffled. But to Roanna who knew him far too well to be fooled, the coldness of his slate gray eyes, the hard line of his mouth, and the jagged pulse beating in the corded column of his throat were eloquent warnings of barely contained rage.

Hastily, she said, "May I present Sir Robert d'Almaric, an old friend of mine from the court in Normandy. My husband, Colin Algerson."

Robert stood up quickly, not sure precisely what it was about the other man that disconcerted him, but fully aware that despite his newly proven skills it was still the height of foolishness to provoke anyone so large and brutal-looking. Bowing stiffly, he muttered, "My congratulations on your marriage, sir. You are most fortunate."

Colin smiled humorlessly. "How kind of you to say so. I'm sure my wife wants all her . . . friends . . . to approve her marriage."

Roanna flushed at his emphasis, but kept prudently

silent. This was not the place to try to convince him that any hopes Robert harbored toward her were completely unwarranted. Nor did she consider it fair that she might have to do so. After all, Colin had all but ignored her for days, making it clear that his brief infatuation with her body was over and that he had no further use for her. What right then did he have to deny her the admiration of another man?

Robert glanced at her worriedly as it dawned on him that he might have caused some problem for her. The thought of Roanna having to face the anger of so formidable a husband filled him with dread. But before he could make any effort to defuse it, Colin took charge of the situation.

Grasping Roanna's arm, her lord informed her, "I will be here for some time yet meeting with William. The escort will take you home." Nodding dismissively at Robert, he firmly propelled his wife out of the room and downstairs to where their guard waited.

Acutely aware of the curious stares they were provoking from the other nobles, she had no choice but to go with him quietly. But the angry glints in her tawny eyes warned that she considered the matter far from settled.

Snatching her arm from him, she lifted herself smoothly into the saddle and seized the reins of her palfrey from the page who held them. Refusing to look at Colin, she nudged the horse forward determinedly.

The clatter of hooves drowned out a low sigh that might have been her name muttered by a frustrated, worried man.

Lady Margaret greeted Roanna upon her return, but the older woman quickly guessed her young friend was in no mood for company. She watched her go upstairs worriedly, wishing there was something she could do to help but knowing that matters of the heart had to be resolved alone. Nonetheless, when Roanna did not appear in the hall for supper that evening, it was Lady Margaret who sent a tray up to her and dropped by her room later to make sure she had eaten.

Roanna greatly appreciated her concern, but she could not speak of her feelings to anyone. Nor could she sleep. Far into the night she lay awake thinking over what she would say to her arrogant, overbearing husband when he at last returned.

But by morning there was still no sign of Colin, and Roanna's anger had long since turned to desperation.

# Chapter Thirteen

"I'M SURE THERE'S NOTHING TO BE WORRIED ABOUT, my lady," Alaric soothed. "Lord Colin had a great deal of business to take care of at Court. If he was delayed very long, he'd most likely just decide to stay over."

Eyeing his young mistress compassionately, the housecarl added, "I warrant he'll be home any minute." Privately, he was not so certain. While it was true that the previous night had been moonless, and therefore so dark as to make even a short journey almost impossible, it was also strange behavior for any new husband to dally so late as to be prevented from returning to his bride.

Alaric did not seriously consider that Colin might be in any danger, although he had already decided to wait only a short time longer before going to look for him. What troubled him most as he studied Roanna's

213

wan face and red-rimmed eyes was the traitorous thought that for the first time in all the years he had known and respected him, his master just might be acting the fool.

Masking any hint of what was in his mind, he reassured his mistress once more before departing to work off his irritation and concern on the hapless men-at-arms drilling in the courtyard.

Roanna had no such ready outlet for her own anxiety. She found only minimal distraction in helping Lady Margaret and the other women clean the great hall. With the assistance of several servants, the matted, filth-encrusted rushes were removed, the floor and walls scrubbed, a fresh coat of whitewash applied, and new tables and benches set in place.

The work was hard but satisfying. With her sleeves rolled up, her hair tucked out of the way, and an apron covering her sensible linen tunic, she managed to expend a little of the nervous energy that threatened to explode within her. But by mid-morning she was still acutely on edge.

Her thoughts kept wandering back to Colin, to the way he had been since the attack on the stronghold, and, most particularly, how he had looked when he found her with Robert. Her temper worsened as she reflected yet again on the injustice of his condemnation. If he meant to punish her by staying away like this, he was succeeding all too well.

The other women stayed prudently out of her way as she fiercely scrubbed and swept. Though their gratitude to Roanna knew no bounds, not even Lady Margaret felt close enough to her yet to offer sympathy. They could only glance at each other worriedly and hope that his lordship would soon return.

Just before noon, he did. Roanna heard the men-at-arms guarding the gate call a welcome as Colin rode in. She straightened in sudden dismay. After the rigorous labors of the morning, she must look a fright. Dropping her broom, she hurried upstairs. If she had to confront an angry, vengeful husband, she would do it looking her best.

By the time Colin entered his wife's chamber, she was seated on a bench near the window looking the perfect picture of serene femininity. Her apparent composure belied the frantic speed with which she had stripped off her soiled tunic, dropped a fresh silk concoction over her head, and hastily combed the tangles from her golden hair.

Her beauty swept over him as he missed nothing of the flush coloring her damask cheeks, her ripe mouth, and the glitter of her amber eyes which he presumed were caused by her pleasure at his return.

In fact, they were the outward evidence of apprehension that had grown throughout the long night and morning. But as Roanna took in her lord's disheveled appearance, anxious dread gave way to pure, unbridled outrage.

Colin's hair was mussed, his eyes red-rimmed, his chain mail soiled, and he sported a night's growth of beard. But none of that accounted for the fury that swept through her. It was the reek of stale ale and wine undercut by a musky perfume clinging to him that brought her to her feet, her small fists clenched and all sense of caution banished.

Sneeringly, she hissed, "I trust you had a profitable stay at court, my lord. It certainly seems to have taken its toll of you."

Colin's smile abruptly vanished. He was very tired, his head hurt, and he had a great deal on his mind. He was in no mood to cope with a spitting termagant.

Sitting down heavily on the side of the bed, he muttered, "Hold your tongue, woman. You have already displeased me far enough without being so foolish as to add to it."

Roanna's eyes widened in disbelief. Her temper, already so severely strained, broke all bounds. She took a step toward him wrathfully. *"I have displeased you!* Why you pompous boor! How dare you speak of my behavior when your own is such a model of indecency!"

For a moment, Colin's broad forehead creased in bewilderment. He had no idea what she was talking about, but that did not change the fact that he would not permit his wife to speak to him in such a way. His voice was dangerously low as he warned, "You forget yourself."

As near to him as she now was, Roanna could make out other telltale signs of debauchery. As though the perfume were not bad enough, there was a streak of vermilion along his jaw. While she had no more experience with face paint than any other lady, she had no difficulty guessing the cause of the stain. The whores who thronged London used just such an artifice on their lips, cheeks, and even the nipples often left exposed by their blatant garb.

Tears turned her eyes to glittering jewels as pain

twisted through her. Ignoring his warning, she blurted, "On the contrary, I have not said enough. Pray tell me, dear husband, how you spent this past night."

Colin paused in the act of pulling off his boots. He looked up at her ominously. "Do you suggest I need account for my actions to you?"

A harsh laugh broke from Roanna's clenched throat. "I can well understand why you do not choose to. But at least enlighten me as to who was so gracious as to offer you hospitality when you found yourself stranded for the night."

Colin shrugged, perplexed as to why she should give such importance to the identity of his host. "I met again with the King and then with Odo. Our talk ran late. So the bishop gave me supper and a bed." More sharply, he demanded, "Does that satisfy your unseemly curiosity?"

It did, all too well. The prelate was renowned for the licentiousness of his household. His holy office did not prevent him from providing the most wanton entertainment for his guests. Far from concerning himself with the state of the souls he harbored under his roof, he counted it a matter of honor that no bodily urge need go unsatisfied. As in Normandy, his table groaned with an excess of dishes, wine and ale flowed in reckless abandon, and whores were ever ready to be tumbled.

More hurt than she would have believed possible short weeks before, Roanna faced him pale and trembling. The knowledge that he no longer desired her had been bad enough. But to be forced to confront his infidelity was more than she could bear.

Recklessly, she lashed out, "What a hypocrite you are! I saw how you looked when you found me with Robert. You twisted our friendship into something shameful and blamed me for it. Well, let me tell you, anything I felt for him was far better than whatever feelings you had for the tramp you dallied with last night!"

Colin's eyes widened in disbelief. For a brief instant he thought he must be dreaming. The furious shrew confronting him bore no resemblance at all to his beautiful, loving wife. But then, he reminded himself grimly, perhaps she no longer had any reason to be alluring with him. Now that she had rediscovered her Norman, perhaps she regretted ever allowing him to touch her.

*Allowing?* His face twisted unpleasantly. She had done a damn sight more than that. He well remembered how frankly she had admitted her desire for him. Was she as forward with other men now that she had discovered the full power of her beauty?

His boots dropped with a thud. Rising swiftly, he crossed the room in angry strides. A flush darkened his rugged face and his eyes glinted like molten silver.

"Do you hope to hide your own guilt by falsely accusing me?" He seized her by the shoulders, shaking her hard. "Was there more than what I witnessed at court? Perhaps you long for that soft-skinned Norman. If so, you are doomed to disappointment. No man takes what is mine!"

Roanna stared up at him in bewilderment. He seemed perfectly sincere in his outrage, yet she could not reconcile his assertion that he was wrongly charged with the lingering evidence of his night's escapade.

Mindless of his harsh grip, she shot back, "Do you think me an addled fool? If you truly thought to trick me, you should at least have bathed before coming up here! The stink of whore's perfume and the mark of her lips belies you!"

Whatever Colin had been about to say died in his throat. He stared at her dumbfounded, the fury slowly dying from him. All that was left was hurt surprise.

"You thought . . ." Easing his grip without completely freeing her, he said slowly, "It is true there were women at the bishop's residence. Apparently, there always are. . . . I may well have picked up their smell . . . and one or two may have gotten close enough to leave some trace. But that does not mean I laid with any of them."

His face hardened again as he demanded, "How in God's name could you believe me capable of such infamy? Whatever have I done that you would think I hold our marriage vows in such low repute?"

Roanna hesitated, wanting desperately to believe him. But the memory of his aloofness over the last few days prevented her. Dismally, she said, "What confidence can I have that you would not take another woman now that you no longer desire me?"

Colin had the curious sensation of having stepped into some twisting maze composed not of serpentine paths but of words that reflected nothing he knew of order or reason. Confounded, he shook himself as though trying to fling the fog from his mind.

"No longer desire you? By all the saints, that is the

most demented charge you have made so far! Have your wits fled entirely?"

Her face was drained of all color as Roanna shook her head dismally. "You have made no secret of your feelings. Throughout the journey here, you could hardly bring yourself to touch me. And only the other night you turned away yet again when there was no reason why we couldn't have . . ." She broke off, the look in his eyes making her forget whatever else she might have said.

After the long, tension-filled hours at court, Colin's temper was strained to the breaking point. The realization of how totally his wife had misunderstood his actions destroyed what little patience he had left.

Between clenched teeth, he muttered, "Sweet Lord! When I think of the nights I lay beside you aching with desire but telling myself you needed time to get over DeBourgnon's attack. Now it seems I should have been less concerned with your feelings and more with my own!"

A mercurial glitter flared deep within his eyes. All restraint gone, he hauled her against him, heedless for the moment of her weaker body. Roanna struggled vainly. Prudence warned her she had better put some distance between herself and her outraged husband, but his overwhelming strength would not permit it.

Lean, brown fingers tangled in the neckline of her tunic. The thin silk gave way shrilly, falling open to fully expose the honeyed length of her body. His molten gaze fell like a burning brand on the soft fullness of her breasts, her narrow waist, and the ripe swell of her hips. Fear splintered through her as she saw his anger turn abruptly to lust.

Twisting desperately, she tried to break free. But his arms were steel bands holding her remorselessly in place. In her struggles, her soft thighs brushed against him. Too late she realized her efforts had only aroused him further.

A low, triumphant growl sounded in his massive chest as he lifted her as easily as a feather. Roanna did not have time to take a breath before she was carried across the room and dumped unceremoniously in the center of the bed.

Colin towered over her. His silvered stare never left the naked loveliness before him. Quickly he stripped off his chain mail and sword. They fell to the floor with a thud, where they were quickly joined by his tunic and loincloth.

The sight of his exposed maleness finally broke through the paralysis of shock that had held Roanna motionless. For the first time, she knew only terror at the thought of being taken by him. His huge, pulsating manhood would hurt her badly.

Frantically, she tried to escape across the bed. But Colin was too quick for her. He dragged her back easily, his weight crushing her into the mattress. A sinewy leg thrown over her soft, slender limbs pinned her in place. Her arms were pulled tautly above her head. One large hand manacled both her wrists while the other moved over her insolently.

His voice was low and thick with anguish as he muttered, "Oh, no, my lady! I have a great thirst which may well take the rest of this day and night to slake. If you have any care for yourself, you will lie still and let me do as I wish."

Roanna had no choice but to obey. Never before had she known the full, unbridled extent of his strength. She was trapped under him, small and helpless. Not even DeBourgnon's attempted rape had made her feel so vulnerable.

Yet beyond her fear was another, even stronger emotion. In the moment before Colin's mouth came down on hers, she caught a glimpse of pain in his eyes, so raw and intense as to stun her. Dimly, it occurred to her that she had done him a terrible disservice. Rather than believing him guilty of such base behavior, she should have trusted him enough to speak openly of her concerns. Instead, she had failed in this, her first test as his wife.

As the acknowledgment of her own part in what was happening burned into her, her last efforts at resistance dissolved. Though it might already be too late, she could at least offer him the comfort of her body.

Yet even as she yielded, Colin's hard, demanding touch softened and grew gentle. He could no more hurt her than he could rip out his own heart. His hand moved tenderly down the silken column of her throat to cup her breast. He took the full heaviness of it in his palm, squeezing lightly, before his fingers closed round the rosy peak which tightened instantly at his caress. A low groan broke from Colin as her response shattered the last of his anger.

"Roanna! I've missed you so!"

Scalding kisses trailed over her shoulders and into the scented hollow between her breasts before his mouth at last closed over the straining bud. Roanna's slender body arched beneath him. Unable to deny the waves of pleasure undulating through her, she could only cry out softly at the warm, moist tugging that brought a piercing core of need to vibrant life within her. She had been so long without him that every part of her yearned for his full possession.

The callous rape she had expected when he threw her on the bed never happened. All rage vanished before the overpowering drive to give pleasure as well as take it. In the burning firestorm of their need, neither could endure extended lovemaking. Her slender hips arched against him, mutely pleading for his possession.

As the full length of his hardness thrust within her, Roanna cried out. She was driven beyond any level of pleasure she had previously known. The world shattered into shimmering fragments. Shards of rapture tore through her. Colin was fully with her at that explosive moment when they shared the furthest limits of ecstasy.

In the aftermath of such utter fulfillment, they drifted easily into sleep, their arms and legs still wrapped around each other. During the night, the air grew ominous with the gathering force of a summer storm. Thick black clouds massed toward the west. Sky-wide fingers of lightning and long, rippling rolls of thunder presaged the sudden rush of rain that brought relief to the parched city.

So violent was the storm that it penetrated even

their deep sleep. Half waking, they instinctively reached for each other. With the first desperate passion satisfied, Colin drove her over and over again to the brink of completion. Roanna writhed beneath him, welcoming the most daring caresses. The fresh-washed scents of fertile ground and verdant life blew over their heated bodies.

Stripped of all restraint and inhibition, she could not resist the need to know his body as fully as he knew hers. Her small hands pressed against his shoulders. "Please . . . lie back. . . ."

Dazedly, Colin obeyed. Powerful tremors racked his body as she bent her head. The silken mass of her golden hair fell across his loins. He could hardly believe what she intended. . . .

"Roanna!"

Her tongue flicked out again, surrounding him with warm, wet pleasure. A purr of delight rippled from her. She loved the way he tasted, loved the musky scent of him, loved how he arched into her. Above all, she loved the freedom he gave her to explore his body as he had hers.

Enchanted, she moved with instinctive skill. Her thumb and forefinger closed around him, stroking rhythmically as her tongue found the ultrasensitive ridge near his tip. The response was highly satisfying. She felt a pulsing inside her mouth before a few drops of salty liquid slid down her throat.

Colin cursed inwardly. He had not meant that to happen. His self-control was perilously close to shattering. Another moment and he would have subjected her to an experience he thought only the most knowing and willing woman should encounter.

His first efforts to pull away were thwarted. She was enthralled by what had just happened and wanted more. Not until Colin grasped her head between his big hands and gently lifted did she reluctantly relinquish him.

A gasp of surprise broke from her when he turned on her stomach. The soft pillows smothered her moans of ecstasy as his hair-roughened thighs straddled hers. Searing kisses fell from the nape of her neck along the delicate line of her back to the lithe curve of her buttocks. Sliding his warm, powerful hands down her belly to the hot, moist haven he sought, he raised her hips. Slowly, carefully his manhood thrust within her, driving them both to tumultuous fulfillment.

When they were at last able to breathe again, Colin laughed softly. Drawing her closer against his massive chest, he murmured, "Did you truly believe I no longer wanted you?"

Roanna blinked dazedly, trying to recapture the fear that had been so piercingly real only a few hours before. Her husband's explosive lovemaking had driven it so far from her mind that she had difficulty recapturing even the memory of her dread. "I . . . it did seem that way . . . although now I can't imagine why I didn't realize you were only thinking of my welfare. I must have been very confused. . . ."

Warm lips brushed her forehead tenderly. "Just because in the last few weeks you've been kidnapped, held hostage, introduced to womanhood, married, and almost raped you feel confused?" Huskily, he muttered, "I think that can be forgiven."

Roanna smiled against the velvet steel of his chest. His willingness to excuse her terrible accusations touched her deeply. She snuggled closer to him as his big hand caressed the silken fall of her hair.

Gently, Colin said, "I'm sorry for the way I acted when I saw you with d'Almaric."

"It doesn't matter." The warm strength of his body made her forget she had ever rankled at the injustice of his jealousy. "So long as you know I could never care for another man."

He was silent for a moment before asking hesitantly, "Can you forgive me also for my behavior this afternoon?"

Roanna could not suppress the soft giggle that broke from her. "Considering what it led to, I will be magnanimous and pardon you."

That earned a soft swat on her bottom. Satisfied that the misunderstandings of the last few days were banished, they were about to drift back into sleep when Colin remembered something he had forgotten to mention. Softly, he said, "I may not be here in the morning when you wake. The King wants me to go down to East Anglia to see if I can convince a couple of recalcitrant Anglo-Saxon lords to come to court."

Half-asleep, Roanna had to struggle to understand him. Thickly, she murmured, "Why is he sending you?"

Colin shrugged. "I suspect he wants a demonstration of my loyalty before he confirms my right to my lands. At any rate, it is not a difficult task. I should only be gone a week or two at the most."

Reassured, Roanna closed her eyes again. She hated the thought of being parted from him even so briefly. But if the journey enabled them to return home soon, it would be worthwhile. Much too content to harbor any concern, she gave up the struggle to stay awake. The dreams that carried her far from shore bore no resemblance to the nightmare about to descend on them both.

# Chapter Fourteen

THE RAIN CONTINUED WITHOUT LET-UP THROUGH ALL the following day and night. Much of it fell in too great a torrent to be soaked up by the parched ground. The dirt-packed roads quickly turned to mud and became all but impassable. Gushes of water poured down the peaked roofs of the houses. Huge puddles formed, spreading into each other until they became rushing streams. By the second day, basements and store-rooms had begun to flood.

Roanna and her ladies were kept busy supervising the servants and what men-at-arms could be spared from guard duty to help carry supplies to safe ground. Despite their best efforts, it was almost impossible to keep anything dry. Precious grain and flour had to be hastily transferred to tin vats lest they become rancid.

Bags of charcoal and stacks of wood had to be stored on the main level above the kitchens, which quickly became unusable. The household was reduced to cold meals that only added to the all-pervasive air of dank misery.

As the rain continued into a third day, Lady Margaret brought the unwelcome news that the backyard latrines were beginning to flood. The stench wafting over the city indicated they were not the only ones with that problem.

Wearily, Roanna said, "As soon as the men finish patching the roof, set them to work with buckets. They won't like it, but there is nothing else to be done."

Lady Margaret nodded calmly. She had not forgotten how to order men to onerous tasks. The retainers might protest, but they would obey.

Fastening a shutter more securely against the sodden grayness, Roanna asked, "What about the stables? How bad are they?"

"At least four inches is on the ground and more coming in."

Neither woman had to be told that the horses and other livestock could not be left standing in so much water. They would have to be moved to the higher ground farther behind the house and a temporary shelter put up for them there. Yet another task for the already overburdened men.

"I'll speak to Alaric about that," Roanna began, only to break off when she saw the quick flash of disappointment in the older woman's eyes. "On second thought, would you take care of it?" She could not suppress a smile at her friend's eager assent. Lady Margaret was a wonder. Even in the midst of such dismal weather, she could find something to be happy about.

Sighing, Roanna wished she could be as good-natured. Since waking alone in her bed after the night of tumultuous lovemaking, she had waited anxiously for Colin's return. Even without the storm, the journey would take at least a fortnight. If the Anglo-Saxon lords proved difficult, he might waste days more convincing them their best hope lay with William. Flooded roads and washed out bridges would further extend the time they were apart. Even a single day without him was too much. She wondered disconsolately how she would get through long, empty weeks.

The flood and all the damage it brought at least provided some distraction. But she could hardly be glad of it when the very basics of life were threatened. Besides the danger to food and livestock, the storm brought an even more serious peril. As the flood spread beneath ground, the inevitable consequence of poor sanitation began to show throughout London.

Rats driven from the burrows along the riverbanks appeared in the streets. At first there were only a few, hardly alarming to a populace accustomed to seeing vermin rooting among the uncollected garbage and carcasses. But their number rapidly increased.

Made reckless by hunger, they quickly took to prowling during the day. Swarms of hundreds, even thousands descended on the city, terrorizing children and horrifying even the most impervious adults. For the first time in living memory, a thriving market developed for the usually maligned cats, who were suddenly worth their weight in gold.

Roanna, whose kindly heart had caused her to begin feeding half a dozen strays when she first moved into the house, was now rewarded by their predatory skills. But as the infestation grew, she was forced to buy several more fierce tomcats who soon found themselves hard pressed to keep up with the teeming mass.

It became a regular morning chore to sweep out the remains of rats killed during the night and beat off with brooms those too bold to withdraw on their own. Food supplies had to be constantly checked against their inroads, no open source of water could be left untended without attracting them, and anyone so foolish as to stick an unwary hand or foot anywhere was liable to receive a vicious bite which quickly became infected.

Unable to bathe or change to clean, dry clothes, too sickened by the constant stench and the rustle of vermin to eat, and so overtired as to make sleep almost impossible, Roanna succumbed to the malaise that inevitably descended upon all the residents of London. Like everyone else, she wanted only to huddle in a corner and not move until she could see warm sunshine and vermin-free streets.

In the midst of all this virulence, Robert d'Almaric chose to come visiting.

He arrived just as she was about to acknowledge a losing battle against the influx of green slime that was spreading in patches over the peeling walls. Wearing a damp, wrinkled tunic, with her hair pinned up haphazardly beneath a kerchief, she hardly thought herself a sight to gladden anyone's eye. But Robert was apparently of a different mind.

Barely had he stepped over the piles of mud and rubble to enter the great hall when his face lit up. Coming hastily to her side, he exclaimed, "I'm so glad you're here! I thought you might have left."

Since that was exactly what Roanna wished she had done, she could only glare at him discouragingly. Long moments passed before she remembered her manners. "Robert. . . . How nice. . . . What brings you out in such weather?"

Her tepid tone did not faze him in the least. Enthusiastically, he said, "Why, you, of course. You've been on my mind constantly." His voice dropped meaningfully. "How are you?"

Roanna's eyes widened slightly. How on earth did he think she was? Tartly, she snapped, "Wet, tired, and disgusted, like everyone else. Aren't you?"

A bit taken aback by such sharpness, Robert retreated a step. "Uh, yes, of course." Gallantly, he added, "But seeing you more than makes up for it."

Fighting down a hysterical urge to laugh, she shook her head. "No amount of flattery will make me believe I look anything but horrible." Seeing his distress, she allowed more gently, "But I appreciate your trying."

Such kindness, Roanna realized too late, was a mistake. Robert took it as license to pursue his cause with unseemly ardor. Seizing her hands in his, he implored, "Please tell me my impetuosity at court did not cause you harm."

Despite herself, Roanna blushed. She recalled only

too clearly where the spur to Colin's jealousy had led. But before she could say a word, Robert misinterpreted her look and struck out angrily.

"By God, if that oversized husband of yours hurt you, I will make him rue the day he was born! He'll answer to me on the field of honor! I'll challenge him to combat, and then I'll . . ."

"Robert! Don't say such things! You have no right to presume there is anything but love and devotion between Colin and myself." Dismayed by the mere suggestion that she might be the cause of a confrontation that could only end with the young man's death, Roanna did her best to soothe him quickly. "I appreciate your concern, but it is misplaced. My husband is all that is kind and gentle."

Unsure whether he was really glad about this, Robert frowned. At length, he muttered, "He had better be, or I'll know the reason why."

Mentally shaking her head over the boastful foolishness of men, Roanna quickly changed the subject. Guiding him to one of the few parts of the house left more or less habitable, she asked, "How are things at court? Are they coping any better?"

"Hardly! No one there has your good sense or skill." Looking down at her adoringly, he continued, "We are all suffering for the lack of a woman's touch. Even the King, who never seems to notice the greatest hardships, has said he would give a good portion of his new realm if Matilda could join him."

Roanna hid a smile as she thought of the changes so spirited and strong-willed a woman would make at William's ramshackle court. The men might quickly find that hot food and clean clothes were a steep price to pay for the end of their rough-and-ready male domain. But she said only, "I'm sure the Queen will come over as soon as the situation is secure. And when she does, she will undoubtedly bring a bevy of Norman ladies to gladden the heart of even the most grizzled knights." Glancing up at him, she added, "Perhaps one of them will catch your eye, if some English girl hasn't already claimed it."

Robert looked away uncomfortably. "You know that won't happen. Especially now that I've found you again."

At a loss as to how to deal with such an inappropriate declaration, Roanna tried to dismiss it lightly. "Oh, you couldn't possibly disappoint the ladies like that. After all, you are now a man of property as well as a respected knight. Naturally, you will want to marry and have children."

Robert did not disagree, but neither did his brooding manner lighten. Anxious to get back to her work, Roanna wished he would take his leave. Good manners required her to be hospitable, but she had difficulty controlling her irritation as he lingered on through a tense hour. Several times she had to head him off adroitly when he showed signs of once again declaring his devotion to her. When he at last departed, her nerves were stretched taut and her head pounded. By comparison, even the trials of the flood were preferable.

But her relief was short-lived. Robert returned the following day, this time determined to be of help. Roanna could hardly turn him away when he made such a show of helping the men-at-arms to drain the latrine, shovel out the stables, and stoke small wood fires in some of the rooms in the hope of drying them out.

Though he appeared to work hard, he still managed to be frequently near her. She would look up suddenly to find him staring at her. The naked yearning in his eyes was a clear danger signal she should not have ignored. But unwilling to hurt an old friend she had already badly wounded once, Roanna told herself she had nothing to be concerned about.

After all, she was in her own home, surrounded by her husband's retainers, and chaperoned by Lady Margaret and her friends, who quickly grasped the situation and were careful never to leave her alone with her callow admirer. With such precautions, she should be able to put up with Robert a while longer, at least until Colin returned. She did not doubt that her husband's presence in the household would be enough by itself to put an end to the visits.

The rain at last stopped, but the overburdened rivers and streams kept the city awash. Roanna was numb now to the constant dampness and the continuing plague of rats, but she was increasingly uncomfortable with the problem Robert posed.

Having worked his way into her household against her better judgment, he was no longer content merely to see her each day. Instead, he found numerous excuses to touch her, never more than on her hand or arm, but enough to make her acutely wary. Again she told herself she should ask him to leave. And again she hesitated in the name of friendship.

Matters finally came to a head ten days after Colin's departure, when she unexpectedly found herself alone with Robert in the family quarters. He had followed her up there on the pretext of bringing more wood for the drying fires. But once the logs were neatly stacked away, he showed no sign of leaving.

Instead, he came over to where she was shaking the lumps from the feather mattress. Glancing over her shoulder, Roanna was startled to find him right behind her. She straightened hurriedly, propelled by the fevered look in his pale eyes. But she was not quick enough to stop his sudden lurch toward her. Embracing her clumsily, he pressed his length against her softness.

"Oh, Roanna! How much longer are you going to torment me? You're the only woman I've ever really wanted. I can't bear to do without you!"

Choking down a panicky scream, which would have brought Colin's retainers rushing into the room and undoubtedly have cost Robert his life, she struggled to break his grip. "Let go of me! Are you mad?"

"Yes! You've driven me to a frenzy! I can't stand the thought of that Anglo-Saxon boor touching you when you were meant to be mine!"

"Don't you dare speak of my husband like that! He's a thousand times the man you are! Why, if he were here, he would . . ."

"But he isn't here! We are, and by God I mean for us to make the most of it!"

Blind rage gave Roanna added strength. She managed to get an arm free and lashed out, striking him solidly in the mouth. A thin trickle of blood seeped from his bottom lip as Robert stared at her witlessly.

"You didn't mean to do that," he whined. "I know you didn't. You just think you have to make some show of defending your honor. But believe me, my love, it isn't necessary. You will always be the most respected and honored woman to me. Only come away with me and let me prove my devotion!"

*"Come away with you!* I want nothing to do with you! You are lower than a swine to try to take advantage of me when I have felt only friendship for you!" Kicking out with a slender leg, she managed to catch him just below the knee. Robert winced in pain as his grip on her loosened. Persevering nonetheless, he attempted to press a wet kiss to her lips.

Roanna evaded him with difficulty. Seizing the first object that came to hand, she brandished a candlestick as she snarled, "A pox take you, Robert d'Almaric! You are a false friend! Get out of my sight before I forget I ever had a kind thought for you!"

He opened his mouth to protest, only to be stopped by the door flying open behind them. Lady Margaret gaped at the pair, hardly believing the testimony of her eyes. Roanna's clothes were pulled askew, her face flushed, and her arm raised threateningly. Robert looked angrily chagrined as he put a trembling hand to his wound. Stumbling past the older woman, he vanished down the stairs without another word.

Roanna collapsed on the bed, torn between tears and laughter. "He was . . . he wanted to . . ."

Lady Margaret quickly sat down beside her, easing

the candlestick from her clenched hand and putting a comforting arm around her shoulders. "Hush, now, it's all right. He's gone, and I warrant he won't be back. At least not if he has any sense. The men would make short work of him, not to mention what your lord would do if he ever got wind of this."

Roanna trembled at the mere thought. Now that her relationship with her husband was back to normal, she could not bear for anything to upset it. "God forbid! He was angry enough when Robert only spoke to me at court. If he found out . . ."

"He won't," Lady Margaret reassured her swiftly. "From the look of it, you managed to send that young whelp packing."

"I should have realized what was going to happen when he kept coming here," Roanna murmured remorsefully. "But I kept telling myself there was nothing to worry about." Looking at her friend, she said, "If you hadn't arrived when you did, I might have been left with no choice but to call the guards. Then Robert would have died, all because of my foolishness."

Lady Margaret privately thought the Norman lout deserved death for trespassing on the friendship of one so kind and giving as Roanna. But she refrained from saying so, not willing to upset the young girl further.

Instead she kept up a soothing chatter as she gently helped her to undress and tucked her into bed. Firmly, she said, "You're going to rest now whether you want to or not. These last few days have been a terrible strain on us all, but you've worked harder than anyone. It's only right we look after you for a bit."

Roanna meant to protest that there was too much yet to be done and that she really needed to be up and about. But somehow the words never passed her lips. Under Lady Margaret's gentle eye, she drifted into the first sound sleep she had known since Colin's departure.

Her rest, though desperately needed, was all too short.

Scant hours later she was awakened with the news that one of Lady Margaret's friends had been taken ill. The woman had a high fever and was barely conscious. There was a red rash on her neck and blisters under her arms. Roanna speedily made a tincture of herbs she remembered her sister-in-law recommending and applied cold compresses in an effort to bring the fever down. But she saw no improvement a short while later when Alaric brought word that two of the men-at-arms were similarly stricken.

By morning, the total number of ill in the household had risen to six with at least one likely to die.

Roanna hurried from patient to patient, changing compresses, brewing more medications, and trying desperately to stem the rising tide of sickness, which threatened to engulf the house.

Because of the flood, there was no ice available anywhere nearby. Unable to find another way to bring the fevers down, Roanna dispatched Alaric with a group of thegns and a wagon to seek out a supply. They returned with a block large enough to serve their needs for several days, but also with the news that the fever was spreading throughout the city.

"It seems to have started down by the docks," the old housecarl explained. "Several shiploads of sailors have died of it and at least a dozen merchants. In the poorer neighborhoods, they say, people are dropping like flies."

"Is there no way to stop it?"

He shook his head sorrowfully. "Not that anyone knows. The few doctors who are willing leave their homes to tend the sick are giving purges and letting blood at a fearsome rate. But that only seems to hasten the fever's course. So far as I have been able to find out, no one who gets it survives."

Roanna set her jaw angrily. She was damned if she would stand by and let death become a triumphant presence in her house. Mustering every ounce of strength and will she possessed, she threw herself into a desperate struggle for life.

But her efforts seemed to have little chance of success. The woman who was first stricken died, as did two of the men-at-arms. Refusing to give their bodies up to the hooded monks whose creaking carts began to make regular collections throughout the city, she arranged for them to be taken to a nearby cemetery, where they were given what was rapidly becoming the rarest of all luxuries, a proper Christian burial. The rites had to take place without her for she was far too busy tending to the ill to leave the house even briefly.

Alaric became her only contact with the outside world. He and those of the thegns who were still on their feet made regular forays for food and other supplies. They brought word of the plague's continued spread. It had reached beyond London, following the path of panic-stricken citizens attempting to flee its clutches. Many nearby villages now refused admittance to any stranger.

William set a stalwart example by remaining in his capital, with the rest of the court having no choice but to stay with him. But many others bribed watch captains to let them slip through the city gates, which were now kept closed day and night.

In the midst of this terrible travail, Roanna gave thanks for her husband's absence. Colin was far enough away that it would still be some time before news of the plague reached him and he could even attempt to return home. His safety was her only comfort as one horror-filled day blended into another.

Several more men-at-arms were stricken and quickly died. The disease seemed to be increasing in virulence. The sorrowful toll of the death bell could be heard at all hours. Those few courageous or desperate enough to venture out found streets littered with unburied bodies, which often lay where they had breathed their last.

Just when she believed the terror could not possibly become worse, Roanna was faced with even greater despair. Lady Margaret, who had worked tirelessly beside her to help care for the sick, joined their ranks.

Alaric found her collapsed in a corner of the family quarters, her gentle face bathed in sweat and her body racked by fever. Choking back his anguish, he carried her swiftly to a pallet.

Through waves of gathering unconsciousness, Margaret tried vainly to reassure him. "It's nothing. . . . I'm just tired. . . . Don't bother Roanna. . . ."

Alaric ignored her. He sent a thegn rushing off to find his mistress before quickly stripping the sweat-soaked clothes from her and wrapping her in warm blankets.

Margaret was not so far gone that she could not still be embarrassed by her nudity. She tried weakly to stop him, only to be flatly told, "For God's sake, Maggie, do you think I haven't already imagined you like this many times? Be a good lass and lie still, else this is the closest you and I shall ever come to what I think we both want."

His gruff frankness succeeded where nothing else would have. With a soft moan, she gave herself up to his care. When Roanna reached them scant moments later, she found her friend nestled in the old house-carl's arms, his head resting on her own and his eyes tightly closed as he sought desperately to pour his strength into her stricken form.

With shaking hands, Roanna set about what was by now the routine of care. Ignoring standard medical treatment, she did not resort to purges or bloodletting. Instead, she meticulously prepared and administered the potions known to reduce fever, lanced the puru-lent blisters, and applied the salve which through trial and error she had found seemed to prevent the rash that presaged death.

As Lady Margaret drifted in and out of delirium, Alaric refused to leave her side. Once Roanna had shown him what to do, he assumed full responsibility for her care. Drawing on the strength that had carried him through countless battles, he waged a remorseless struggle with the skeletal shadow hanging over the woman he loved.

The few others who also appeared immune to the plague took their turns beside the sick beds so that Roanna could snatch a few hours' rest. But it was on her, as mistress of the household, that the burden of treating the victims fell.

At first, the struggle was solely to stave off the specter of death. But slowly, imperceptibly, in tiny victories won from moment to moment, the tenor of battle began to change. Despite the leaden sense of doom hanging over the city, Roanna found a few tremulous signs of hope.

Lady Margaret and many of the others she tended did not die. For a while they seemed simply to hang between one world and the next as the fierce battle went on to drag them back from the precipice. But then, so gradually that she could hardly believe it, they began to heal.

Fevers hesitantly abated, resurged, then departed for good. Blisters shrank and vanished. The deadly rash withdrew, not to be seen again. Patients regained consciousness, blinked with surprise at finding themselves still in this world, and weakly called for water. There was a sudden need for nourishing broths that could be spooned down parched throats.

A week after the plague first struck, Roanna dared to believe it might be lessening. She still heard the death bell and the creak of carts outside in the streets. But inside, in her own domain, the shadow of doom was rescinding.

Two of the most seriously ill thegns recovered sufficiently to leave their pallets. Lady Margaret was still weak, but able to take solid food. Alaric sat beside her hour by hour encouraging her to eat, talking with her gently, or simply watching her sleep.

Others continued to improve slowly but steadily. Roanna was able to rest more and restore her strength. The day came when she could take time out to bathe, wash her hair, and don clean, bright clothes in a gesture less of defiance than impending triumph.

As the plague retreated, so did the effects of the flood. Those so busy caring for the ill hardly noticed that the sun had reappeared. But as the muddy roads and sodden buildings dried, the rats withdrew back to the riverbanks, and the stench of rotting waste was blown away by a fresh breeze. Hesitantly, the survivors turned their eyes to heaven and dared to ask if the cataclysm might be over.

Roanna herself declared it at an end on the day the last of her patients was able to rise from his bed and stand under his own power. In the aftermath of terror more profound than what any human force could cause, there was a natural desire to rejoice. Though the closing of the market had stretched their food supplies to the limit, she directed that a special meal be prepared. Divisions of rank were temporarily forgotten as servants and retainers alike gathered in the hall to celebrate their victory over death.

No food ever tasted better, no drink was ever sweeter than that which reaffirmed life. Roanna received glowing praise as man and woman alike credited her for bringing them safely through an ordeal which had destroyed thousands. Her embarrassment was acute as she tried to convince them that everyone had helped make their survival possible, but no one would listen. She was the living symbol of their triumph, and they would not be denied the right to honor her.

In the midst of so much joy, there was yet more. Alaric shyly announced that the Lady Margaret had agreed to become his wife. This pronouncement brought cheers from the household that threatened to shake the rafters. It was the cue for yet more courses to be brought out and additional kegs of ale and wine to be cracked open.

The old housecarl came in for some gentle teasing, which he took with high good humor. The least comment was an excuse for laughter. Musical instruments were brought out, and voices just a bit creaky from disuse lent themselves to love ballads.

As the revelry proceeded, even the most routine precautions taken in times of peace were temporarily waived. It was unthinkable that any of the guardsmen should miss the celebration. They left the posts they had maintained even during the pestilence to join in the rejoicing.

So it was that the armed men approaching the keep found their path unimpeded. Even the door to the hall was unguarded, allowing them to enter without first announcing their presence. Their grim faces hardened even further as they took in the signs of merrymaking. Not until their leader rapped hard on the floor with his scabbard was their intrusion realized.

Montague FitzStephen gazed about him contemptuously. Everything he saw about him seemed to reaffirm his low opinion of the Anglo-Saxon waste infesting the country. It made the task he had come to perform all the more pleasant.

With measured strides, the tall, powerfully built knight crossed the hall. His armor glittered darkly and the plume in his battle helmet was dyed blood-red. Onyx eyes gleamed as he threw a rolled document on the table before Roanna.

Only her quick signal stopped her men from reaching for their weapons. She had caught sight of the seal holding the parchment together. However treacherous FitzStephen might be, he came on the King's business.

Rising, she faced him calmly. "What is this?"

The Norman looked her over narrowly before he responded. "A warrant for your arrest."

"That's preposterous!" Alaric exploded. The other housecarls and thegns joined him in repudiating such an absurdity.

Roanna had to raise her hand to quiet them. Somehow managing to keep her voice steady, she asked, "On what charge?"

FitzStephen allowed himself an icy smile as he said, "Witchcraft."

# Chapter Fifteen

"THIS REALLY COULDN'T HAVE HAPPENED AT A WORSE time," William complained. He turned from his perusal of the scene out the window to regard Roanna glumly. "You must believe me, I didn't want to have you arrested. But I had no choice."

Trying hard to look sympathetic, she refrained from mentioning that whatever inconveniences he might be suffering could hardly be compared with her own plight. Instead, she said softly, "I still don't understand how this happened. What did FitzStephen tell you to prompt such action?"

The King's black eyes focused on her intently, as though trying to judge the degree of her sincerity. He must have been convinced because at length he said, "You honestly don't know, do you?"

Roanna shook her head mutely. She sat up straighter in the hard, wooden chair, her hands clasped tightly in her lap and her features rigidly composed. Whatever was coming, she meant to confront it with dignity.

"Robert d'Almaric is dead." Seeing the shock this blunt statement wrung from her, William went on more gently. "He was one of the first to succumb to the plague. He died crying out that you were responsible. I believe his exact words were to the effect that you had summoned a pox on him. Now ordinarily I wouldn't have paid any attention to that. But with thousands dead throughout the city and your own household relatively untouched, FitzStephen has a rather compelling case."

Struggling against an almost overwhelming sense of disbelief, Roanna blurted, "You can't be serious! Robert was a disappointed suitor liable to say anything for vengeance! And as for my household, only skill and good fortune saved us from taking losses as severe as anywhere else! In the name of God, would you condemn me for being able to heal!"

"No, no! But you must try to understand my position. FitzStephen is an old and valued retainer. He is also the leader of the faction that wants to see all the Anglo-Saxon nobility destroyed. As such, your husband has become his prime adversary." Shaking his head, William concluded, "It didn't take much cunning to realize that Colin is most vulnerable through you. FitzStephen hopes to provoke him to some enraged act that will make it impossible for me to let him keep his lands."

"Colin is far too intelligent to fall for such a trick," Roanna declared firmly.

"Perhaps, but if that fails, FitzStephen has a fallback position. He knows that it is in large measure Colin's marriage to you that predisposes me to believe him capable of loyalty. If that marriage ends, I will be more inclined to replace him with a Norman lord."

"Ends? But how . . . Only the Pope can dissolve a marriage."

William sighed regretfully. "I am not speaking of dissolution. Witchcraft is a capital crime."

Cold fingers of fear crawled through Roanna. For the first time since assuring her retainers it was safe for her to answer the King's summons, she wondered at the wisdom of her action. Would William actually stand by and let her die?

There was no clue in his expressionless features. Studying him in the vain hope of comfort, Roanna was reminded of the merciless expediency he had always shown in matters affecting his own power. From the moment he first put foot in stirrup to win for himself the lands his father could not leave to a bastard son, William had let nothing and no one get in his way. He had triumphed over almost insurmountable obstacles, and in the process had won a well-deserved reputation for ruthlessness. She would have to be a fool to believe the habits of a lifetime would be suddenly ignored for her sake.

Caught in the middle between those of his followers

who wanted an accord with the conquered and those who looked forward only to more bloodshed, William would not willingly alienate either. Instead, he would seize any opportunity for the conflict to be settled by seemingly divine intervention. All unwittingly, she had provided him with just such a chance.

Dimly, she said, "I gather you mean to try me?"

William nodded, privately relieved that she was intelligent enough not to need everything spelled out. In the back of his mind, he regretted that it had to be Roanna who was caught up in such a mess. Besides the genuine fondness he felt for her, there was the far deeper bond of affection for her brother. But Guyon was miles away across the width of the country, and FitzStephen could no longer be put off. Regret it though he might, he knew she could not be spared the confrontation that would at last decide which policy would rule in England.

"It is necessary." Reassuringly, he added, "But nothing will happen for at least several days. There is much to be arranged."

"I hope," Roanna murmured tightly, "that some of those arrangements will include notifying my husband and brother of this outrage."

Impervious to her angry tone, William surprised her by saying, "Messages are already on their way."

Roanna had to be content with that. Escorted from the King's presence, she was taken to a small, barred room high in the keep. There she was locked in with a sleeping pallet, blankets, a container of water, and her thoughts.

The tedium she had suffered during her first days as Colin's captive proved as nothing compared to what she now had to endure. Days that only a short while before had been far too short to accomplish all that needed to be done dragged by in relentless monotony relieved only by bouts of fear.

Her cell, she swiftly discovered, was precisely twelve paces long and ten wide. The small, barred window was set too high in the wall for her to be able to look out comfortably. But if she stood on tiptoe and pulled herself up by her hands, she could just see the bailey below. The effort, however, strained her back and leg muscles, which quickly began to ache.

The jailers who guarded her in three shifts night and day were at first not inclined to talk. They seemed to take the charge of witchcraft seriously, at least to the extent of crossing themselves each time they came anywhere near her and refusing to meet her eyes. But that behavior fortunately did not last.

Before very long they apparently decided she was simply a young, beautiful lady who through a set of extraordinary circumstances found herself in their care. This new attitude proved far more pleasant than the other. All three men were sensible enough to treat her with rigorous propriety. But they did unbend enough to express their growing support in a multitude of small ways.

Little treats began to appear on her trays. From one of the taverns across the road, which provided far better food than the stronghold's own kitchens, came fragrant barley soup and fresh-baked white bread. A handful of daisies appeared next to brighten her drab surroundings. Softer blankets replaced the regulation issue. Hot water was provided twice daily.

Her modesty was respected to the extent that none of the guards would enter the cell without knocking first. When they did, their conversation was unfailingly cheerful. They brought welcome word of life outside her prison, but no news was as eagerly received as the announcement that William had decided to allow her visitors.

Alaric and Margaret came first. Their anxious faces brought a lump to Roanna's throat. She embraced them warmly, hastily reassuring them that she was all right.

"There's no reason to look so grim. I'm being quite well looked after."

Her friends were less certain, but they were not about to inflict their worries on her. Stalwartly, Margaret said, "Well, you'd better be or there'll be hell to pay. The King has given strict orders you are to be treated with all honor and respect."

Roanna had suspected William was behind her good care but she was glad of this confirmation. Surely if he was as neutral as he pretended, he would not show any interest in her circumstances.

"If he thinks that makes up for imprisoning you," Alaric growled, "he's an even bigger fool than he seems. Word of your arrest has already spread beyond the city. I've had offers of help from every Anglo-Saxon lord in the area. With Colin away, every one of them is ready to take arms in your defense."

"Oh, no!" Roanna exclaimed. "There mustn't be any trouble. We would be falling right into FitzStephen's trap."

Alaric nodded somberly. "That's what I figured. So far I've been able to keep them under control. But I'm not sure how much longer that can last. Our own men are chomping at the bit. They're all for marching on this keep and taking it apart log by log to get to you. If you aren't released soon, William's going to have a full-fledged battle on his hands."

"Tell the men they must be patient," Roanna instructed firmly, "and say the same to those who have offered help. I deeply appreciate their concern, but we must look to the future. Even if you did manage to free me, we would only have convinced William he cannot count on our loyalty, which is exactly what FitzStephen wants him to believe. That must be avoided, at all costs."

Lady Margaret and the housecarl glanced at each other worriedly. The older woman's eyes were dark with concern as she took Roanna's hand. "Not at all costs, my dear. Your life is far too precious to us to allow it to be threatened."

More confidently than she felt, Roanna insisted, "It will not come to that."

"Pray God you are right," Alaric muttered. "A few weeks ago, I wouldn't have thought anything could make the remaining Anglo-Saxon lords work together. No matter how much they all hate William, they were still far too independent and contentious. But between their respect for Colin and their horror at what's happening to you, they're coming close to the point of joint action." He shook his head wonderingly. "FitzStephen may succeed where no one else has before. Thanks to him, the lords may be truly united for the first time."

Roanna's face was strained as she listened to him. Nothing could be worse than for the Anglo-Saxon nobility to rise against William so belatedly. "It's too late for that. The King's liegemen hold all but a few of the most strategic points in the country. The castles they've built to secure their positions are all but impenetrable. Any rebellion now would only be the excuse FitzStephen and his kind need to finish the job begun at Hastings. By the time they were through, there wouldn't be an Anglo-Saxon lord left alive."

"Then Colin had better get back here quickly and convince them of that," Alaric muttered. "Otherwise the hotheads will prevail."

Thinking of her husband and how he would react when he learned of her imprisonment, Roanna bent her head. It seemed as though she had brought him little good since their marriage. Softly, she asked, "Do you think he has heard yet?"

Alaric nodded. "If our own messengers haven't reached him yet, it's likely the King's men have gotten through. They left a day earlier with instructions to stop only to change horses." Gently, he added, "His lordship won't let anything stand in his way. As soon as humanly possible, he'll be here."

But the rest of that day brought no news of Colin's

arrival, and on the following morning her trial began.

For the occasion, the great hall of the keep was cleared out, a dais constructed, and a large table hauled in to accommodate the dignitaries. Some effort was made to create an atmosphere of proper solemnity by draping the rough-hewn walls in war banners and stationing staightbacked men-at-arms at regular intervals. The guards were not there for mere ceremonial purposes. They were needed to keep down the press of curious observers, who clearly viewed the proceedings as a welcome distraction from the everyday monotony.

Awakened early in her cell, Roanna bathed before donning the dark blue tunic and bliaut Margaret had brought. The somber color was well suited to her mood. With shaking hands she combed the silken mass of her hair until it fell in golden waves to her waist. Securing the transparent veil in place with a plain circlet, she glanced into a small polished metal mirror.

The young woman who stared back at her was unnaturally pale. Beneath thick fringes, wide amber eyes had the look of a wounded animal. Her mouth was set tightly and the firm line of her chin trembled slightly.

That wouldn't do at all. Determinedly, Roanna pinched color into her ashen cheeks and bit her lips until they were once again rosy. Lifting her head proudly, she made her gaze as hard and unrevealing as was possible. The result, while not all that she might have wished, was still a great improvement. Only someone who knew her extremely well would be able to suspect the clawing dread bottled up inside her slender body.

Certainly the officials who watched her enter the hearing chamber saw only a remarkably beautiful, apparently serene young woman. William sat at the center of the table, dressed in a black velvet tunic embroidered in silver. His garb was at once unrelentingly somber and regal.

Beside him, Odo's scarlet robes were in sharp contrast. The bishop was seated at the King's right, a position required by his rank but which Roanna hoped also signified William's silent choice between the two contending factions of his followers.

To his left sat Montague FitzStephen. His lean, vulpine features might have been a mask for all they revealed of his thoughts. Only his narrow black eyes showed any life as they followed Roanna's every move. The dark green tunic he wore was cut to emphasize the power of his battle-hardened form. Almost as tall as Colin and certainly as fit, he had none of the other man's inherent grace. He shifted impatiently as she neared, apparently anxious to get on with it.

A clerk called the assembly to attention. "Oyez, oyez! Be it known the King's court is now in session. All those having business before it draw near."

A guard gently guided Roanna to her position in front of the table. Staring at the men who would judge her, she thought William met her gaze for just an instant. But he looked away so quickly that she couldn't be sure.

FitzStephen, who apparently would lead off, consulted some papers before him, more for effect than any need. His voice was sonorous as he declared, "We are come to consider the matter of the Lady Roanna Algerson, nee D'Arcy, lately charged with witchcraft in the parish of St. Elbert's, city of London, dominion of his most gracious majesty, William the King." His sharp, relentless eyes locked on the young woman before him. "What is your plea?"

Roanna had seriously considered her response. She might be able to delay the proceedings by refusing to enter any acknowledgment of guilt or innocence. But that would be a direct challenge to the legitimacy of the court and as such would constitute an attack on William, who, as presiding judge, was lending the full weight of his authority to the hearing. Reluctantly, she had decided it would be better to go along for the time being in the hope that Colin would soon return and the whole awful business could be settled peacefully.

Her voice was low but firm as she said, "I am not guilty."

FitzStephen frowned. He had hoped that after several days in prison she would be less spirited. But it seemed he would have to wait a bit longer to see her cower. Irately, he gestured to the clerk. "Call the first witness."

Roanna turned round, curious to see who accused her. Her eyes widened as she encountered the Norman matron from the market making her ponderous way to the front of the chamber.

When the woman was at last settled in place before

the judges, FitzStephen began the questioning. Rapidly he drew out the witness's name and circumstances and established the fact that she had encountered the accused only once, several weeks before.

"And what happened at this meeting?" he inquired considerately.

The matron sniffled. She cast a fearful look toward Roanna. Her voice was shrill as she proclaimed, "That one . . . over there . . . the witch . . . she put the evil eye on me! Barely had I left her than I was struck down by a gripping pain in the stomach. Oh, it was agony! For days I could not move from my bed or take any nourishment. Ask anyone in my household, they will tell you how I suffered. Just when I thought I could not endure another moment, a priest recognized my illness for what it was. He read the rites of exorcism over me and a devil leaped from my mouth! A hideous, twisted thing put there by *her!*" A trembling finger pointed at Roanna. "She's a witch, she is! As I live and breathe, she should be burned!"

FitzStephen, having listened attentively to every word, nodded sympathetically. "Yes, indeed, it must have been horrible for you, my good woman. Thanks be to the Lord for preserving you so that you could give testimony before this court. Now you may go in peace."

"Uhhh . . . just one moment." Bishop Odo smiled benignly. "If you wouldn't mind, dear lady, a question or two."

The matron looked uncertain and glanced at

FitzStephen for guidance. He shrugged vexedly. "If you really think that is necessary . . ."

"I do," Odo said firmly. His smile was gone as he addressed the woman. "Where exactly did you meet the Lady Roanna?"

"Why in the market, not that I see what difference that makes."

Ignoring her objection, the bishop continued. "And how did you come to speak with her?"

"We were in the same shop. She got angry when I wanted the merchant to wait on me. And that's when she did it. That's when she cursed me with her evil eye!"

"Yes, yes, you've already mentioned that. But what happened first? Did you argue?"

"No . . . not exactly. She was impatient, arrogant . . . didn't know her place. Praise God I had the sense to get away from her as quickly as I did. If she'd had more time to work her devilish ways, I don't doubt I'd be dead by now!"

"But you aren't, are you?" Odo observed mildly. "In fact, you were far less ill than those who contracted the plague. Unless I am mistaken"—his gaze wandered over her ample form—"your health is, shall we say, robust."

A dark flush stained the woman's jowls, made all the worse as the bishop went on, "You were at the market to buy food, no doubt. How is your appetite, madam? Vigorous? I will hazard a guess that you tend to eat more than is good for you. Do you suffer often from stomach complaints?"

"No! That is . . . I certainly don't eat more than is needed to hold body and soul together!"

"And in your case," Odo concluded, "that's quite an undertaking, isn't it?" Before the matron could sputter out another word, he raised a hand dismissively. "Thank you, madam. Your conscientiousness in appearing here today is appreciated. But you'll do well to take my advice and try a bit of peppermint water next time your stomach acts up. Like as not the devil you spit out was a fine, fragrant *belch!*"

Not even William attempted to hide his laughter as the outraged woman hastily withdrew. The guffaws of the highly amused crowd followed her into the bailey.

Roanna began to feel a great deal better about everything. FitzStephen was undoubtedly a dangerous enemy, but if all his witnesses were as easily demolished by the rapier-tongued bishop, she had nothing at all to worry about. She was almost smiling when a small, wizened man was summoned next.

He shuffled reluctantly to the front of the chamber, his head bent and his gnarled hands clasped before him. Lank hair of indeterminate color fell into his red-rimmed eyes. Startled to recognize one of the many itinerant peddlers who frequented the area around the Algerson residence, Roanna waited anxiously to hear what he would say.

With a fine grasp of the distinctions between a matron of slight but still noble rank and a common drifter, FitzStephen addressed the man gruffly.

"Name?"

"Uh . . . Peter . . . Martin, may it please you . . . sir. . . ."

"Occupation?"

"T-this and that . . . whatever brings a penny. . . ." Toothless gums grinned obsequiously. "I turn my hand here and there, your worship. Why you might be surprised what I can—"

"Just tell us how you came to notice the Lady Roanna," FitzStephen snapped.

The man recoiled at the reprimand. Haltingly, he explained, "Uh, well, you see, I collect old clothes, rags and the like. Been slim pickings lately what with one thing and the other." He cast a quick eye at William before continuing, "But I still can find something good every once in a while. Enough to make it worth lookin'. Anyway, I was on the road by the house where the lady lives and I noticed her there in the yard. Well, I mean, after all . . . what man wouldn't? . . ."

He paused for an instant, silently calling on the gentlemen to understand how he had come to stand in a public thoroughfare gaping at a radiant vision whose golden hair, perfect features, and exquisite figure had played a major role in his dreams ever since.

An impatient glare from FitzStephen prompted him to continue. "So I was standin' there, see, and I couldn't help but notice what she was doin'. There were these cats, maybe half a dozen of 'em, all around her." His bulbous nose wrinkled. "Mangy beasts. Can't stand 'em myself. But there she was, smilin' and talkin' to 'em. And they were listenin', they were! All the time they were brushin' up against her, gulpin' down the food she'd brought, even lickin' her hands, you could tell they were takin' in every word she was sayin'.''

His voice rose meaningfully, "I looked away for just a second. Not more. When I looked back, the lady was gone. And in her place, standin' just where she'd been, was a soft, sleek she-cat with golden fur the same color as her hair!"

Pausing to relish the shocked gasp of the crowd, which by now was hanging on every word, the peddler went on importantly, "And that's when I knew what I was *really* lookin' at. I crossed myself, said a 'Hail Mary' and ran down that road prayin' to the good Lord to protect me and all the faithful from witches what go about in the bodies of cats and turn a poor man's rest to a torment of unholy thoughts!"

Stunned silence greeted this dramatic conclusion. Even Odo seemed briefly at a loss for words as he struggled to come to terms with the peddler's charges. Long moments passed before the bishop gathered himself sufficiently to murmur, "Remarkable . . . absolutely remarkable. . . . We are asked to believe the testimony of an addle-brained idiot who I sincerely doubt can remember to pull down his hose before pissing!"

Turning on FitzStephen, the bishop demanded scathingly, "Is this the best you can do, sir? Over-stuffed matrons and lecherous rag pickers? God's breath, do you imagine this court has no truly serious matters to attend to?"

"This is serious!" the warlord protested fervently.

"We are dealing here with a matter of witchcraft! This woman is in league with the Devil!"

"Then prove it!" Odo roared.

Drawing himself up stiffly, FitzStephen glared at the bishop. He knew there was no help to be had from William. The King was leaning back comfortably in his chair, his hands held in front of him with the fingers pressed thoughtfully together, and his expression inscrutable. Only one seated very close to him could see the tiny smile curving his sensual mouth.

With gathering dismay, FitzStephen realized that if he could not turn the trend of events around quickly, he would lose all chance to influence his master. Indeed, he was in real danger of being made a figure of mockery and derision, something his overweening pride would never bear. As his hatred for Roanna and everything she represented reached new heights, he summoned the final witness.

The monk who came forward was a somber-faced, iron-backed old man whose spare frame and austere robes gave him an air of unshakable sanctity. Alone of those who had so far spoken, he looked unimpressed by the high lords ranked on the other side of the table. His thoughts were clearly on a higher plane as he spoke quietly but determinedly.

"I am Father John Manus, abbot of St. Bartholemew's in the west minster of London."

A low murmur ran through the crowd. The monk was one of the most respected men in the city. As leader of a Benedictine abbey, he had tirelessly led the effort to help the plague victims. When most doctors and priests were trying to bar their doors against the infection, he and his fellow monks risked death countless times over as they brought food and medicine to the sick, gave last rites to the dying, and collected the remains of the dead.

Not even Roanna, who desperately wanted to believe there could be no convincing testimony against her, could remain unaffected by his presence.

Ignoring FitzStephen, who tried to launch into his usual questions, Father Manus looked directly at the King. "My lord, I wish there to be no misunderstanding about why I am here today. I do not accuse this woman. Neither her guilt nor innocence have been revealed to me. I come only to provide information to this court which is relevant to your proceedings."

William had straightened up in his chair. His face was grave as he motioned the abbot to continue.

"As you may know, sire, it was monks from St. Bartholemew's who during the plague gathered the corpses of the victims so that the natural course of decomposition would not spread further sickness. I will not send others to do such sorrowful work without sharing the burden myself. Therefore, it became my custom to drive the cart which collected bodies each day from the area in which the Algerson residence is located."

"And were there many?" the King asked softly.

"Indeed, several hundred from that neighborhood alone. There were days when we had to make two or three trips to bring them all in. Some households were wiped out entirely."

"And how does this pertain to the charge of witchcraft?"

Father Manus hesitated. He glanced at Roanna somberly. "There was only one house in all the city from which we never gathered a single corpse. While all about were dying like flies, we took no bodies from this lady's home."

"And yet," William said sharply, his voice rising over the anxious mutterings of the crowd, "the Lady Roanna has reported that two of her retainers, two servants, and one female guest perished of the plague."

"So she may say," Father Manus agreed calmly, "but what then happened to their bodies? The facilities for private burial were quickly overwhelmed, and no one other than monks of St. Bartholemew's would take the corpses. If there was death in her household, why is there no evidence of it?"

It was not a question William could answer. Mutely he turned to Roanna, as did everyone else in the court.

She had to swallow hard to get past the obstruction in her throat. What a short time before had begun to look like no more than a bad joke once more assumed the shape of deadly menace.

So softly that she had to stop and begin again, Roanna said, "The abbot is wrong when he says there were no private burials. They were difficult to arrange, but not impossible. In the mass internments that took place to prevent contamination, much had to be overlooked. I wanted to make sure those who had been in my care received the full Christian rites."

"Where then were they buried?" William prompted quietly.

"At a small church on the outskirts of London, called St. Ethelbert's."

"If that is true," Father Manus pointed out, "there should be records."

Roanna nodded, only to have her hope quashed by FitzStephen's triumphant announcement. "An effort has already been made to find any documents related to private burials arranged by the Lady Roanna anywhere in London or its environs." He paused significantly before adding, "There are none."

"But that's impossible!" Roanna exclaimed. "Even during such terrible times, no priest would bury someone without at least noting the name and place. There have to be records!"

FitzStephen shook his head flatly. "Not in London. Not anywhere nearby." His black eyes glittered with deepest satisfaction. "Whatever you arranged, Lady Roanna, it was not Christian burial carried out by human agents of the Lord. Only Devil's imps will do your bidding, and they can not serve you here, witch!"

Not even William could prevent the pandemonium that broke out following FitzStephen's revelation. Nor was the warlord the only one to denounce her so vehemently. The dreaded cry of "Witch!" reverberated through the chamber as those who only a short time before had been more than willing to think her falsely accused now adroitly shifted sides and wallowed in righteous fear.

The King and bishop murmured anxiously to each other. Things were not going as they had hoped. To dismiss the charges now would be to invite the vengeful fury of the mob.

Regretfully, William took the only course left to him. He stood, commanding silence through the sheer force of his presence. Without looking at Roanna, he declared, "Only God can judge this woman's innocence. We will submit it to His hands."

Roanna paled. She barely heard FitzStephen's gloating demand. "Let it by ordeal! Submit the witch to the burning brands, and if her skin is marked we will know her guilt!"

The crowd shouted its approval for this hideous custom conceived in the demented belief that divine intervention would guard the innocent. Experience showed that it was but a brief step from the brand to the stake.

Though her legs threatened to give way, she managed to remain upright, facing the King. A tiny spark of relief surged through her as William firmly shook his head.

"No! It will be trial by combat. Her champion against her accuser." Turning, he eyed the warlord who was on his feet with the rest of the blood-thirsty crowd. Tauntingly, the King demanded, "Unless, FitzStephen, you are afraid to fight?"

Taken aback, the Norman could only shake his head. "No . . . of course not. I would be honored to take the field in such holy work. . . . But she has no champion."

"That," a low voice announced from the back of the chamber, "is not correct."

The crowd parted instinctively for the tall, powerfully built man who strode forward. Covered in dust and weary from his desperate race, Colin nonetheless presented a threatening vision of barely leashed rage. His features were set in harsh, unrelenting lines as he faced his wife's accuser with deadly intent.

"Find a priest to hear your confession, FitzStephen," he grated. "For by tomorrow eve, only one of us will still be in this world."

# Chapter Sixteen

"If THERE'S ANYTHING ELSE YOU WOULD LIKE, MY lady," the guard said softly, "you've only to ask."

Roanna smiled as she shook her head. "No, thank you. You've already worked wonders."

Flushing at her praise, the guard withdrew. He was glad to do everything possible for so lovely a lady. But he couldn't prevent a quick stab of jealousy as he thought of the man who was sharing her cell.

Nor was the guard the only one who would be happy to change places with Colin, at least until dawn. The other men on the watch had eyed him enviously as he accompanied Roanna back from the hearing chamber. Few of them thought it odd that he chose to remain with her when he still had his freedom and could have gone anywhere he liked. Confinement in the small room high in the keep was a small price for the delights he would undoubtedly enjoy. Although come morning, he might have to pay far more dearly.

"You'd think he'd want a good night's rest before fighting FitzStephen," one of the guards muttered.

"There's more important things than sleep," an older and wiser compatriot informed him. "Any man worth the name would choose to spend what could be his last night on earth just the way Algerson's doing." He whistled softly. "I'll tell you this much, by tomorrow there'll be no doubt left in his mind about why he's fighting."

"Some say it's a mistake to lie with a woman before battle," a young sentry suggested. "Weakens a man, it does."

The older guard laughed bluntly. "You sure haven't been around much, lad, if you believe that. Before, after, or during, any time's a good time for f—"

"All right, now!" the watch captain intervened hastily. "There'll be no talk like that with a lady about. Get back to your posts." The men went off grumbling, but with no real malice. Although they would be reluctant to admit it for fear of being thought womanish, each was privately glad that the Lady Roanna was not spending this night alone.

Outside in the courtyard before the keep, a high wooden stake had been pounded into place. Tinderdry faggots were piled around it and bleachers were set up to accommodate what would undoubtedly be a large crowd of eager spectators. The men who had come to have such affection for their beautiful prisoner could only pray that God would intervene to prove her innocence before it was too late.

Seated at a small table covered with linen and illuminated by a brace of candles brought by the thoughtful guards, Colin silently echoed their hope. He spared no concern for the possibility of his own death. If Roanna was not saved, the world would become a joyless desert in which he had no wish to endure.

His eyes followed her unswervingly as she moved about the cell, unpacking the food brought by Lady Margaret. No detail of her appearance went unnoticed. Each was cherished as further evidence that despite all the horror she had passed through, her spirit and beauty remained indomitable.

By tacit agreement, neither spoke of the desperate events that had brought them to this point. Their time together might be all too short to waste even a moment of it in fruitless recapitulation.

"Margaret has outdone herself," Roanna declared, her voice deliberately light. "This is a feast."

Colin's answering smile did not reach his eyes, which remained intently focused on her. Rising, he helped lay out the fresh bread, roast chicken, cheese, wine, and honey cakes Margaret had apparently thought essential to their well-being.

Though he had barely eaten since leaving East Anglia three days before, he had no interest in the food. But conscious of Roanna's anxious glance, he would try to do justice to it.

When the meal was ready, they both sat for a moment in strained silence as each searched for some innocuous topic of conversation. Under such tense circumstances, it was difficult even to remember the ordinary, commonplace things they had once talked about. After he had silently rejected half a dozen gambits, Colin was relieved when Roanna said, "Tell me what happened in East Anglia. Were you successful?"

He nodded swiftly. "I met with both the lords William asked me to see. They're willing to come to court provided he guarantees their safety, which he has already said he will do."

"That is good news! Now if only a few more will be as sensible, this talk of war can be stopped."

The moment the words were out Roanna bit her tongue. She would have given almost anything to recall them, but could not. Nor could she avoid Colin's inevitable question.

Abandoning all pretense at eating, he demanded, "What talk? Has something new happened?"

Reluctantly, she nodded. "Alaric says some of the lords are very upset about my being accused. He's had a hard time preventing them from challenging William. I told him that's just what FitzStephen wants, and that it must be avoided at all costs. But he is doubtful about how much longer peace can be maintained, especially if . . ."

She broke off, unable to go any further. Unspoken between them was the knowledge that if the battle the next day went against Colin, the cry for vengeance would be irresistible. Many more lives, both Anglo-Saxon and Norman, would be lost because of their deaths.

The succulent repast had lost its flavor. Even the wine seemed bitter. Colin put down his cup, noticing as he did so that Roanna's scant appetite was also gone. The small portions she had taken lay almost untouched before her. Her slender hands trembled slightly, and her face, which had been unnaturally flushed but a short time before, was now ashen.

"I . . . I guess I'm not hungry," she murmured, catching his eyes on her.

Colin nodded gently. "Neither am I." He studied her bent head for a moment before suggesting, "Why don't we see if the guards have better appetites?"

Once the men were convinced their lovely prisoner and her lord really did not want the food, their windfall was eagerly accepted. Excited exclamations filtered down from the guard post as the cell door closed behind the sentries.

When they were alone again, Roanna and Colin faced each other. There was no need for words. Silently he opened his arms and silently she went into them.

For a long moment, they were content simply to touch. She nestled into his chest as his proud head rested against the silken fall of her hair. The powerful arms that held her were gentle but firm, mute reminders of the immense strength leashed within him. But though Roanna longed to take comfort from it, she could not forget his vulnerability.

FitzStephen was a highly skilled and experienced warrior. Moreover, he would have the added advantage of fighting in a manner to which he was well accustomed, against an opponent used to different weapons and tactics. Colin would need all his ability, and a large measure of luck, to carry the day.

The image of him battered and bloodied, on the verge of death, rose all too easily in her mind. Roanna shivered convulsively, prompting Colin's instant concern.

"You're cold! You should be abed."

Even as she opened her mouth to assure him she was perfectly warm, Roanna thought better of it. He was, after all, only taking her where she most wanted to be. Carried across the room, she was gently lowered onto the sleeping pallet stuffed with straw and covered with clean, soft blankets.

Colin hesitated before reluctantly withdrawing his hands. He wanted so badly to touch and hold her, to lose himself in the full possession of her womanhood. But he believed she must be exhausted after her ordeal. The fear he had briefly seen in her tawny eyes the last time they made love had left him more acutely aware than ever that his own desire depended on hers. The mere thought of forcing her made him feel only revulsion and self-disgust.

But for Roanna, there was no question of force. Her body was already on fire with desperate need for him. Mutely, she reached out, following the path of his retreating hands. Seizing them in her own, she drew them loving back to the ripe curve of her breasts.

"Colin . . . please . . . don't leave me. . . ."

The slate gray eyes fastened on hers turned to molten silver. A low groan broke from him as he slid down on the pallet beside her. "Roanna . . . are you sure? . . ."

Her answer was the touch of petal-soft fingertips stroking across his brow, over the hard ridge of his high cheekbones, along the stubble-roughened line of his firm jaw. Her lips, light as a butterfly's wings, followed the path of her caress. By the time they settled gently against his mouth, Colin was shaking with the force of his desire.

"The guards . . ." he muttered thickly into her mouth.

"Are very discreet."

Willingly convinced, Colin rose swiftly. He stripped off his clothes, vividly aware of Roanna's gaze fastened on him. She could not bring herself even to blink as the full length of his magnificent male beauty was revealed to her. A soft moan rippling from her, she opened her arms to receive him.

Big, urgent hands slid under her tunic, slipping it swiftly over her head. The tumult of her golden curls fell in wanton disarray over the straw mattress as she stretched languorously. Colin's breath caught in his throat. No matter how often he saw her like this, his wife's loveliness never failed to stun him.

Despite the gathering crescendo of his passion, he could not resist the need to savor her lingeringly. His strong, skilled hands drifted down her satiny length, stroking and caressing until she thought she would go mad from the sensations he provoked. A hot, moist tongue circled the glowing globes of her breasts before at last flicking repeatedly over her aching nipples. She whimpered softly as his mouth closed on her, suckling the swollen buds erotically.

Languid warmth grew within her, flaring ever brighter as his lips wandered over her silken belly to tease the soft inner flesh of her thigh. Trailing fiery kisses down the full length of one slender leg, he followed the path of the other back to the nest of honeyed curls sheltering her womanhood.

Pulsating with need, Roanna tried to draw him to her. But Colin resisted. He brought her repeatedly to the burning edge of fulfillment. Her soft cries and unbridled response fanned the already white hot flames of his desire. But not until he had sent her spiraling again and again into near-painful rapture did he at last give in to his own almost intolerable passion.

The surging power of his manhood thrusting within her shattered Roanna's last slim grasp on consciousness. She cried out helplessly as the dissolving mist of ecstasy engulfed them both.

Colin loomed above her, huge and dark in the candlelight. She could not make out his features, save for the quicksilver gleam of eyes that stared down at her adoringly.

Her body was the flesh-and-bone expression of her spirit, and as such he found it beautiful far beyond mere physical bounds. The all-encompassing love he felt for her made him at once humble and exultant. Surely the God who had granted his creations such wonders would not now abandon them?

His love became a living prayer flowering in his soul as he reached for her. Roanna melted against him. Her body was an instrument of joy that had but one purpose, to hold off for some little time the darkness threatening to engulf them. Soft where he was hard, yielding where he demanded, she merged with him in an eternal dance of consecrated union. Together they reaffirmed the infinite power of life even while surpassing all mortal limits.

Much later Colin stirred under the blankets he had dazedly dragged over them both in the aftermath of their passion. Roanna was snuggled against him, soft and delicate beneath his hand. The thick fringe of her lashes cast shadows over the pale curve of her cheeks. Her breath was warm against the bronzed column of his throat. He knew by the gentle rise and fall of her breasts brushing his chest that she was asleep. His embrace tightened around her carefully. Throughout the remainder of that night, he held her close against him, cherishing each precious moment.

Too soon the first faint rim of light showed against the eastern horizon. As the burning eye of the red sun climbed into the sky, Colin rose to arm himself. His hands were steady and his face resolute as he prepared to do combat for the life of the woman who was more to him than life itself.

# Chapter Seventeen

THE ENCLOSED FIELD IN FRONT OF THE KEEP WAS crowded. William and the other dignitaries occupied the small grandstand draped with heraldic banners. The bleachers on either side were packed so tightly that hardly a breath of air could move amid the occupants. Those not fortunate enough to get seats were jammed into the far side of the bailey, behind a bulwark of men-at-arms who knew they would be hard pressed to keep the mob under control once the action began.

Though it was not yet noon, the day was already warm. Barely a cloud showed in the cobalt sky. A flock of ravens perched on the palisade, peering balefully at the strange goings-on. Along the nearby river, the tide was heading out. A soft summer breeze carried the fecund scent of rotting vegetation and salt spray.

A few square-sailed merchant vessels drifted past, but most ships were securely tied up at anchor. The usual crowds were missing from the dockyards and markets. Most people had chosen to stay inside, waiting with differing degrees of fear and anger to hear the outcome of the great event taking place within the royal stronghold.

The eyes of all those privileged to witness it were fastened on the door of the tower through which the accused would be brought, along with the two men who would be the means by which God decided her fate.

Though wholly Norman, the crowd was divided in its sentiments. Some confidently expected to see FitzStephen triumph. They made derisive comments about the lack of fighting skill among the Anglo-Saxons and offered contemptuously high odds in the betting that quickly sprang up.

Others were less certain. There were those who remembered the prowess Colin had shown at Hastings and recalled that it had taken half a dozen Normans finally to bring him down. They suspected he would fight even more fiercely today, and were not anxious to predict the outcome.

Many were not so hesitant. The large faction of the crowd that sided with the Bishop Odo in his desire for accord with the Anglo-Saxons were frank about who they wanted to see win. They detested FitzStephen not merely for his political stance but for his willingness to attack Colin through Roanna.

When the tower door at last swung open, the mob pressed forward eagerly. Boos almost drowned out the cheers as FitzStephen strode forward. His long, hard body was encased in black armor. A massive war sword was strapped to his side. Behind him, a squire carried his plumed battle helmet, while another held the shield emblazoned with a fiercely snarling wolf's head. The horse he would ride was a massive ebony stallion whose glistening hooves pawed the ground impatiently as steam shot from his flared nostrils.

The Bishop Odo appeared next. His usually smooth features were distorted by a worried frown, the product of his unsuccessful struggle to convince Colin to wear Norman armor. It was bad enough that he had only recently learned to fight from horseback. To go against FitzStephen without full protection was, in the bishop's opinion, sheer madness. He had even tried to lend his own equipment, only to have the offer politely but firmly rejected.

"It would only hinder me," Colin had explained calmly. He had deliberately decided to make no concessions at all to Norman ways. Instead of the heavy metal armor that would both protect and weigh down FitzStephen, he wore his usual leather jerkin and chain mail. The coppery pelt of his hair still hung to his massive shoulders, defying the new, much shorter style. His powerful legs were bare beneath his short tunic. Only soft leather boots covered his feet and calves. Even his weapons appeared lighter and less threatening than those of his foe.

If he lived, there would be time for compromise later. But on this day he would fight purely as an Anglo-Saxon chieftain defending what was his. When he triumphed, as he was certain he would, the myth of the conquerors' invincibility would be shattered forever.

Odo shook his head despairingly. "The first part of the combat will be in the lists, with unsheathed lances. FitzStephen is renowned for his prowess there. He can hit almost any opponent, no matter how quickly they are both moving. Should he strike you as poorly protected as you now are, you will be killed instantly."

Colin shot the bishop a warning glance, reminding him that Roanna was listening to every word. She was pale but composed. He intended for her to remain that way.

"FitzStephen will not hit me."

In a gesture that was not the least pious, Odo looked heavenward. "It is fine to be confident, but this is sheer recklessness!"

Colin smiled faintly. He tested the edges of his longsword and the shorter blade that hung across from it before fastening both in place around his taut waist. Each was sharp enough to split a hair placed over them, a fact which did not go unnoticed by Odo, who fell abruptly silent.

No shadow of doubt darkened Colin's eyes as he said softly, "We shall see."

Forgetting the bishop for the moment, he took Roanna's hand in his and pressed a kiss into her palm. His eyes told her everything that was needed. Instead of the plain white robe that was the expected garb of accused witches, she wore the raiment of her wedding day. The gold silk tunic and amber damask bliaut were the perfect accompaniment to her radiant beauty. Her hair fell unrestrained to her waist. A jeweled circlet proclaimed her rank, though no such declaration was truly necessary.

The regal self-possession with which she carried herself was eloquent proof of her true nobility. Never had she looked more strikingly lovely, or more stalwartly courageous. Strength flowed through Colin as he considered that, come what may, he was honored to fight for such a woman.

The crowd thought so, too. Ribald jeers from FitzStephen's supporters were easily overwhelmed by admiring shouts and praise for the couple who seemed at that instant to represent all the best that anyone could hope for.

Even William was not immune to the vision they presented of masculine power perfectly complemented by feminine grace. He had to fight down the urge to put an end to the whole absurd business right then. Only the knowledge that the fulfillment of his most precious dreams depended on keeping the support of all factions forced him to maintain a pose of neutrality.

Yet despite his best intentions, he had to look away as Colin touched his wife's face for just an instant in a gesture of boundless tenderness and comfort. Even the raucous crowd was momentarily silenced, though their excitement resurged swiftly when the hooded monks who would guard Roanna until the matter of her guilt or innocence was settled by God escorted her to the waiting stake.

By the King's order, she was not tied to it as was usually done. Instead, she was allowed to stand a few yards away, just near enough to smell the dryness of what could be her funeral pyre and hear in her imaginings the fierce crackle of the flames.

The moment she was led from him, Colin began the essential struggle to put her from his mind. All thought, all energy had to be absolutely focused on the task ahead. There was no room for even the faintest distraction as he faced what was easily the severest test of his life.

At a signal from William, both combatants strode to opposite ends of the lists and mounted their war horses. FitzStephen's huge roan was almost as heavily protected as his master. To carry the weight of both rider and armor, he was specially bred for girth and endurance. By comparison, Colin's ebony stallion looked smaller and less formidable. As the massive, razor-sharp lances were handed to each man, the crowd pressed forward. The last bets were placed, with the odds now even more in favor of the Norman, who smiled malevolently as he closed the visor of his battle helmet.

A white cloth appeared in the King's hand. The crowd hushed. In an instant that seemed to stretch out forever, the very air reverberated with tension. Then the cloth fell, the mob surged to its feet, and the heavy thud of pounding hooves shattered the stillness.

Colin and FitzStephen galloped directly at each other, the huge, heavy war lances held straight out before them. A man in full armor stood a chance of staying in the saddle despite being struck by such a formidable weapon. But Colin's only hope seemed to lie in evading the blow aimed directly at his chest.

At the last instant, when it seemed inevitable that FitzStephen would strike him, he twisted lightly in the saddle. Roanna had to put a hand to her mouth to hold back a scream as he just managed to escape the piercing lance point. But his own aim was also knocked off enough to leave FitzStephen untouched.

The crowd cheered his agility, but Colin did not hear them. Returning to the start of the list, he concentrated strictly on what he had just learned about his opponent. In the moment before the lance had almost struck home, FitzStephen had slightly raised his right shoulder, as though better to absorb the blow's impact. Was it a fluke, or did he unconsciously do the same thing each time he charged?

Colin soon had his answer. Twice more they went at each other at full speed, their lathered horses snorting wildly as clumps of dirt flew up from their hooves. Twice more he just managed to evade the Norman's lance and in the process noticed the same, slight movement.

A faint smile touched his mouth as they prepared to charge yet again. The crowd was stirring restlessly. It was all well and good to see how agile the Anglo-Saxon was, but a real man did not depend on avoiding blows. Rather he concentrated on striking his own. Scattered jeers rose from the mob. Only a few of the most experienced fighters understood what Colin was doing. They leaned forward eagerly, forgetting for the moment whatever faction they happened to belong to. If he could actually pull it off . . .

Again the horses were spurred forward, the war lances lowered to maim and kill. Again Colin swerved in the saddle, but this time his weapon did not move with him. It remained steady, pointed directly at the seam in FitzStephen's armor just above his right shoulder.

The impact stunned the Norman. Though the metal plating laid over toughened leather was enough to protect him from being wounded, he was knocked drastically off balance. His own lance flew from his hand, spinning harmlessly away, as he was hurled from the saddle. The ground came up in a rush beneath him.

Dazed and winded, FitzStephen had difficulty rising. His heavy armor weighed him down. He barely managed to get to his feet before Colin was out of his saddle and approaching with sword drawn.

Roanna watched ashen-faced as the two men circled each other warily. Under his closed battle helmet, sweat streamed down the Norman's face, stinging his eyes. The massive blade he wielded had to be held with both hands. Whirled above his head and slammed down with crushing force, it could slice a man's head from his body or crush his chest with a single blow.

But without the burden of armor, Colin was able to dodge it repeatedly even as he searched out an opening for his smaller, lighter sword. FitzStephen was soon panting hard. He was not accustomed to fighting an opponent who turned his most formidable advantages against him. At Hastings, all his killing had been done from horseback, leaving him with the conviction that the English were inferior warriors. But now, matched face to face with a relentless enemy, he was quickly discovering such was not the case.

His chest tightened painfully as he raised his weapon yet again. Once more, Colin neatly sidestepped it. He darted behind FitzStephen, who turned lumberingly. Razor-sharp steel flashed in the air. A cry tore from the Norman as the English blade cut through his armor as though through butter. Blood ran red against the gleaming black metal.

The crowd gasped. In the grandstand, William leaned forward. His professional curiosity briefly overshadowed even the political implications of the clash going on before him. Colin seemed intent on giving a demonstration of the weaknesses of Norman fighting methods. The King, who aspired to greatness far beyond the limits of his homeland, was willing enough to learn from him.

FitzStephen, however, had no intention of becoming an object lesson. A red mist rose before his eyes as he raised his blade yet again. Colin noted the effort almost distantly. He thought the exercise had gone on long enough. Moving with the agility of a wrestler, he linked a leg around the Norman's and pulled firmly. FitzStephen's feet flew out beneath him. He landed in the dirt, sprawled like a beached whale.

This time, there was no chance to rise before Colin reached him. Almost insolently, he yanked the red-plumed battle helmet off and threw it to the ground. FitzStephen's small black eyes widened in shock as the point of the English blade came to rest against his throat.

Colin's features were coldly implacable. With his massive chest rising and falling only lightly from his exertions, his powerful legs planted firmly apart in a rock-like stance, and his quicksilver eyes glittering menacingly, he might have been some legendary war god come to shake the world.

Not even William could suppress a shiver of primeval fear as Colin stared down at his fallen foe. Harshly, he grated, "Do you yield?"

FitzStephen hesitated, hardly daring to believe he was being given the chance. Slowly, reluctantly, he nodded. A mocking smile curved Colin's hard mouth. Well aware of the insult he delivered, he said clearly, "Then rise, for you are not worth the killing."

From his awkward position, FitzStephen had to crawl to his feet. His once glorious armor was stained and dented. The wound in his shoulder still bled copiously. His face was ashen, but his eyes burned with hatred that was fueled even higher by the mocking shouts of the crowd. Even those who had supported the Norman forgot their disappointment long enough to hail the victor.

William was grinning broadly as both men approached. He was well pleased, so far, with the outcome. Even those who had wanted to destroy all the remaining Anglo-Saxon lords could not help but be impressed by Colin's display of skill and courage. The sheer, relentless ferocity of his attack would compel serious reconsideration of their position. By sparing his opponent's miserable life, he had provided them with the excuse they needed to change their views and accept a peaceful accord.

Responding to William's summons, Roanna stepped forward quickly to stand beside her husband. Her eyes glowed as she stared up at him in the most profound relief and love. With his compelling gaze locked on hers, she hardly heard the King begin to declare her innocence. But she became abruptly aware when he was stopped by FitzStephen's sudden interruption.

In the rapid hush, the vanquished Norman shouted, "I challenge the outcome of this combat! The accused's champion must be sworn to chivalry before he can render God's judgment. The Englishman took no such oath. The decision is meaningless, for he had no right to meet me on the field!"

In the pandemonium that followed this shocking assertion, William remained strangely aloof. He appeared deaf to the shouts of those who supported FitzStephen's charge and equally oblivious to those who hurled insults at the Norman for so abusing Colin's mercy.

The King waited until some semblance of order could be restored before stepping forward to address the crowd. With apparent reluctance, he said, "FitzStephen is quite correct. The decision of trial by combat is valid only if both the opponents are sworn to God's service as knights."

Odo opened his mouth to protest, vehemently, only to be stopped as his half-brother continued calmly, "However, I see no great problem in this." A royal hand reached out, beckoning Colin. He came at once, having anticipated what was to happen.

As the crowd gaped in disbelief, the victorious

chieftain went down on one knee before the King whose vision of peace he shared. William calmly unsheathed his own sword. Laying it across Colin's right shoulder, he said loudly and clearly, "I accept you as liegeman to serve me well and loyally all the days of your life, and in return I pledge myself to the defense of our lands, families, and mutual honor."

Pausing for just an instant, as though to savor the moment, he concluded firmly, "Rise, Lord Algerson, Earl of Hereford."

# Chapter Eighteen

"TELL ME THE TRUTH," MARGARET PLEADED ANXIOUS-
ly. "Do you think I'm being foolish?"

Roanna smothered a laugh. Her eyes were gently
teasing as she studied her nervous friend. Despite all
she had lived through and triumphed over in her
forty-some years, Margaret was acting like a timid
young girl.

"Not at all," she assured her kindly. "Anyone who
suggests such a thing is only envious of your great
happiness. Few ever find true love. It's not to be
turned aside at any age."

As she spoke, her mind flew unerringly to the man
who was the source of her own limitless joy. Colin was
downstairs with the rest of the household, waiting for
the festivities to begin. His deep laughter reached her
even over the voices of the other men.

A faint blush stained her cheeks as she remembered the passion-enthralled night they had just spent together. Since his terrible clash with FitzStephen, and its remarkable aftermath, their lovemaking had been especially ardent and tender. In the privacy of their chamber, they could not resist the need to celebrate the continuance of life in the timeless way of lovers everywhere.

Shaking her head ruefully, Roanna considered that given her recent lack of sleep she had no right to look so good. A quick glimpse in the mirror revealed a radiantly beautiful young woman whose skin glowed lustrously and whose tawny eyes shone with sublime satisfaction.

The lavender tunic she wore seemed to fit more snugly than usual. Her eyes narrowed slightly as she wondered if her breasts were indeed somewhat fuller. The faint, tentative hope that had first occurred to her several days before arose again. She touched a wondering hand to her still flat belly, breathing a silent prayer that she was right.

Too quickly for Margaret to notice, Roanna hid her preoccupation. She resumed brushing the older woman's luxurious chestnut hair lightly sprinkled with silver. The soothing motion eased some of Margaret's nervousness. She even managed to smile as Roanna slipped the veil in place and secured it with the golden circlet that was Alaric's bridal gift.

Shaking her head slightly, she murmured, "If anyone had told me a few months ago that I would be doing this . . ."

"But a few months ago," Roanna reminded her gently, "you hadn't met Alaric."

"That is true," Margaret admitted ruefully. "I really had no idea I was capable of reacting to a man so . . . uninhibitedly. . . ." She blushed lightly as she added, "It isn't that I didn't love my late husband. He was a good man and I was very fond of him. But we were married so young and what with the children and all the problems of the estate, we never seemed to really get to know each other. Whereas with Alaric, I felt as though I knew him the moment we met." She looked up, her soft gray eyes uncertain. "Does that sound impossible?"

"Not at all. I felt the same way when I met Colin. Well . . . perhaps not the first instant. . . ." She laughed, remembering her initial impression of him as a marauding Viking. "But very quickly, once I realized how strong and gentle he was, I knew he was the man I wanted to spend my life with."

"It must be startling enough to make such a discovery at your age," Margaret said softly. "But at mine. . . . I shudder to think what my children think."

"They all seem quite happy," Roanna pointed out. Colin had sent an escort to bring Margaret's two sons and three daughters to London in time for the marriage. They had arrived several days before and showed no sign of being other than delighted at their mother's good fortune. Alaric's concern about how they would receive him faded quickly as he realized that the children who ranged in age from twenty to barely five genuinely wanted his help and support. For the first time in his life, he was discovering the pleasures of fatherhood.

"It is good of your lord to give my youngest boy a position with his guard," Margaret said. "He can hardly believe he is to serve so great an earl."

Roanna laughed gently. "I think Colin can hardly believe it, either. It's taking him a while to get used to his new rank."

"I should think so! Imagine, the first Anglo-Saxon earl. Not, of course, that he isn't perfectly suited to it." Loyally, Margaret said, "The King is lucky to have such a man holding lands for him."

"Lucky, and wise," Roanna murmured. "Colin will keep the peace as no one else could. And because of his authority, many others who might have rebelled will instead be inclined to accept William."

Margaret agreed. Many of the men waiting downstairs were the same who had attended that supper during which Colin explained his views and held forth for accord with the new ruler. Only a short time before, when Roanna was awaiting trial, they were ready to attack William and everything he stood for. But with their pride more than restored by the outcome and everything Colin had promised seeming more possible than ever, they were of a different mind. No matter how unlikely it would have been only weeks before, they were now willing to give the new King time to prove himself.

Which was just as well, considering that William would be arriving shortly.

Smoothing a last tiny wrinkle from Margaret's gown, Roanna silently ran down the list of preparations, confirming that everything was ready. The Earl of Hereford's London residence fairly glistened in the summer sun. Freshly replastered, with new roof tiles, shutters, and doors, it was a model of gracious elegance. The yard both front and back was swept clean, the ramshackle stables replaced by a far sturdier structure, and not a hint of dirt or disorder allowed anywhere.

Inside, the rooms were perfumed with the scents of fresh flowers and the aromas of the wedding feast being prepared in the sparkling kitchens. Long tables covered in white linen were set up in the great hall. Musicians were tuning their instruments and making their final selections of the melodies they would play.

In the men's quarters, a last polish was being given to chain mail and ceremonial swords, a last brush to unruly hair and unaccustomedly grand clothes. All the retainers had new tunics and cloaks in the bright emerald and scarlet Colin had selected for his heraldic crest. The colors, he had told Roanna, signified that their land was worth any sacrifice, even to the cost of blood. They were a subtle reminder to William and everyone else that the Algersons held what was theirs.

Only a few days before, the new King's court had received another, more direct warning about the futility of challenging the implacable Earl of Hereford. Having been given an opportunity to wind up his affairs in England, Montague FitzStephen departed in disgrace, carrying with him the promise that if he ever set foot in the realm again his life was forfeit.

Since there was not a man anywhere who would

support him after his disgraceful attempt to steal Colin's victory, he was unlikely ever to be stupid enough to return. Stripped of his wealth and rank, FitzStephen was little more than a broken shell. Roanna could almost, but not quite, pity him.

Putting aside all thought of the hapless Norman, she accompanied Margaret downstairs to where the bridegroom waited with his boisterous friends. The two greeted each other self-consciously. Alaric's gaze was infinitely gentle as he took his lady's hand. Together they stepped outside to greet the arriving King.

Standing beside Colin, Roanna watched as the royal entourage approached. Since this was one of the few times he had left his stronghold for purely peaceful purposes, William was determined to put on a good show. Banners flew and trumpets blared, caparisoned horses pranced smartly, and row upon row of lords and knights lent a festive air to the usually drab city streets.

The crowd lining the King's route cheered wildly. For too long, London had been denied the pleasure of such a regal spectacle. Old King Edward, though his memory was revered, had been far too pious to indulge in such displays. And Harold had hardly had the chance during his brief, tumultuous reign. It was left to William to restore to the people their sense of pomp and pageantry.

Convinced at last that he truly wanted an accord with them, their delight was unrestrained. For the first time, William heard English voices raised in his tribute. The sound elated him. He was smiling broadly as he dismounted before the Algerson residence.

"Quite a turnout," he exclaimed to Colin. "I had no idea the people could be so enthusiastic."

The earl smiled drily. "All they needed was a chance, my lord. Alaric and Margaret have been kind enough to provide it."

William glanced at him understandingly. Both men knew full well it was not the wedding the people cheered. They might be glad enough of the couple's happiness, but it was their own great joy in the vastly improved state of affairs that sparked their welcome.

Nodding silently, the King turned to greet his hostess. A soft sigh escaped him as he drank in the sight of her beauty. He missed his wife terribly and hoped they would soon be reunited.

Some glimmer of his longing reached Roanna. She made a special effort to make him feel at home as they entered the great hall garlanded with bridal wreaths and lit by dozens of tall, white candles.

"You are a lucky man," William told his newest earl. "Your lady is not only remarkably lovely, but she possesses rare strength and grace." More softly, he added, "I can well comprehend why you guard her so fiercely."

Colin graciously accepted what he knew to be a sincere compliment. "Thank you, my lord. But in all truthfulness, I will be glad to take her home to Hereford. London palls on us both."

"I share the sentiment," William admitted, "despite today's showing. Being shut up inside city walls is no way to live."

Talking of the pleasures of country life, the two men proceeded to the chapel where Alaric and Margaret would be wed. Only a few of the guests, those who would fit inside the small chamber, followed them. The rest were content to wait in the great hall, where kegs of ale and wine had already been opened and the drink flowed freely.

Odo had been asked to bless the union. Highly pleased by the invitation, he had been reluctant to admit that in his twelve years as a bishop he had never performed a marriage and was in fact unfamiliar with the rite. A quick study of the prayer book borrowed from a young priest who managed to hide his surprise at his superior's ignorance sufficed to make him sufficiently eloquent.

Whatever the prelate lacked in piety he more than made up for with thoroughness. Having gotten through the mass with only a few pauses to consult the missive held up by an assistant, he blessed the couple and admonished them to cleave together in loving fidelity all their lives.

"Marriage," Odo reminded everyone firmly, "is a holy state endowed by God for the comfort of souls and the procreation of children." It was not to be entered into lightly or, as was regrettably too often the case, for material gain.

The silver-tongued bishop did such a convincing job of expressing her own feelings about the beauty and meaning of matrimony that Roanna found herself wondering how she had ever believed him capable of leading anyone astray. Not a trace of the unbridled sensualist showed in his somber features as he joined the bridal couple's hands and announced them wed.

The congratulations afterward were as much for

Odo as for Alaric and Margaret. He had given a superb performance, which his audience, knowing him as well as they did, was fully able to appreciate. Still marveling over his magnificent delivery, the guests followed their host and hostess, their liege lord, and the new couple into the hall.

Their arrival was greeted with jovial shouts as the celebration got underway in earnest. From his seat at the high table, William rose to announce he wished to honor the marriage with a gift. Handing a document bearing the royal seal to Alaric, he declared that henceforth all the lands and property in Norfolk that had belonged to his wife and her family were restored. The news brought especial joy to Margaret's eldest son, who fairly beamed with delight as his stepfather, after thanking the King, asked the young man if he would be so kind as to manage the estate, which would now one day be his.

No one in the hall was so naive as to think this meant all Anglo-Saxon claims would be upheld. But it was an indication that William would at least be fair in his judgments, and as such it gave hope to all.

Through the long, enthusiastic merrymaking which followed, Roanna was surprised to discover she had little appetite. The seemingly endless parade of dishes carried from the kitchen made her feel slightly queasy. Only the blandest offerings were at all tolerable to her, and she could eat little even of them.

Far from detracting from her pleasure in the event, this further proof of her most cherished hope only made her all the happier. Colin, noticing her lack of appetite, looked at her with concern. The beaming smile she gave him made him blink, so joyful was it. Reassured that she must be fine, he nonetheless kept a careful eye on her throughout the remainder of the meal.

Very sensibly, Margaret had claimed one of the few privileges of age and insisted she could do without any bedding ceremony. She and Alaric simply contrived to slip away unnoticed as a troupe of acrobats distracted the company. When their absence was noted, there were some goodnatured complaints from the guests, who hated to be cheated out of any excuse for ribald jokes and suggestions. But with the food and drink more than making up for any lack, the revelries quickly resumed. It was well past midnight before the last amply fed, tipsy lord stumbled to his horse and took his leave.

Even then, Roanna's tasks were not complete. She checked to make sure all the fires were safely banked, the candles snuffed and torches gutted, and the remnants of the feast removed so as not to attract vermin. Not until the last servant was abed did she retire to seek her own rest.

Upstairs in the family quarters, it was very quiet. Only a faint light shone from the room she shared with Colin. Opening the door softly, Roanna had to bite back a peal of laughter. Caught in the act of relaxing in a tub of steaming hot water, her lord looked up in dismay, only to settle back promptly when he realized who was at the door.

In the dim candlelight of the chamber, his skin glowed like polished bronze. Thick coppery curls clung to his massive chest. His freshly washed hair hung damply around his broad shoulders. A long, pointed moustache framed the sensual mouth that was drawn in a far tighter line than usual.

"I thought it might be one of the servants," he admitted ruefully. "Wouldn't do to let them know I'm still hurting."

Roanna nodded understandingly. Her brow furled as she took in the lingering evidence of his struggle with FitzStephen. Livid bruises marred the smooth bronze expanse of his shoulders and arms. Angry abrasions shone along his furred chest and powerful thighs. He moved gingerly, owing to the strain of pulled muscle and sinew. Before everyone else, he felt compelled to hide his discomfort and maintain an indomitable air. But with her he could let down his guard and admit that the contest had cost him dear. Neither had to point out that but for his vast strength and agility, the price would have been far higher.

Kneeling beside the tub, Roanna reached for the small keg of soap. Gently, she massaged his corded back, arms, and chest. Her hands lingered on each bulging muscle and flat, hard plane. Colin's eyes drifted closed as a soft sigh of contentment escaped him. But his sense of ease turned to something very different as Roanna's soft, skillful touch drifted down his flat abdomen toward the thick nest of hair where his burgeoning manhood lay.

Her breath became tight and rapid as she stroked his steely thighs before rubbing lather over his heavily muscled calves and long, slender feet. Cupping handfuls of water, she rinsed him carefully, heedless of the fact that her snug-fitting tunic was splashed in the process. By the time she finished, her nipples shone tautly through the thin fabric.

Shakily, she held out a towel for Colin. He stepped from the tub, streams of water flowing off his huge, supremely male body. His molten silver gaze locked on her as Roanna reached up to dry his head. The motion further strained the silk over her high, pouting breasts. He could clearly see the outline of hardened peaks surrounded by generous aureoles, whose velvet smoothness beckoned his touch.

Though he bent over to give her easier access, she still had to stand on tiptoe to reach him. Briskly drying his hair, Roanna continued on to brush the clinging droplets from his shoulders and chest. But before she got more than midway down his torso, Colin's big hands seized hers.

"Enough, my lady," he growled. "The heat you've sparked will dry me from within!"

Laughing throatily, she allowed the towel to be taken from her. It was tossed forgotten in a corner of the room as Colin reached for his wife. Arching her back over his arm, he gently nuzzled her breasts before his mouth closed on a straining nipple. Through the thin fabric, his tongue flicked over it again and again.

Roanna moaned helplessly. Her hands clung to his massive shoulders as waves of pleasure rippled through her. When he at last raised his head, she was panting and her heart slammed painfully against her ribs. Determined that she would not be the only one to feel such acute pleasure, she straightened against him. A soft, teasing smile curved her lips as she brushed them lingeringly against his. For just a moment, their eyes met. Colin's gaze held a challenge she could not resist.

Trailing scalding kisses down the long expanse of his chest, Roanna slowly sank to her knees before him. Her small hands kneaded and stroked the hard contours of his thighs and buttocks. Not until she had wrung a groan of desperate need from him did her petal-soft fingertips at last brush against the pulsating fullness of his manhood.

Drawing out her own anticipation to the utmost, her soft pink tongue slowly followed the path of her touch. Colin's big hands tangled in her hair as he trembled convulsively. Only after she had fully savored him did Roanna finally allow herself to be drawn upward into her husband's arms.

The damp tunic was swiftly stripped away. Her skin shone against his darkness like cream sweetened by the faintest drop of honey. Laid on the bed, she welcomed him joyfully. Colin delayed only long enough to be sure she was ready for him before bringing them together in a tumultuous explosion of pleasure that sent shards of white-hot rapture tearing through both.

With the first shattering burst of passion eased, they were free to explore each other at length. Roanna was almost mindless with joy before Colin drew her to him again. Thrusting deep within her, he drove them both to soaring fulfillment.

Much later, lying with her husband's burnished head against her breast, Roanna smiled softly. When they had first begun to make love, she had thought to tell him of the child and to ask him to take special care. But her intention was lost in the firestorm of her own need, and at any rate it had not been necessary. Colin was far too gentle and loving a man ever to harm her even inadvertently.

Her smile deepened as she stroked the rough silk of his hair. There was time enough to tell him of the baby later. Joy and a deep sense of peace filled her as she at last allowed herself to believe that for them there would be time for everything.

# Epilogue

"THERE MUST BE SOMETHING WE CAN DO," COLIN insisted. "She can't just go on suffering like this."

Brenna touched his arm gently. "You know there's nothing to be worried about. Roanna is strong and healthy, and the birth is proceeding rapidly. Your son—or daughter—will be here quite soon."

"You said that an hour ago," he reminded her tightly.

Nodding patiently, she reassured him yet again. "It won't be much longer now."

A soft moan came from the bed, claiming their attention. Roanna's face was pale. Tendrils of damp hair clung to her forehead. Her amber eyes were shadowy with pain, but they nonetheless shone with determination.

"Listen to Brenna," she said firmly. "I'm fine."

Colin took her hand in his, holding it as though he was afraid she might break. "It's been going on so long."

A slight smile curved her mouth. "It only seems that way. Nothing really started until this morning."

He nodded morosely. Throughout the previous night, she had been troubled by occasional aches and a growing feeling of pressure in her burdened belly. Colin had piled pillows behind her, rubbed her back, and talked to her soothingly. He was as anxious as she for their child to be born, but the knowledge that she had to suffer to bring it forth tormented him.

When the new day's light at last began to reveal the early spring landscape, her labor started in earnest. He had hastily summoned Brenna, who had arrived the week before to help care for her sister-in-law. She took charge immediately, summoning servants with fresh linens and hot water and doing her best to convince Colin he should go downstairs. But he would have none of it, stubbornly remaining at his wife's side. Acknowledging that he had as much skill at healing as she did herself, Brenna relented. Together they made Roanna as comfortable as possible and settled down to wait.

Or at least, the two women remained calm in the face of what gave every appearance of being a perfectly normal delivery. The knowledge that there were no apparent problems did not reassure Colin at all. He alternated between sitting anxiously beside Roanna watching her every move and pacing the room in increasing frustration, until Brenna seriously considered asking Guyon to knock him over the head and drag him away.

Only the memory of her own delivery a few months before stopped her. Guyon had not behaved any differently from Colin. Having missed the birth of their first child, he had insisted on remaining at her side through every moment. Fortunately, this baby came much more easily. So quickly that she could hardly believe it, Brenna had found herself holding a beautiful little daughter. Guyon, however, had not appreciated the swiftness of her labor. He had gone around for days horrified by her suffering and had required great persuading after she healed to resume their intimacy.

Throughout the long afternoon, Roanna's increasingly anguished moans had mingled with the sharp ring of hammers against stone and the shouts of men working on the castle construction. Like Guyon, Colin was building himself an impenetrable fortress that would dominate the countryside for miles around. Though neither man was concerned any longer about Norman raiders, both their holdings were too close to the Welsh border to take security for granted.

Thinking of her husband, Brenna hoped he had found some way to distract himself, perhaps with little Alain and Meri, who were an endless source of fascination to their doting father. But she knew nothing could really take his mind from the chamber where his sister labored to bring forth their child.

"You're doing fine," Brenna told her gently, mopping the perspiration from her brow.

Roanna smiled faintly. Caught in the throes of yet

another contraction, she could not speak. The torches lit hours before against the late night darkness shone on her strained features. Colin held her hand tightly as pain tore through her. When it was over, she lay panting. All too soon the agony struck again. Her back arched in a frantic effort to throw off the torment as a scream broke from her.

"Quickly," Brenna ordered, "it's almost time."

Ashen-faced, Colin obeyed. Taking her place at the foot of the bed, he was infinitely relieved to see that the child was indeed about to be born. "Just once more," he urged huskily. "Push, Roanna, push!"

Strengthened by his voice, she summoned all her energy to expel the child. Another tearing pain ripped through her, but she was suddenly almost unaware of her own suffering. With Brenna helping to hold her up, she could see Colin's face. His rugged features were suffused with wonder and overwhelming tenderness.

As he glanced up, their gazes met. An adoring smile lit his eyes before he quickly looked back down. "Almost there, my love. Push . . . that's it . . . again. . . . Good!" With infinite care, Colin reached forward to receive his son, who slid long and perfectly formed into his father's hands.

Roanna fell back against the pillows. Exhausted, she could only stare in astonishment as Brenna rapidly cut the cord and cleaned the child before wrapping him in a soft blanket.

Once the afterbirth was safely released and the bleeding stopped, Colin gently removed the stained linen from beneath Roanna, washed her, and slipped her into a warm sleeping robe. His hand shook slightly as he filled a cup with nourishing broth into which he had mixed herbs to ease her soreness. He held it as Roanna sipped, noting gratefully that much of her normal color had already returned.

"What a beautiful babe!" Brenna exclaimed as she laid the child at his mother's breast. Neither parent could disagree. The son they had already agreed to name Kenelm in honor of Colin's late father had his sire's coppery hair and features, except for the eyes that amid the blue of all newborns already showed amber glints.

The adults watching him laughed indulgently as he rooted around for a moment in search of Roanna's nipple before clamping down on it determinedly. Soft sucking noises announced Kenelm's success as his mother's milk began to flow.

His appetite was barely satisfied when Roanna's eyelids fluttered. Sleepily, she allowed Brenna to take the child and place him in the cradle Colin had lovingly made. For a few moments longer she watched her son with awed fascination before sleep gently claimed her.

Brenna tiptoed out, leaving Colin to watch over his wife and son. Though he had been up since the previous night and should have felt weary, he was aware of nothing but soaring exultation. Not only had Roanna come safely through the ordeal he had so dreaded, she had also given them both a beautiful, healthy son.

After checking once more to make sure she was really all right, he strode over to the cradle. Kenelm blinked at him curiously. Very carefully, Colin lifted the baby into his arms. He could not resist the urge to show his child to the world.

The late night air was warm enough for the shutters to be opened. Standing by the window, Colin gazed out over the countryside just visible in the predawn light. The gently rolling hills and tranquil valleys were already verdant with the promise of spring. The scars left by war and defeat which he once thought beyond repair had vanished. There was no sign of the terrible upheaval begun little more than a year before. The land, and the people, were too busy now with the future to worry about the past.

Cradling his son to him, Colin looked down into the small, puckered face. The future. Bright with the promise of peace and joyful with the knowledge of love. Smiling, he turned back to the woman who had made it all possible. Sitting down on the bed beside her, he laid their son nearby. His eyes, quicksilver in the gathering light, never left them as slowly the new day broke over the land.

# Tapestry

## HISTORICAL ROMANCES

### Breathtaking New Tales

of love and adventure set against
history's most exciting time and
places. Featuring two novels by the
finest authors in the field of romantic fiction—every month.

### Next Month From
### Tapestry Romances

**SNOW PRINCESS**
by Victoria Foote

**FLETCHER'S WOMAN**
by Linda Lael Miller

POCKET BOOKS